JOURNEY
ACROSS THE
HIDDEN
ISLANDS

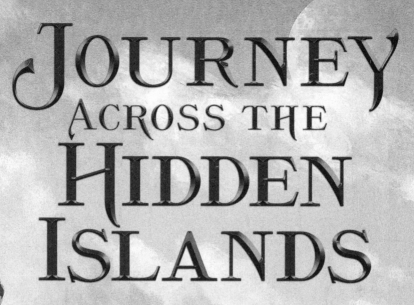

JOURNEY
ACROSS THE
HIDDEN
ISLANDS

BY SARAH BETH DURST

CLARION BOOKS
Houghton Mifflin Harcourt
BOSTON NEW YORK

CLARION BOOKS

3 Park Avenue, New York, New York 10016

Clarion Books is an imprint of
Houghton Mifflin Harcourt Publishing Company.

www.hmhco.com

The text was set in Warnock Pro.
Title page illustration © 2017 by Brandon Dorman

Library of Congress Cataloging-in-Publication Data
Names: Durst, Sarah Beth, author.
Title: Journey across the Hidden Islands / Sarah Beth Durst.
Description: Boston ; New York : Clarion Books,
Houghton Mifflin Harcourt, [2017]
Summary: "When two princesses—twin sisters—travel to pay
respects to their kingdom's dragon guardian, unexpected monsters
appear, and tremors shake the earth.The Hidden Islands face
unprecedented threats, and the old rituals are failing. With only
their strength, ingenuity, and flying lion to rely on, can the sisters
find a new way to keep their people safe?"— Provided by publisher.
Identifiers: LCCN 2016016161 | ISBN 9780544706798 (hardback)
Subjects: | CYAC: Princesses—Fiction. | Sisters—Fiction. | Twins—Fiction.
| Fantasy. | BISAC: JUVENILE FICTION / Fantasy & Magic. |
JUVENILE FICTION / Action & Adventure / General.
JUVENILE FICTION / Family / Siblings.
JUVENILE FICTION / Girls & Women.
Classification: LCC PZ7.D93436 Jo 2017 | DDC [Fic]—dc23
LC record available at https://lccn.loc.gov/2016016161

Manufactured in the United States of America
DOC 10 9 8 7 6 5 4 3 2 1
4500644193

For my son, with love

Journey Across the Hidden Islands

CHAPTER
ONE

*D*ON'T FALL, DON'T *fall, oh no, I'm going to fall . . .*
Crouching, Ji-Lin raised her sword over her head. She counted to thirty and then straightened to standing, without falling. Slowly, she lifted one foot to her knee. Her other bare foot was planted on the top of a pole, on the roof of the Temple of the Sun, at the top of a mountain.

Sweat tickled the back of her neck, under her braid. She was supposed to be calm, like a bird on a breeze or a leaf in summer or some other very calm nature image she could never quite remember. But she felt too jittery, as if all her muscles were vibrating.

If she passed this test, she'd be one step closer to being like the heroes of the tales she loved.

She'd also be one step closer to her sister.

Tomorrow was her and her twin's twelfth birthday, and if she passed this test, then maybe, *maybe* she'd be allowed to spend the day with her. They could steal a lucky orange from the palace kitchen and climb the spires and watch the gondoliers steer through the canals . . .

I'll pass, Ji-Lin thought. *No matter what I have to do.*

Twisting on the pole, Ji-Lin faced north, then east, toward the rising sun. Yellow light bathed the mountains, soaked the trees, and tinted the streams and waterfalls. In the sunlight, the water looked like liquid gold as it cascaded over the rocks and crashed into the mist that hid the valley below. Fire moths flew in and out of the mist, streaking it with glowing red-orange dust, and a pair of flying monkeys chased one another before disappearing into the soft whiteness. *Calm,* she told herself. *Focused. Fierce. DO NOT FALL.*

When the attack came, it was fast. A shadow darkened the sky. At first, it was a speck like a bird, and then it rapidly grew larger and larger, until the silhouette of a winged lion blotted out Ji-Lin's view of the rising sun.

The lion hurtled down from the sky, his wings folded for speed. Sunlight caught his mane, creating a halo. Roaring, he stretched his claws toward her, and it didn't matter that it was almost her birthday or how much she missed her sister. All that mattered was that the test had begun.

Ji-Lin held the sword point out with both hands as she kicked the pole beneath her. The lion veered to avoid the tip of her sword as the pole broke and Ji-Lin dropped to the roof. She landed, kicked the pole up with her foot, and caught it in one hand. *Yes!* she thought, and then she hurled the pole at the lion's belly without lowering her sword.

He bashed the pole out of the air with his paw, then swiped at her, but she was already in motion. *Go, go, go!* Her bare feet were soundless on the clay tiles as she ran across the roof. The lion filled the air with thunderous roars to rattle her bones and make her afraid. But she'd heard too many roars during her lessons to be shaken.

Balancing, she ran along the roof and then leaped onto the next building. A tile shifted under her feet as she landed. The winged lion dove for her again, and she scooped up the broken tile and threw it. Spinning in the air, it hit the lion's face. He turned his head before it could strike his golden eye. *Uh-oh,* she thought. *Too close!* Ji-Lin ran again. He was right behind her. She imagined she felt his warm breath on her neck.

She had to try something else. The goal was straight-forward: she had to jump onto the lion's back and ride him before he forced her off the roof to the ground. But how to do it?

Be swift. Be bold. Be unexpected.

How many times had she heard those words? Ji-Lin had come to the temple the day after her eleventh birthday, and at least twice a day the drummers would chant them as they beat out the rhythm of morning exercises; then the masters would repeat them during the ritual to welcome sunset. So a full year of hearing those words meant . . . *It means think,* she ordered herself. *And run faster!*

Pivoting, she raced down the roof. She pushed harder with each stride until she was leaping. It wasn't going to be enough. He was going to catch her! *Time to be unexpected,* she thought. As the lion dove for her, she threw her sword at him. It flashed as it spun through the air.

The lion caught it, trapping the hilt between his front paws, at the same moment Ji-Lin reached the edge of the roof. She jumped off the roof as the lion fumbled the sword, hurling herself into the air, and she landed half on and half off the lion's back. She hung on to his wing and, twisting her body, pulled herself upright. Burying her hands in his mane, she wrapped her legs around his broad chest.

I did it!

Surprised by her sudden leap, the lion dropped her sword. It fell, flashing in the dawn light, until it clattered in the courtyard below. There it lay, silver against the black stone, glistening like a dead snake between the obsidian sculptures.

Roaring, he soared over the temple. Ji-Lin felt the wind batter her face. The wind roared in her ears as loudly as the lion himself. The lion aimed for a trio of green mountains. His wings pumped beneath her, and she felt his powerful back muscles strain. Sunlight pierced her eyes, and she squinted until the lion plunged into a cloud. Mist swirled around them, erasing any sense of up or down, sky or ground. She heard the cries of birds screaming warnings about the sudden appearance of a large cat in their sky. The winged lion twisted and swooped.

They burst out of the cloud, high above the mountains. Below, between clouds, Ji-Lin could see her island, the imperial island of Shirro, the largest of the Hundred Islands of Himitsu, a green jewel in the midst of blue ocean.

Beneath her, she felt a rumble as the winged lion, Alejan, spoke: "You are going to get in so much trouble. Granted, it was brilliant. But so much trouble! Never fear, though; I will defend you and tell them you are brave beyond brave, exactly like Master Shai when she defeated two —"

Ji-Lin interrupted him before he could wax on about his hero. As much as she loved that tale of Master Shai, this was *not* the time. "I played the game! You were the evil *koji*, and I tamed you." He'd taken the role of a monster intent on throwing her from her perch, and he'd had instructions to not go easy on her.

"Your *sword*, Ji-Lin. You threw it! It's your claws, your teeth! You know how they feel about students who lose their weapons. *I* think you were clever and inventive and brave, but you know they like their rules."

He was right, of course. She might have succeeded in "taming" him, but they weren't going to like the way she'd done it. She groaned. "They'll make me clean the toilets, won't they?"

"For this crime, they'll have you clean them with a toothbrush."

"Or no brush," she said glumly.

"Or your tongue."

Extending unbroken to the horizon, the sea glittered in the morning light. Close to shore, within the protective barrier that surrounded the islands, fishing ships with red sails drew lines through the waves. "I think that would kill me."

"I will mourn you," Alejan said solemnly.

"I expect loud wailing and tearing of clothes."

"But I don't wear clothes."

"You could shed a lot."

His fur quivered beneath her: he was laughing.

She leaned her cheek against his mane, feeling his laugh through her body. He smelled like fresh dirt, as if he'd been rolling around in a field . . . which he could have been. She wondered where he'd gone yesterday while she'd been stuck inside the classroom. To a farm? To the shore? To another island? She wished she were allowed to go with him, traveling the islands instead of staying behind to study. She could do it! She was ready! But the masters said no. Extended journeys were for older students. In a year, she'd be allowed to explore more, but only if she passed all her tests, which wouldn't happen if she failed so badly they punished her, like they might after today's performance. *Certainly they aren't going to reward me with a trip home.* She thought of her sister and the lucky orange they should have been sharing tomorrow. *I'm sorry, Seika.*

"Can we fly a little farther before we head back?"

"If we do, can I have chicken for breakfast?"

"You already had breakfast."

"I have a healthy appetite! I'm a growing lion. Someday I might grow as huge as Master Shai, who is said to be directly descended from the lion who flew Emperor Himitsu from Zemyla—"

"All right. You can have a second breakfast." She scratched him behind his left ear, his favorite spot. He'd probably already helped himself to snacks. He liked to visit the harbor before dawn, when the night fishermen returned with their catches. To be fair, he didn't smell like it this morning — after a trip to see the fishermen, his fur smelled like spices and rotted fish, but this morning he smelled like earth and olives. *He must have rolled in an olive grove,* she decided. "I'll ask the cooks to put gravy on it."

"You are not only clever and brave, you are also wise and kind."

Through the mist below, between the spirals of fire moths, she saw the sparkle of the imperial city, which spanned the gap between the mountains. She used to live there, with Seika, until their father said it was time for them to train on their own: Seika to be the emperor's heir and Ji-Lin to be her imperial guard. They'd be reunited when — *if* — they both trained hard and passed all their tests. Until then, Ji-Lin would only see her home from above: the graceful curves of the palace suspended over the water, the canals with their elegant black gondolas, and the spires of the libraries.

The mist closed over the city and hid it from view. Soon the sun and the fire moths would burn the mist away, but for now, the city was shrouded in wisps of white, as if it were still asleep and hiding between white sheets. She wondered if Seika was awake or asleep.

"I guess we should head back," Ji-Lin said at last. "I have to get my sword."

"And my chicken," Alejan reminded her.

"Of course."

"And your toothbrush."

"Hah. Very funny."

Tilting to the right, Alejan soared toward the temple. Its white walls gleamed in the rising sun. His wings caught the wind, and he rose higher. Ji-Lin felt the sun warming the air. A sea hawk circled near them, watching the lion.

The Temple of the Sun was perched on the peak of a mountain on the imperial island. It was set into the rocks, and its many buildings were connected by steep steps that led to courtyards. Alejan circled the training courtyard, an octagon of black stone. It was ringed by statues of their heroes, the first winged lions and riders to fight the koji, all carved from obsidian, with smooth faces and angled bodies. Ji-Lin's sword still lay in the center of the courtyard where it had fallen. Several of the masters sat, wings folded, in a circle around it. Curious students perched in the olive trees and filled the verandas. As Alejan spiraled down, Ji-Lin felt her heart sink. Everyone was going to know about this.

The most embarrassing moment of my life is about to happen, she thought, *and I can't do anything to stop it.* Maybe she could die of shame right now and skip all the humiliation.

Paws extended, Alejan landed. He sank onto the stone, cushioning the landing so he was as silent as the fall of an autumn leaf. Ji-Lin slid off his back, bent to one knee, and bowed her head. Out of the corners of her eyes, she saw herself reflected in the blank faces of the obsidian statues.

No one spoke.

She heard no sound except the breeze in a nearby flowering olive tree. Leaves whispered, and a few white blossoms fell. They swirled down onto the stones around her, and onto the sword. One of the masters could have composed a song about the moment: the white blossoms crying, the sky lightening with dawn's kisses . . . or not. Ji-Lin had almost failed her composition class. She'd been saved by her punctuality. She just didn't see the point in playing with words when there were races to be won, games to be played, and lions to be flown. She was training to be a hero, not a court lady.

"Ji-Lin."

It was Master Vanya, the eldest of the masters. She was a stately lioness with silver wings and white fur tinged with gold around her muzzle. According to legend, she once defeated three koji on her own, a vicious trio that had eluded hunters for years. In another story, she saved an entire village from a lava flow by diverting it into the sea. Over her life, she'd trained many famous lions and riders, including Alejan's beloved Master Shai. Alejan knew at least a dozen different tales about Master Vanya and her star student. A few were even true. Ji-Lin bowed lower.

"Child, why did you throw your sword?"

Her mouth felt dry, and her thoughts scattered. She latched on to the words that came with the memory of drumbeats: *Be swift, be bold* . . . "I wanted to be unexpected."

"Your sword is your life."

"Yes, Master."

"You would throw away your life to win?"

There was no anger in her voice. Only curiosity. Ji-Lin raised her head to look into the tawny eyes of the lioness. Master Vanya had broken the circle of masters. She stood only a few feet from Ji-Lin, in front of Ji-Lin's sword.

"My choice was unexpected," Ji-Lin said, trying to keep her voice calm and measured, as she'd been taught, "but his wasn't."

"A foolish risk," another master rumbled. Eyes locked on Master Vanya, Ji-Lin didn't see which one spoke. "She is a child in body, heart, and mind. The emperor will be displeased."

Ji-Lin bowed her head again and wondered how many more classes would be added to her schedule after she failed today's test. At this rate, she'd be eighteen before she was allowed to visit Seika. She told herself she would *not* cry, no matter what they said. "I won't drop it ever again."

"She won," Alejan said. "She caught me midair, exactly as

she was supposed to. She was brave and clever, like Master Shai when she faced a sea koji —" Ji-Lin shot him a look, and he stopped. He shouldn't speak so freely to the masters. He was still in training too.

"Perhaps. Or perhaps not." It was Master Fen. He was in charge of teaching Ji-Lin and the other students how to read the sacred texts and how to memorize the maps of the islands. "Regardless, it is not enough to justify —"

"Explain, child," Master Vanya interrupted. "What did you mean by 'his wasn't'?"

Ji-Lin took a deep breath and reminded herself she had nothing to fear from the masters. Their disappointment wouldn't kill her. In the end, they wanted the same thing she wanted: for her to be a hero, like in one of her and Alejan's favorite tales. "I knew Alejan would catch it."

"A real koji —" another master began.

"But she was not fighting a real koji," Master Vanya said. "She was fighting her partner *pretending* to be a koji, and she adjusted her strategy accordingly. Rise and take your sword, child. You have passed our test." The lioness pivoted, shifted her weight, and leaped into the air. Her wings flapped once, and olive blossoms flew from the trees. They rained on the courtyard as the lioness flew above the temple.

One by one, the other lions left.

Ji-Lin still knelt on the stones. She felt as if she heard singing in her ears. She'd expected to be yelled at, lectured, or at least assigned more lessons or chores. She had not expected to pass! Slowly, she stood. She looked down at her sword. Tears teased the corners of her eyes.

The curve of the silver blade looked like the crescent moon. Curled designs, shaped like waves, were carved into the steel, and the hilt was braided with ribbons of black leather. Ji-Lin wormed her bare toes under the hilt and kicked up. The sword flew into the air. She reached with one hand, and the hilt landed in her palm. She held it for a moment, studying the blade. Orange and gold flashed in her eyes — the sunrise reflected in the silvery steel. "I passed," she said, tasting the words. She felt as if she had wings, and she wanted to stretch them out and fly. She'd really passed!

"Tomorrow, you will fly to the city and join your sister." Master Vanya spoke from the roof of the temple. Her voice was a rumble that washed over the courtyard. Her wings were extended, and she looked as regal as the twin statues that guarded the path to the temple.

Ji-Lin wanted to cheer. Home! A real visit! A real birthday!

But Master Vanya continued, "Your imperial father has called you to service. Your training is over. Congratulations, and do us proud." She then rose into the air again and flew toward the triple mountains.

If Ji-Lin had been flying, she would have crashed.

The sword in her hand felt suddenly heavy. She lowered it until the tip touched the stones. She heard whispers around her from the students in the trees and on the verandas. "Alejan," she said, and then her voice failed. How had that . . . What had just . . .

She couldn't have heard correctly. Master Vanya couldn't have said she was done — she hadn't taken all the classes! She hadn't passed all the tests! Students, especially not-so-obedient ones, weren't supposed to be done early. That *never* happened. Traditions were always followed. Rules were never bent. Not by the emperor.

Father never, ever broke a rule. He wouldn't have thrown his sword. He would have hated that she'd thrown hers.

Alejan was beside her. Nudging her hand with his head, he placed his mane under her fingers, which curled into his soft, thick fur. "Congratulations! Ji-Lin? You don't look happy. Why don't you look happy? I thought you wanted to see your sister."

She *did* want to see Seika. But for a birthday treat, not . . . This was too fast. She was supposed to endure many more trials before she was pronounced ready to be her sister's guard. She hadn't proved herself, not against any serious challenge.

"Are you all right?" Alejan sounded anxious.

Ji-Lin shook herself. Ready or not, she was going home! Tomorrow! One more night, and then she was going to see Seika, live in the palace, sleep in her own bed, eat her favorite foods . . . Sheathing her sword, she jumped on Alejan's back. "Come on, let's celebrate! Fly, Alejan!"

"To breakfast!" he cried, and launched into the air.

Squashing down her doubts and worries, she laughed as they flew into the wind. Below, the temple drums began to sound, and the flying monkeys played in the tops of the olive trees.

CHAPTER
TWO

S EIKA LIFTED THE mask over her face. It took her three tries before she knotted the ribbons behind her head correctly. She stepped in front of the mirror. The mask was covered in snow-white owl feathers and boasted the spiraled horn of a mountain unicorn. (Or more accurately, a sheep — it was illegal to hunt unicorns.) Drops of jewels were tied to silver threads that draped from the mask. She looked as if she'd been caught in a rainstorm of diamonds and sapphires.

Scowling at herself, she added another strand of crystals to the horn. It was the night before her twelfth birthday, and she was supposed to be ready by now. The Spring Ritual was already under way, and she was to join the dance as one of the seven unicorn maidens, the Heralds of Spring.

"You look ridiculous," she told her reflection. She imagined what her sister would say if she saw her in this costume. Mimicking Ji-Lin's voice, she said, "Look, it's a sheep that fell into a jewel mine. *Baaa-baaa-baah.*"

"Your Highness?" A startled voice interrupted her *baah*s.

Seika felt her cheeks blush as red as a pomegranate. Trying to sound dignified, she called, "You may enter!" Belatedly, she realized the court lady was already inside.

Catching a glimpse in the mirror, she corrected herself: six court ladies, all in identical unicorn costumes, all staring at her with identical expressions of horror. "Vocal exercises. *Baa-baah.*"

"Of course, milady." The lady bowed with her hands clasped at her waist and then scurried over to Seika. As if her bow had released the others from their frozen state, they fluttered around her, oohing and aahing over her mask and her hair. They added more necklaces to her throat until she felt as if she'd choke, and they shoved more bracelets onto her arms and rings onto her fingers. She stood motionless in front of the mirror, as she was supposed to.

When they finished fluttering around her, she looked even less like herself and more like a living feathered jewel, some strange and dangerous creature that had come from the outside world through the barrier. She stared in the mirror at herself and at the court ladies, all of them dressed the same, awash in feathers and draped in jewels.

We're beautiful monsters, she thought.

She wondered what it would be like to see a real monster, and then she pushed the thought aside. That wasn't likely to happen. Thanks to the lions and riders, the koji had been hunted to near extinction on the islands. She needed to focus on tonight's ritual — and then she had another tradition to complete. Years ago, she and her twin sister had promised each other they'd always share a lucky orange on their birthday. Seika didn't break her promises.

But this year that promise was going to be hard to keep. Very hard.

I can do this.

When she and Ji-Lin were little, they used to sneak away from the Spring Ritual, hide in the balcony, and watch and whisper and giggle all night. She planned to do the same thing tonight . . . except that Ji-Lin was farther away than she used to be. But princesses were supposed to be bold and daring and fearless, weren't they? *It's time to see if that's true,* she thought.

Pretending she was braver than she felt, Seika swept out of the bedchamber with the ladies in a V behind her, like a flock of beautiful yet artificial birds. They murmured to one another, and Seika thought they sounded like birds as well. She wished at least one of them were her age. But they weren't supposed to be her friends. Which was part of why Seika wanted to see her sister so badly. Ji-Lin was not just her sister. She was her best — and only — friend.

Out in the halls, Seika saw that the palace had been decorated for the Spring Ritual. The marble statues wore masks, even the stodgiest of the old emperors and empresses. The only statues that had not been touched were the two winged lions that flanked the entrance to the Bridge of Promises. Carved out of Zemylan purple wood, the statues were incalculably precious because that tree didn't grow on the islands. Maybe they were too irreplaceable to be messed with. Or maybe the decorators were scared of annoying the real winged lions. She hoped the lions at Ji-Lin's temple weren't going to be angry with her when she showed up on their steps.

First things first, though: she had to successfully sneak out of the palace.

Easier said than done.

Made of black and white stone, the Bridge of Promises arched over a canal, connecting two wings of the palace. Windows let the night breeze whistle through. Stone winged statues guarded the spires. Seika and the court ladies glided over the bridge. Their slippered feet were soundless on the marble path. On the other side was the heart of the palace, with the Hall of Seasons and her father's celebration dais with its flower-strewn throne. She could hear the strains of music drifting over the water and knew the ritual had already begun.

At the peak of the bridge, Seika slowed by a window. Cracks ran through the sill, from one of the recent tremors that had shaken the island. She touched the cracks, tracing their veinlike pattern. In a few days, they'd be filled in and painted so they wouldn't show.

The palace was only ever allowed to be beautiful.

Like a princess, with every flaw hidden.

Outside, the city sparkled with hundreds of lanterns hung on both sides of the canals. Their light glistened on the dark water. Boats slipped through the water, shadows that passed silently, and the waterfolk — the merpeople who lived under the bridges — were singing softly to summon fish for their dinners. Seika wished she could bring Ji-Lin home for their birthday. Ji-Lin hadn't seen this sight in an entire year, nor heard the song of the city's waterfolk. She must miss it. *This* was where Ji-Lin belonged, not at the top of a mountain, far away from her twin.

"Princess Seika?" one of the ladies asked.

Leaning on the windowsill, Seika looked out without replying. The palace sprawled on either side of her, its spires and turrets reaching high, as if they wanted to touch the mountains. Master Werr, her history tutor, said that two hundred years ago, when her ancestors fled from the mainland, these islands were empty wilderness: new islands, born from the sea, summoned by dragon magic. In the years that followed, safe within the protection of the dragon's magic barrier, her ancestors had carved this city into the rocks and suspended it between the mountains. The water that used to rush between the mountains had been tamed into hundreds of canals. Beyond the city, she knew, the water ran free, tumbling in waterfalls and spilling down mountainsides into the ocean.

She wanted to see it. Maybe someday she would. Maybe she and Ji-Lin could see it together, when they were done with their training, when they were ready to explore! Until then, every year, the palace felt smaller, the walls closer, and the sky wider.

Behind her, one of the ladies spoke. "One legend says

that the Bridge of Promises was built to the specifications of Emperor Himitsu himself, in honor of his promise to the dragon. Another says it was built by the third emperor for his daughter, in honor of his promise that she would be his heir. The empress Maiyi went on to build many of our greatest cities and temples."

It would be nice if the ladies didn't turn every moment into a lesson. *I was being meditative and introspective.* A tutor had once said those were good traits for royalty. "Which is true?" Seika asked obediently. Politeness and obedience were also good traits, and she knew what the court ladies wanted to hear.

"Both or neither. It is also said that when a promise is broken, the statues on the bridge cry, and it is their tears that fill the canals below — and that is why the canals are salt water."

Ji-Lin would have pointed out that the canals were salt water because they connected to the sea — she'd always been the one to dare argue and question — but Seika just smiled at the court ladies and withdrew from the window. *I'm the good girl*, Seika thought, *which is why Father will understand why I have to do this, right? I promised Ji-Lin.* She crossed the rest of the bridge without another glance at the glittering city.

At her approach, guards threw open the doors, and in seconds, she stood at the top of a wide curved staircase, overlooking the Hall of Seasons. This hall was used four times a year, to mark the turning of the seasons. According to her favorite tutor, the quarterly rituals were supposed to comfort the islanders as they confronted the passage of time.

Ji-Lin had always called them ridiculous, but Seika thought they were beautiful.

Musicians, clad in purple to represent the flowers that bloomed on the mountainsides of Shirro in springtime, played the traditional music of spring with an array of five- and seven-stringed instruments. Their music swelled and fell like waves, punctuated by bells. Below, the court was performing the traditional dance. In sets of four, the lords and ladies looked like petals on a flower. The colors swirled as they danced, and all the masks glittered with jewels.

Across the hall, on a dais, on a throne of gold wreathed in white roses and orange blossoms, was her father. He was dressed as a winged lion, with a mane of gold threads around his face, his skin painted gold, and wings made of swan feathers on his back. He sat stiff and silent as he watched over his court.

After a moment, he lifted his face and looked directly at Seika.

And then his gaze swept on, without any hint of recognition.

She knew she shouldn't be disappointed — she was in the same costume as the court ladies. In fact, the whole point of escaping *now* was that she was indistinguishable from the other unicorn maidens. Tonight, the palace guards wouldn't know her, and she'd be able to slip away during the ritual.

Seika swept down the stairs with the other unicorn maidens, and the dancers parted to allow them onto the floor. Instantly, they began the pattern of the dance. Each set was supposed to ensure verdant growth across the islands. Seika's feet knew the steps well, and she was free to watch around her as she swirled with the others, joining the blossoming flower patterns on the floor.

Her father did not look at her again.

As the music changed, she switched partners. Her slippered feet were light on the marble, and she spun and danced, until the music died midnote.

All the dancers froze like statues — arms raised or lowered, legs stretched or bent, toes pointed or flexed. Seika was midspin when the music stopped. As she'd practiced, she smoothly dropped one foot to the floor to halt her spin and held herself as still as the rest, as the hourly ceremony known as the Procession of Time began.

Three men in black hooded robes emerged from a plain wooden door opposite the dais. Silent, they weaved through the dancers. Each man carried a black lacquer box decorated with pearls. Each wore his hood over his head, and a polished silver mask. When they reached the dais, they knelt as one before the emperor and held up the boxes.

The boxes sprang open, and jewel-colored birds flew out.

Seika tilted her head, just slightly, to watch them fly.

The birds spiraled to the ceiling and out the skylights into the star-speckled night. The boxes closed, and the Time men filed back through the statuelike dancers. When the door closed behind them, the music started, and the dancers continued as if they'd never stopped. Seika continued her spin.

Seika danced and danced through the night, completing the patterns of the Spring Ritual and halting every hour for the Procession of Time. She counted the hours as they passed. As midnight approached, she felt her heart beat faster. *Almost time,* she thought. She spun closer and closer to the edge of the hall.

At midnight, the music died once more.

The dancers froze, and so did Seika, one foot in the air and one arm outstretched. She waited and watched and tried not to wobble.

The wooden door opened.

The silver-masked men marched toward the emperor, who still sat rigid on his throne. As one, they knelt and opened the boxes. Darkness fell as every lantern was shuttered and every window was shaded simultaneously by servants around the ballroom. A curtain was drawn across the ceiling to block any light from the stars. Rehearsed for a month, the midnight ritual happened in only an instant.

And in that instant, Seika slipped through the wooden door.

It was so quick, this moment she had planned for days, but she was quick too. She heard the music begin again and knew the lights had been relit and the curtain withdrawn, symbolizing the way midnight switched the world from growing night to growing day.

Suppressing the urge to giggle, she hurried through the narrow corridor. She was doing it! Really doing it! Ahead, she heard the flutter of wings and snippets of bird songs. The cage of jeweled birds was at the end of the hallway. Hundreds of songbirds flew around the cage, swirling like flowers blowing in the wind. Behind the birds was the entrance to the Time men's chambers.

She'd chosen this escape route because it connected to the capital's old koji shelters. Every town and city on all the islands had a koji shelter: usually a collection of tunnels or caves, built for escape from the koji. They weren't used much nowadays, of course. But Seika had learned about them in her lessons, and she knew the tunnels were both accessible and safe. *I doubt Master Werr ever expected those lessons to be so practical,* she thought. She imagined sending a thank-you note to her history tutor and suppressed another laugh.

Seika found the entrance to the tunnels exactly where it was supposed to be: in the center of the Time men's room, underneath a rug. Throwing back the rug, she pulled up a stone. It shifted easily. She pulled a string from a hidden pocket in her dress and tied it to the corner of the rug. As she lowered herself into the hole and replaced the cover, she tugged on the string. The rug unrolled again, hiding her escape.

Only seconds later, she heard the Time men return to the room, murmuring to one another in soft voices and cooing at the birds.

I did it!

Now she just had to find the boat. She knew one was stored here — she'd glimpsed the tip of it from her window during low tide. This tunnel *should* lead her right to it.

While the Time men chattered above her, Seika crept down the ladder. It creaked, but she moved as silently as she could. Holding her skirts up so they wouldn't snag on anything, she silently hurried through the tunnel, which smelled like rotten cabbage. She counted her strides and tried not to breathe deeply.

At ten steps, she halted, and she felt along the wall. Around her, she heard the scurrying of rats. Yuck. She hoped they weren't nearby. Or hungry. "I don't taste good," she whispered into the darkness. At the sound of her voice, the rats skittered away. She was glad she'd never been afraid of the dark.

Soon she located a lantern — all the koji shelters were stocked with lanterns and other supplies. If she kept going, she'd find abandoned rooms with cots and stores of old food and water, but that wasn't her destination. She lit the wick with a flint that lay next to it. Soft shuttered light spilled into the tunnel, and the oil smelled musky. With the lantern, she continued.

She felt a smile pulling at her face. She was doing it! Really, really doing it! Ji-Lin was going to be so surprised. And happy. *I keep my promises.*

She hurried. Up ahead, she saw it: the elegant curve of the black gondola.

She also saw a figure in the boat.

He had painted gold skin, a fake lion's mane, and swan-feather wings, and he was sitting calmly, legs crossed, hands on his knees, as if he'd been waiting for her for hours.

"Father?" Seika said, slowing.

The Emperor of Himitsu inclined his head. "Daughter. Care for a boat ride?"

But . . . But . . . She'd been so quick and so clever! How did he . . . How could he . . .

He signaled one of his guards, who stepped out of the shadows and into the gondola. He held a polelike paddle for steering. Seika glanced around and saw more of her father's guards blended in with the dark walls of the tunnel. Hitching up the hem of her skirt, she climbed into the boat. It rocked as she settled into a seat directly across from her father. She set the lantern between them.

She peeked up at him. He didn't *look* angry.

Standing on the back of the gondola, the guard rowed

them out of the tunnel. Above, the night sky was dressed in stars. "If I may ask, how did you know?" She kept her hands in her lap, eyes respectfully down. She thought her voice sounded admirably calm and steady, considering she'd just been caught.

"Spies," he said bluntly. "I had you watched."

The gondola slid through the water. "Oh." She should have known. She was watched all the time, of course, but she'd thought that during the Spring Ritual she'd be lost in the crowd, indistinguishable from the other unicorn maidens.

"I am disappointed in you, Seika."

Ouch. His words felt like rocks dropped on her toes. She slumped in her seat. She'd thought he might be annoyed, but she hadn't thought he'd be disappointed. "I'm sorry, Father."

"Someday you will be empress, and all of Himitsu will look to you for guidance and inspiration. You will be responsible for the rituals that give our people's lives meaning, that elevate them from primitive animals to enlightened beings, that ensure safety for both the young and old."

With every word, she felt as if she were sinking lower and lower. She wished she could sink into the water and disappear. She shouldn't have left during a ritual. But it was the one time she'd thought there were no eyes on her. "I'm sorry," she repeated.

"I must be able to depend on you to respect our traditions.

You *must* complete our rituals. They are important to our people and our way of life. Promise me you will never abandon one again."

"I promise."

His eyes bored into hers. "Promise me you will always do your duty. You will think of our people, and you will do what is needed."

"I will! I promise! I won't let you down again." She hadn't thought he'd be *this* upset. She'd only meant to spend the day with her sister. She was going to come right back. "I just . . . missed Ji-Lin." Her voice was so small that she wasn't sure he heard her.

When he replied, he did not give the answer she expected. "You'll see her tomorrow."

She straightened so fast that the gondola rocked from side to side, water sloshing against it. "Really?" Her voice squeaked. "Oh, Father, that's the most wonderful—"

He held up one bejeweled hand, stopping her. "Tomorrow, you will begin the Emperor's Journey. You will go alone, with your sister-guard and her lion, as in the tales of old. You will follow the path of our most beloved ancestor for five days to Kazan, the island of the Dragon's Shrine. You will speak with the dragon before the sun sets on Himit's Day, and you will keep our people safe, as generations have done before you."

She couldn't stop staring at him, even though she knew it was not proper manners. Her mouth was hanging open too, in a way that would have caused her etiquette tutor to tap her jaw with a fan. "But I . . . But that's . . . I don't . . . Truly?" The Emperor's Journey?

"Truly." He clasped her hands. His palms felt smooth, soft, and cool. "Fly straight and fast. Do not linger. Do not veer. Follow the path of Emperor Himitsu. Our people will ensure you have all you need as you travel — food to eat, places to sleep, wisdom to share."

"But . . . I'm not ready!" She hadn't completed enough lessons, hadn't memorized enough of the rituals, hadn't ever ventured that far away from the palace or Father before.

"Remember what you have promised: you must do your duty. All of Himitsu depends on it."

Seika swallowed hard. "I will keep my promise." Ready or not, she had no choice. *Please, please let me succeed!*

CHAPTER
THREE

FLYING ON ALEJAN, Ji-Lin heard the drumbeats. And then she saw the drums themselves, at the top of the palace spires, poking through the mist that covered the city. Each drum was so large that it looked as if it was going to topple off, and each drummer was strapped on with ropes so she wouldn't fall. Kicking off the roof, the drummers swung up and out, away from the spire, raised their drumsticks with both hands, and then swung back, crashing drumstick and feet first into the drum. Swerving between the spires, Alejan flew between the drummers. The beats were so loud they echoed into Ji-Lin's bones. "Are we late?" she called.

"Exactly on time," Master Vanya said, flying beside them. "They herald our arrival."

"Oh." Ji-Lin had never been greeted with drums before.

"It's really loud," Alejan complained. "Can I roar at them?"

"No," Ji-Lin and Master Vanya said.

"Just one roar?"

"No."

"A little roar? A meow?"

"Imperial guardians are always dignified," Master Vanya said. "You would do well to remember that. People will look

to you, and to you, Princess Ji-Lin. It is the role of the imperial family to be the spirit of Himitsu. If you do *not* act as you
should, uphold our traditions, and lead our rituals with confidence, our people will feel fear." She circled a spire. "Fear is
our enemy. Fear leads to stupidity. Stupidity leads to danger,
death, and destruction. Therefore, you must both be on your
best behavior, no matter what comes."

"Yes, Master Vanya," Ji-Lin and Alejan said.

"Good. You will learn, as you age, that the world is more
fragile than it seems, unbalanced by a single poor decision
or broken promise. Now, follow me." Master Vanya flew
down into the mist above the palace. Alejan followed, and
Ji-Lin leaned forward against his mane. Droplets hit her face
as they plunged through the low clouds.

A streak of red-orange flame darted in front of them.
And then another. And another. As the clouds began to
lighten, Ji-Lin saw a trio of fire moths twisting around her,
breathing tiny flames, burning away the mist with every
exhale. One zipped past Ji-Lin's shoulder, and she flinched.
She patted her shoulder to be sure there weren't any flames.
Yay! I'm not on fire. Must mean I'm doing something right.

Alejan spiraled lower, and soon they dropped through
the bottom of the layer of mist. Below, the imperial city was
suspended between two green slopes with dozens of bridges
and canals, so many that it looked like a maze.

In the center of the city was the palace.

Ji-Lin always felt a jolt of awe when she saw it from above.

All the spires, all the courtyards, all the tiered roofs — so elegant and so huge. *I'm home!* she thought.

They circled above a courtyard. Like the temple courtyard, it was stuffed with art: statues of past emperors and their finest victories. It was also stuffed with people: lords, ladies, guards, magistrates, cooks, cleaners, craftsmen . . . all of them crammed onto balconies and rooftops, hanging out windows, and crowding into doorways. All the people were shouting and waving and cheering, but Ji-Lin couldn't hear them over the drums and the conch-shell trumpets. She just saw their mouths moving and hands flapping around.

She scanned the crowd, looking for Seika. Her sister should be here. It wasn't like she could have missed all the fuss being made for Ji-Lin's arrival. But where . . .

There!

She saw Father first, on a throne balanced between two rocks. He was smothered in purple and green silk and draped in dozens of gold tassels. Behind him were his guards, all dressed in identical ceremonial armor, with swords crossed on their backs. And beside him, to his right, was a smaller figure, also swathed in purple and green. Seika!

Ji-Lin waved at her. But her sister looked at Father and didn't wave back.

Master Vanya landed in the dead center of the courtyard. Wind from her wings blew the scarves that hung from every window. The drums fell silent. Trumpets, silent. People, silent.

Startled by the sudden hush, Alejan dipped his wing too far, faltered, and landed hard. Ji-Lin was jolted forward, her face into his mane, fur in her mouth. "Oof!"

"Sorry! I'm sorry, Ji-Lin! Are you okay?"

She spat out fur as she sat up. "Fine. I'm all right."

Everyone was staring at them. Her father's face was immobile. He might as well have been carved from stone. Ji-Lin heard Master Vanya sigh lightly. "Go and greet your sister. I must address the emperor. Remember: *dignity*."

Ji-Lin slid off Alejan's back and ran across the courtyard, toward Seika, who bounded toward her. Her sister looked longer, as if she'd been pulled by her head and stretched. Even her face was longer, and her hair had been brushed back into three tight braids that were wound together with gold string. But she had the same Seika smile on her face.

Ji-Lin opened her arms to hug her sister . . . but Seika skidded to a stop and said quickly, the words tumbling over each other, "You're supposed to greet me with a bow, and then I bow back to you. Everyone's watching, so it has to be done correctly."

Ji-Lin clasped her hands together and executed a sloppy bow. She straightened quickly, but Seika was already bowing back to her, gracefully and slowly, as if she'd practiced it a thousand times.

The crowd cheered.

Seika smiled again, looking at the crowd. "They're happy! That means we did it right! I wasn't —" The rest of her words were swallowed by noise from every direction, including the roof. Some of the audience had come with their own horns and drums, which added to the shouting and clapping.

"Seika . . ." Ji-Lin began, but she was drowned out by the crowd.

Over the cheers, in a voice as loud as a roar, Master Vanya said, "Your Imperial Majesty, I have come to tell you a tale."

"And I have come to hear it," the emperor said, his voice carrying across the courtyard.

Everyone fell silent again — all the lords, ladies, guards, cooks, everyone. Ji-Lin hadn't known that that many people could quiet so quickly. She shot another look at her sister. On her tiptoes, Seika was watching the crowd. She seemed far more interested in the ritual than in a reunion with Ji-Lin.

The emperor repeated, "I have come to hear it, for I am the Keeper of Stories and the Guardian of Memory." This was the role of the emperor, retelling the old tales and leading the most important rituals.

She should have guessed there would be a whole ritual around her homecoming. She tried to look interested, even though all she wanted to do was grab Seika's hand and run into the palace and shout, *I'm home! We're together!* She didn't want a ritual right now. Couldn't it wait?

"Once, long ago, my people were not free," the lioness said. "Enslaved by the cruel emperor of the vast land of Zemyla, they were his warriors. They fought whom he told them to fight. They killed whom he told them to kill. They were given no choice, offered no trust, shown no respect, but only fear. They were his blade and his hammer, his mindless tools."

Seika was still watching with rapt attention. Ji-Lin tried —and failed—to catch her eye. She wanted to tell her sister about the test she'd taken, the flight here, her winged-lion companion, Alejan.

Standing, his robes swirling around him, the emperor said, "Once, long ago, my people, too, were not free. Ruled by the cruel emperor of the vast land of Zemyla, they thought what he told them to think. They loved whom he told them to love. They were given no choice, offered no trust, shown no respect, but only contempt. They were his bowl and his brush, his mindless conveniences."

"Until one of my kind befriended one of yours," Master Vanya said. "And together they began to dream of peace and freedom and harmony."

The words finally caught Ji-Lin's attention. *Wait a minute—this doesn't sound like a homecoming ritual.* It was the Tale of the First Emperor, which was saved for the most important occasions. *Why are they telling this now?* Ji-Lin wondered. Her coming home wasn't *that* momentous—at least, not to anyone but her and Seika.

She opened her mouth to ask her sister, but before she could, Seika whispered, "Are you really here? Is it really you? Can I pinch you?" Her hand darted out of her sleeve.

Ji-Lin felt a pinch on her arm, just above her elbow. "Ow! I'm real."

A cymbal chimed, and acrobats poured through a curtained doorway. Silk billowed behind them as they spun and flipped in the air, acting out the story of their ancestors. *Wow, Father really pulled out all the stops,* Ji-Lin thought. *Could it be he missed me?*

She shot another look at her father. He wasn't looking at Ji-Lin. He was studying the acrobats as if they were priceless. He'd barely acknowledged Ji-Lin.

No, he'd sent her away because she wasn't the one who mattered. She wasn't the heir. She wouldn't lead any of the all-important rituals, and she didn't want to. She wanted to be *in* the tales, not telling them.

"You look different," Seika whispered. "Strong."

Ji-Lin thought of the hours spent raising her arms and legs into proper defensive position, only to have one of the lions swat them with his or her tail until she moved them exactly right. She'd run up and down the temple stairs countless times. She'd swung arm to arm across ladders. Yes, she'd grown strong. "You look . . ." She couldn't think of an adjective to match it. "Pretty."

Seika giggled. "The court ladies did my hair." She pointed to the piles of braids. "I think birds are going to want to nest in it."

At least Seika still laughed. They used to laugh together

all the time. *Nothing's changed,* Ji-Lin told herself, and hoped it was true.

Master Vanya spoke again in her grand, trumpeting voice. "'Let us take to the sea,' my ancestor said, 'and find our people a new home, a safe home.' And together, they flew: the lion and the man, with the man's warrior-sister as his only guard, until they found a string of newborn islands, beyond the eastern shores of Zemyla."

"New islands, summoned from the sea by a rare and remarkable koji: a dragon," the emperor said. "Created with the dragon's power, for the dragon's purpose. Cooled and hardened by the dragon's will." He swept his right arm open wide, and firedancers emerged from another doorway.

Running to the center of the courtyard, the firedancers swirled torches. Flames streaked as they spun faster and faster. Tossing the torches into the air, they somersaulted and then caught the torches again.

"Wow," Ji-Lin said.

"They must have been practicing this for days," Seika whispered.

"But that doesn't make sense. No one could have known I'd pass the test." She shot another look at Father, who was watching the firedancers with a polite expression. He wasn't looking at the princesses.

"Everyone must have expected it," Seika said. "You can't pull together a performance like this without a lot of preparation. And the banquet, too—that takes at least a week of planning."

A week ago Ji-Lin hadn't even known she was taking the test. She'd been in classes, memorizing maps and practicing her sword exercises. No one could have known she'd pass. *Unless it wasn't a real test,* she thought. If this performance was already being planned, Father could have ordered Master Vanya to pass her, regardless of what she did. The test could have been just for show.

Ji-Lin looked at Master Vanya. The lioness *had* overruled the others. But if it wasn't a real test, if it was fixed . . . did that mean they didn't think she was ready for the actual test? And if they thought that, then why had she been allowed to come home? What was going on? Seika was still talking. "I wish they'd told me sooner. But even if I'd had days, I still don't think I'd be ready for the Journey."

Ji-Lin stared at her, test forgotten, firedancers forgotten. "You mean the *Emperor's* Journey? To the Shrine of the Dragon? But that's—" Before she could finish, the acrobats joined the dance right in front of the princess. Three of them spun around the firedancers, close enough that their scarves touched the fire and burst into flame—they'd doused them in oil.

Blazing golden red, the fire danced with the acrobats as they swung the burning scarves in circles and figure eights. Ji-Lin felt the heat as they twirled past her, and she backed up against Alejan. Seika was swept sideways, away from the flames — and from Ji-Lin.

Craning her neck to see Seika, Ji-Lin applauded with the crowd as the acrobats and firedancers bowed, and the emperor and Master Vanya continued the tale:

The dragon koji had created the islands, calling on the lava deep beneath the sea, to be her own. She planned to encase the islands in an impenetrable magical barrier to protect herself while she healed from a mighty battle. And so the man bargained with the dragon: let our people stay within your barrier; in return, we will protect you while you heal.

"It's getting near our part," Seika whispered. She was back next to Ji-Lin.

We have a part? Ji-Lin thought. She didn't know what she was supposed to say or do. The Emperor's Journey! It was the most important ritual that the heir, her sibling-guard, and a winged lion were ever called to perform, but they weren't supposed to go on it for years. Why hadn't Master Vanya warned her? Ji-Lin shot a look at the ancient lioness before whispering to Seika, "What's our part?"

"We have to say our names when he calls for us."

"That's it?"

"Don't miss the moment, or Father won't be happy." Seika looked as if she wanted to bolt. She kept wiping her hands on her skirt and shooting glances at the exits.

"Father is never happy." Ji-Lin looked closely at Seika. "Hey, don't panic. If all we have to do is say our names, that's not so hard."

"I'm not panicking." Her eyes were wide. She looked like a cornered mouse. "Princesses don't panic. All right, maybe they do a little bit. It's just that I want to do it right. If I mess this up, I might die of humiliation." Her voice was such a soft whisper that Ji-Lin had to piece together the words.

"You can't die of embarrassment. Trust me. I've tested it out."

Master Vanya said, "The islands were encased in a magical barrier, with the man, the lion, and all the people and lions who followed them within. The man became Emperor Himitsu, the first emperor of the Hundred Islands of Himitsu, named for him; his sibling, who had accompanied him, became the very first imperial guard, responsible for leading all the warriors on the islands against the koji that remained; and the winged lion founded the Temple of the Sun, dedicated to the teaching of future generations."

The emperor continued, "Every generation, the emperor's heir journeys across the hundred islands and renews our bargain with the dragon, ensuring the continuation of the barrier for another generation. The heir travels only with her or his sister or brother and one winged lion, as Himitsu himself did long ago. I ask: where is the one who calls herself heir?"

Seika took three steps forward, toward the dais but still

in the center of the courtyard, and spun in a slow circle so that all could see her. Every eye was on her, Ji-Lin saw. "I am here," Seika said. Her voice shook at first, and then, as if she drew strength from the audience, she continued in a stronger voice, "I am Seika d'Orina Amatimara Himit-Re, first-born daughter of Emperor Yu-Senbi of Himitsu."

"And where is your sister, the one who will protect you on this journey?"

Ji-Lin thought of all the times she'd dozed off in ritual class and wished she could wake her old self up. She imitated Seika, turning in a slow circle, hoping she was doing the right thing, hoping her father and Master Vanya didn't regret bringing her here. She was supposed to be the warrior, the hero who protected the heir, not front and center in the ritual. "I am —" she began.

And then a tremor shook the courtyard.

It ripped like a wave through the water. A few people screamed as they were knocked against walls or off the edge of a crowded roof into the bushes below. The stones beneath Ji-Lin's feet buckled, and she crouched down.

A moment later, the quake ended, and everything quieted again.

A few people were brought inside, to be tended to. No major injuries that Ji-Lin could see. Just scrapes, bruises, and sprains. There were murmurs, a few excited voices, and then the emperor boomed, "Continue."

Straightening, Ji-Lin stood. "I am Ji-Lin a'Tori Eonessa

Himit-Re, second-born daughter of Emperor Yu-Senbi of Himitsu."

"And I, Alejan of the Temple of the Sun, will fly with them!" Alejan added a roar to punctuate his words. His mane was fluffed out, the way it always was after the earth shook — he hated quakes, even the little ones — but other than that, he appeared strong and confident, exactly the way an imperial guardian was supposed to look. Ji-Lin hoped she looked as strong and heroic. *You can do this,* she told herself. *You are a hero. Or will be. Someday.*

The crowd cheered wildly.

Seika waved, and the crowd cheered louder.

Again imitating her sister, Ji-Lin waved at the crowd — she wasn't nearly as graceful as Seika, but the people didn't seem to mind. They were throwing flower petals. The wind caught the petals and swirled them across the courtyard; they landed on the dancers, the mosaic tiles, and even the emperor himself. The drums and trumpets started again.

Soon Ji-Lin found herself waving more enthusiastically. Listening to all the cheers, she wanted to cheer too. The Emperor's Journey! She was going to do it! Cross all of Himitsu! Meet a dragon! *The* dragon!

Looking up at the petal-filled sky, she saw blue against the sharp green lines of the mountains. Birds flew: herons with their broad wings soaring in wide curves, fish hawks circling the canals, and songbirds darting from spire to spire.

She saw them scatter, startled by the drums and trumpets. And then she felt a poke in the middle of her back.

Master Vanya had tapped her with a claw. "You're supposed to mount."

Hurriedly, Ji-Lin climbed onto Alejan's back. He unfurled his wings. "Isn't there going to be a banquet?" Alejan asked in a mournful voice.

Master Vanya rolled her large yellow eyes at him. "You must begin your journey. We will feast in your honor. When you have reached the island with the Shrine of the Dragon—"

Alejan's ears pricked forward. "I'll meet Master Shai! Do you think she'll tell the tale of when she defeated—"

"Dignity, Alejan," Master Vanya reminded him.

He subsided, but his tail continued to twitch.

The emperor crossed toward them, and for an instant Ji-Lin thought he was going to speak to her, greet her, say something about how he'd missed her or how she'd grown, but he didn't. He knelt and swept his arm under Seika, lifting her as if she were a baby. He then placed her on Alejan's saddle, behind Ji-Lin. Two guards stepped forward and affixed straps around her.

"Fly straight and fly fast. Take no unnecessary risks," their father told them. "You will journey for five days and four nights in order to speak with the dragon on Himit's Day, as is tradition. The following dawn, I will meet you on the volcano island in the fortress home of the Guardians of the Shrine — the lioness, Master Shai, and her rider, my brother, Balez — to celebrate the end of the ritual. Do not fail, my daughters."

Ji-Lin wanted to say that she would not fail. She'd prove that even if the test had been just for show, she'd deserved to pass; she was ready, she could do this — but the conch-shell trumpets crescendoed, the drums boomed, and the cheers echoed louder and louder.

With a lurch forward, Alejan launched himself into the air. As they rose above the courtyard, the cheers began to fade away. "Can you believe we're doing this?" Seika squeaked in her ear.

Honestly? No. She couldn't. But they were! And she felt like crowing as loud as a rooster. She and Seika, with Alejan, together on their first real adventure!

Alejan spoke, his voice a soft rumble beneath them. "Please tell me no one peed on me."

There was a pause.

"It was an orange," Seika said. "A birthday orange. I think . . . I sat on it."

Ji-Lin snorted and then laughed out loud. Below her, Alejan shook, laughing also. After a moment, Seika joined in, and suddenly it felt as if no time had passed — as if they were little kids again, sneaking away to a balcony to watch the Spring Ritual.

And they flew, laughing together, away from the palace.

CHAPTER
FOUR

SEIKA LOVED FLYING.

She'd imagined it a hundred times, but this . . . ! She loved the way the wind rushed around her and against her and through her. It pulled at her skin and at her hair as if it wanted her to play. Every time she breathed in, she felt the wind chase down her throat. It tasted fresh, like mint leaves crushed in water — she hadn't expected the wind to have a taste. She loved the way her heart raced, fast as a hummingbird's, and the way the sky felt so much wider and deeper and bigger than it ever had before. And she loved how the world beneath looked like art, displayed for her to admire.

Below, the imperial island of Shirro was laid out like a court lady's dress. The lacy mountains were the shoulders, the farms were the embroidery, the villages were the bead-work, and the blue sea was the hem. Alejan dipped into the wind, and Seika bit back an unprincesslike shriek as she squeezed Ji-Lin's waist.

"He won't drop you," Ji-Lin called back.

Seika wanted to ask, "Are you sure?" because it felt like he was about to let her fall to a messy, squishy death, but she knew it would be rude to imply she didn't trust him. Instead, she twisted, trying to see if the straps were still tight around her.

"It would help if you didn't fidget," Ji-Lin said.

Seika froze.

"You need to relax. Enjoy this. Alejan and I have flown together lots of times."

Lucky, she thought. "You've already flown across the islands?" Seika hadn't been allowed out of the palace. So many times, she'd slipped away from her tutors and climbed to the tops of the spires, but cradled between mountains, she hadn't been able to see out of the valley. In comparison to what Ji-Lin must have seen, Seika felt as if she'd been shoved into a closet for a year.

She told herself not to be jealous. She was here now, with the wind all around her and the world spread below her. Besides, jealousy was definitely unprincesslike, according to chapter five of *The Examined Lives of Emperors and Empresses.*

"Only over the imperial island. Students aren't allowed to fly beyond Shirro until we've passed all the tests. Tomorrow, we'll be flying farther than I've ever flown." Letting go of the lion's mane, Ji-Lin gestured toward the west, beyond the mountains and the sea, where dozens of tiny, mostly uninhabited islands lay. Seika wanted to grab Ji-Lin's hands and force her to hold on again, but she didn't dare release her own grip. Falling, she was certain, would not be nearly as wonderful as flying.

"I'm an excellent flier. Everyone says so," the winged lion said, his voice a rumble beneath her. It felt so strange when he spoke. She could feel his voice through her legs. "I even did the Unmei Run in sixteen minutes, which is only one minute thirty-two seconds slower than Master Shai herself. Oh, Ji-Lin, do you think we'll see her fly?"

"Alejan, focus," Ji-Lin said. To Seika, she said, "What he means to say is that you don't need to be afraid." She sounded full of confidence, as if she'd aged five years instead of merely one, outpacing Seika.

"I'm not afraid." Princesses weren't afraid. Terrified, maybe. Her tutors would be appalled if she felt anything as common and small as fear. She *was* permitted to be terrified, though — but she was terrified in a good way, in a way that made her feel as if all the blood in her veins were singing. "Has he carried two people before?"

Alejan snorted. "We train with weights far heavier than you, little princess. I've *eaten* things that weigh more than you. Relax and enjoy the view. It's pretty."

She didn't want to relax. They were *flying!* And it was more than pretty. It was beautiful: green mountains, blue sky, darker sea. Olive trees and fig trees, as well as rows and rows of grapevines, were growing on the slopes of the mountains. Houses were tucked into crevasses and built into cliffs. The tiled roofs were blue to match the sea and sky, and the walls were white, reflecting the sun. Right below them, Seika saw a woman in a garden, shooing away a flying monkey that was nibbling on her fruit trees. She also saw a sunbird perched on a roof, with its wings spread wide — it was glowing nearly as bright as the sun itself, exactly the way her books had described. A kind of phoenix, it burned with a magic fire that consumed its own feathers, which then were supposed to instantly regrow. Craning her neck, she watched the sunbird, hoping to see it burn and regenerate. It didn't, but she thought she saw sparks dancing over its back, which was spectacular enough.

She could do this. Five days of flying, seeing new and wonderful things! She'd always wanted her own adventure. It was only that she hadn't expected to leave the palace so soon, before she finished her training, before she was ready. But maybe Father wanted it to be a surprise, so she wouldn't over-worry. She liked surprises, didn't she?

Without warning, Alejan flattened his wings against his sides and dove. Shrieking, Seika squeezed her eyes shut, squeezed her legs around the lion's torso, and squeezed her arms even tighter around Ji-Lin's waist. Wind screamed past her ears until she wasn't sure what was louder, her voice or the wind. She cracked her eyes open and saw the ground — *Oh no, we're going to crash!* It came toward them, growing larger, the hillside rapidly approaching. She saw Alejan reach his front paws out. They were —

His paws closed around a rabbit, and then he swooped higher, higher, until the island receded behind them again. She swallowed her next scream but didn't loosen her grip.

Her heart was beating so fast it was like a string of fireworks inside her ribs.

"Alejan, you scared her," Ji-Lin scolded.

"Sorry." He didn't sound sorry; he sounded as if his mouth was full. "Peckish."

"You can eat when we eat."

"All right." He sounded sulky. "I'll drop the rabbit."

"Don't!" Seika cried.

"All right, I won't." His body convulsed as he swallowed.

Ji-Lin sighed. "You shouldn't reward him for scaring you."

"He surprised me, not scared me," Seika corrected. Now that it was over . . . She liked the way her heart was pounding and her breath felt caught in her throat. She wondered if this was how the acrobats felt when they danced with fire. "Besides, imagine if you were one of those farmers down there and you were hit on the head by a half-eaten bunny that fell from the sky." That was *not* the way to make a good first impression on their people.

"Oh. Yes. That would ruin anyone's day." Ji-Lin sounded as if she was on the verge of laughing. Seika grinned into the wind. It pulled at her cheeks.

Alejan rumbled, "A future empress should care about her people's feelings. It's admirable that you think of them, Princess Seika." And then he burped.

"I won't be empress for a long time."

"You're on the Emperor's Journey. Once you renew the

bargain with the dragon, everyone will celebrate and honor you. There will be banquets, with fish and roasted chicken and rare beef and lamb . . . Mmm, lamb, with fresh fig sauce and a side of goat brains . . ." He shook his mane as if shaking off a daydream. "Sorry. I mean, it's good that you already think of the people."

"Um, thanks." She just thought half-chewed food was disgusting, but if he wanted to be impressed with her, that was fine. Lots of people liked to be impressed with virtues she wasn't sure she had. The court ladies often claimed she was "elegantly reserved," when in reality she was busy trying to figure out what to say to them. Her tutors praised her for dedication to her studies, when the truth was she had little else to do but read the old histories and tales.

The only one who'd ever seen her as just Seika — not Princess Seika d'Orina Amatimara Himit-Re, firstborn daughter of Emperor Yu-Senbi and heir to the imperial throne, long may her father live — was Ji-Lin.

And now they were together again! On their own quest! Flying on a winged lion! "If you wanted to dive down again, that would be fine," Seika said.

"Happily," Alejan said.

Seika laughed out loud as he swooped and soared.

They flew until the sun began to set in front of them. Seika stared at the silken yellow as it faded to orange, then red, spreading across the sky. She'd seen sunsets from the palace, the sun burning the tops of the mountains in a red glow, but she'd never seen it scald the sky like this. Clouds darkened around them, and the sea in the distance deepened to a blue-black. *So beautiful,* she thought. Forget a five-day journey — she could fly like this forever.

"Alejan, keep an eye out for the village," Ji-Lin called to him.

"Only one, or can I look with two eyes?"

"You can look with three, if you want."

"Master Shai once fought a koji with a hundred eyes."

"Are you going to talk about her the entire flight?" Ji-Lin sounded amused, and Seika felt a tiny pang of jealousy. She wished she'd had someone to tease after Ji-Lin left.

Alejan was silent for a moment, as if seriously considering the question. "Yes. I think that's very likely. Come on, Ji-Lin, you know she's your hero too. You're the one with a sketch of her in your room."

"It's a nice sketch," Ji-Lin admitted. "She's fighting a sea monster."

"After we complete the Journey, I'll talk nonstop about how lucky I was to carry two of the bravest, best princesses ever on my way to meet Master Shai, the hero of the Hundred Islands and the greatest Guardian of the Shrine."

Seika smiled. He seemed like a sweet lion, even if he was prone to exaggeration. "You know, our uncle, Prince Balez, is the other Guardian of the Shrine. And Master Shai's rider." She remembered him as a friendly uncle who smiled much more than Father did and brought them presents: little animals carved from volcanic rock, books with pictures of Zemyla, and fresh *kimi* fruit. It would be good to see him again; he hadn't visited in a few years.

"I'm sure he's very heroic too," Alejan said grudgingly.

"Just watch for the village, Alejan," Ji-Lin said.

They were supposed to stop for the night in one of the fishing villages, a town named Tsuri that was founded just after Emperor Himitsu's reign — Seika had read about it. The villagers would feed and house them. Each town on their route was supposed to play a role by performing part of the Journey ritual. It was, her tutor had once said, a way for the people to feel connected to the imperial traditions and to the imperial line. It was their first chance to meet the next heir.

Seika wasn't sure she was ready to be met. They'd be expecting someone older, more experienced, more prepared. Not a twelve-year-old princess who had never taken the lead in a ritual before, much less a ritual as important as this. She wished they could just keep flying. "Is that it?" Seika pointed toward lantern lights flickering in the distance.

"Do you think they know we're coming?" Ji-Lin asked.

"Of course. Father sent messenger birds to all the villages we'll be staying in," Seika said. "We'll be greeted with a warm welcome." She told herself she didn't need to worry. The townspeople would know exactly what to do. The princesses would be offered food and a bed and entertained with tales and songs, and at dawn the villagers would celebrate the continuation of the Journey with the ritual dances.

Veering into the wind, Alejan aimed for the village. Seika watched the houses grow larger as they approached and began to feel excited. *So long as I don't mess anything up or forget what to do, it will be fun.* She'd never stayed anywhere other than the palace. She wondered if the pillows would be scratchy or soft, if she'd hear the buoy bells in the harbor at night, and if she'd have different dreams.

Tsuri was nestled against the rocky shore. A pier jutted out into the water, and an array of boats were moored around it. Sailors were tying their sails against masts and unloading nets and traps onto the dock. The town itself was a crescent, with one tall, spired building in the center and a collection of tiny white-and-blue homes around it. As they flew closer, she saw lines of laundry stretched between the houses like colorful flags, catching the last of the setting sun and flapping in the breeze. The lion aimed for the spire.

Alejan circled to land, and Seika saw the townspeople heading toward a square by the tall building. Fishermen left their catch on the dock and hurried over. Children dropped their jump ropes and balls and ran to join them. Men and women poured out of their houses.

"See?" Seika said. "Warm welcome."

She wished there weren't *quite* so many people for her first official appearance on her own. *Be brave,* Seika told herself. *You studied this.* She knew what she was supposed to say. She took a calming, cleansing breath, the way her meditation tutor had taught her.

Everyone was cheering as Alejan's paws touched the cobblestones. He landed in front of a fountain with a statue of a winged lion and rider. The rider was holding a sword aloft in one hand and the head of a koji in another, its monstrous face frozen in a marble scream: fangs extended and many tongues sticking out. Folding his wings, Alejan held his head up in a proud position, a replica of the statue. He looked every bit as noble, Seika thought.

"Knock it off," she heard Ji-Lin whisper. "You look ridiculous."

He lowered his front paw and settled his wings on his back.

Seika moved to unbuckle the straps, fumbling with them until at last she heard the click. She slid off Alejan's back, intending to bow to the townspeople ... and her knees caved. She caught herself on the saddle. Straightening, she hoped no one had noticed, even though every eye was fixed on her, Ji-Lin, and Alejan. The cheering had died down as the townspeople got a better look at the princesses. She felt a flopping inside her stomach, as if she'd swallowed a fish, when she realized how many people were staring at her.

Their expressions weren't as friendly as before, though she couldn't imagine why. The princesses had arrived exactly when they were supposed to. She hadn't messed up yet.

The crowd began to murmur. Seika felt her stomach flutter again. She was used to people talking about her, in front of her, and around her. This was the first time she'd have to address them directly herself. *Don't panic,* she told herself, but as the crowd buzzed around them, she suddenly couldn't remember what she was supposed to say.

I'm not supposed to speak first, she remembered. The townspeople were supposed to be expecting them. They should be the ones speaking, welcoming their imperial guests and continuing the ritual. She forced herself to smile her best princess smile.

One boy, about six years old, was staring at her with his jaw dropped wide. "Are you here to kill the monster?" he asked.

Seika's smile vanished. "Monster?"

CHAPTER
FIVE

J I-LIN DISMOUNTED NEXT to her sister. "Do you mean a koji?" She looked at the faces of the townspeople — tight lips, worried eyes — and knew she'd guessed correctly. She felt her heart beat faster.

"But that's impossible," Seika whispered.

She's right, mostly, Ji-Lin thought. When the magical barrier first went up around the islands, plenty of koji had been trapped within. Over the years, the lions and their riders had hunted them down. Still, it was always possible there were more, hiding in caves or under the sea. Every once in a while, a few would emerge. That was why lions and riders trained.

"Not impossible," Ji-Lin said. "Just unlucky." *Or lucky,* she added silently. If she could defeat a real koji, it wouldn't matter if her last test was fake, if she hadn't completed her training, if she'd only passed because Father and Master Vanya wanted her to. *This* would be her real exam! She could prove she *was* ready.

The crowd parted as a woman hurried forward. She wore robes that brushed the seashell-paved street and a pendant around her neck that marked her official position: she was this town's leader, their "caller." Callers were chosen by the townspeople to be the voice of the town, to "call" out decisions that affected them. In addition to the pendant, she wore decorative chains with charms in the shape of a fish — the town's symbol. The caller bowed, hands clasped, and Ji-Lin and Seika returned the gesture. Alejan inclined his head.

"I am the caller of the village of Tsuri," the woman said. "And yes, we might have a koji in the area. We were getting ready to send a messenger bird to the temple, but we haven't sent it yet. How did you know to come?"

One of the nearby villagers, a young girl, gasped. "She's wearing a tiara! Mommy, I think she's a princess!" She tugged on a woman's sleeve.

"Nonsense." The woman shushed her. "The princesses are too young to be out on their own. Look at their winged lion — he's young too. They're students from the temple, probably sent to assess the danger before the real warriors come."

Ji-Lin bristled. She was a real warrior! Just unproven.

Seika swallowed so loudly that Ji-Lin could hear her, but then she raised her voice and recited in a clear, ringing voice: "I am Seika d'Orina Amatimara Himit-Re, firstborn daughter of Emperor Yu-Senbi, many times descendant of Emperor Himitsu, he who delivered us to freedom and peaceful beauty, and these are my companions, Ji-Lin, second-born daughter —"

"By eleven minutes," Ji-Lin muttered.

"— of Emperor Yu-Senbi, and the noble Alejan from the Temple of the Sun."

The crowd burst into louder murmurs, and there was a flurry of bowing and kneeling. The caller bowed even more deeply as she said, "Princesses? Here? Oh, Your Highnesses, we are honored!" Mimicking her, the others bowed as well. One little girl, maybe four years old, jumped up and down. And the girl who'd noticed Seika's tiara was so happy that she was hugging herself.

Ji-Lin saw that her sister's face was flushed pink, but her every move was graceful as she acknowledged the greetings. She looked every inch a princess. Ji-Lin wondered if Seika even knew how regal she looked. Maybe their arrival hadn't started the way it was supposed to, but Seika had gotten it back on track. *I couldn't have done that,* Ji-Lin thought.

The murmurs grew louder, the men, women, and children all talking at the same time, asking questions of one another, of the caller, of the princesses. The excitement was like a buzz that hummed through the village: *The princesses are here! The princesses — here!*

"If you have a koji in the area, then my kin should have been contacted immediately, as sworn and promised to the first emperor's sister, the first imperial guard," Alejan said, louder than the excited whispers.

More chattering.

"What kind of koji?" Ji-Lin asked, raising her voice to be heard over the people. Her voice squeaked on the last syllable, and she knew she didn't sound as regal as her sister. Nearby, a woman was wringing her hands, but her children were dancing around in a circle and singing about princesses. "Has it threatened the town?"

"No one has seen it," one man said, "but we've lost several sheep. This is a town that exists on fishing and herding. We can't afford these losses." His neighbor elbowed him, and he subsided. "But these are not your problems, Your Highnesses. And the koji—or whatever it was; maybe it wasn't even a koji—may have moved on already."

Ji-Lin felt her sword's hilt, a comfortable pressure against her waist. She and Alejan could fly above the town, locate the monster, and subdue it. It was what a hero would do. "We can help you—" Ji-Lin began.

The caller gasped. "Oh no, Your Highness! We couldn't think to ask it of you. It's much too dangerous. If it truly is a koji . . . We will release a messenger bird at dawn, whether there's proof or not, and the temple will send warriors. You cannot risk yourselves! The islands need you!"

I am a warrior, Ji-Lin wanted to say. *I will protect you!* But before she could get the words out, the caller asked, "Please tell us, Your Highnesses: if you weren't sent here for the koji, what brings you to our humble town?" She bowed again.

Seika spoke in her crystal clear princess voice. "We are

on the Emperor's Journey. We hope to spend the night in your town, sharing in the ritual of the Journey. Can we count on your hospitality?"

The crowd began to cheer.

Clasping her hands over her heart, the caller exclaimed, "The Emperor's Journey! Oh! Oh my! Yes, of course you may count on our best hospitality, Your Highnesses. You honor our town."

I don't need hospitality, Ji-Lin wanted to say. *There's a monster out there!* "You go ahead while Alejan and I find your koji—" Ji-Lin began.

"Please don't concern yourself. It's probably merely a wolf, or a mountain lion, or just our overactive imaginations. Nothing worth interrupting the Journey! Oh my, the Emperor's Journey, so soon! Come with me, and I will see you are given quarters and food."

"But—" Ji-Lin protested.

The caller bowed again. "It would be our honor, Your Highnesses. Our children and our children's children will sing of this day." She sounded so anxious, as if worried that Ji-Lin and Seika would be angry.

Ji-Lin clapped her mouth shut and bowed when Seika bowed.

Shepherding them along, the caller led them through the town. A few townspeople trailed behind them, but most drifted off back to the docks or their houses. The little boy who had asked about the monster stuck with them, his mother holding tight to his hand. He was staring at the princesses.

"I should hunt this koji," Ji-Lin said under her breath to Seika.

"Ji-Lin, the Journey is a great responsibility. You see how excited these people are! They know the bargain *must* be renewed, or the magical barrier will fall and the islands will be laid bare to all the dangers of the world." Seika sounded as if she was quoting something — some lesson, Ji-Lin guessed. She wasn't looking at Ji-Lin. Her eyes were fixed firmly ahead, at the back of the caller's robes. "They want us to continue on."

"I'm not saying we should stop the ritual," Ji-Lin said. "Alejan and I could fly over the village while you do whatever is needed with the people. You don't need me for listening to old stories —"

"No!" Seika said.

The caller looked back at them.

Lowering her voice, Seika said, "It's too dangerous. You could be hurt. Or eaten!"

Ji-Lin snorted and opened her mouth to reply —

"Over here, Your Highnesses, if you please!" Up ahead, the caller waved to them by the entrance to a blue house. Four stories tall, it looked like a tiered cake coated in frosting, each floor smaller than the one below.

Seika strode forward, and Ji-Lin trotted after her. Again in her princess voice, Seika said, "Thank you for your hospitality." The caller bowed even deeper than before, and the princesses returned the bow.

They were ushered inside.

It was an inn. Ji-Lin had never been in one, and from the way Seika was looking around, apparently neither had she. Judging by the long tables, the first floor was a dining area. Each table had been set with napkins folded into the shape of birds.

The innkeeper bustled over to them and ushered them to a table in the middle of the room. Other patrons — who Ji-Lin suspected had come to gawk at the princesses and the winged lion — filled tables around the edges of the room, so that Ji-Lin felt as if they were on a stage, even though it was the villagers who prepared to perform.

Stepping out of the crowd, one villager, a woman in a dress painted with white blossoms and fish, bowed and said, "We would be honored to tell you a tale."

"And we would be honored to hear it," Seika said graciously.

"And to eat," Alejan said.

Ji-Lin shushed him.

The woman in the painted dress was handed a harp — clearly an antique, Zemylan-made, of a metal that couldn't be found on the islands and was thus irreplaceable, likely brought out only for special occasions. She plucked the strings, and Ji-Lin tried not to wince. The sound should have been mellow, but instead, it was as shrill as a bird chirp. "It is our duty to tell this tale, as prescribed by your father, the Emperor of the Hundred Islands. This is the Tale of the Three Brothers."

Ji-Lin felt her jaw drop in surprise.

"But Father hates that story!" Seika said.

It was about Father and his brothers. He refused to tell it himself — she and Seika had heard it from their tutors when Father was not nearby.

"It is his will that we tell it and that you hear it, Your Highnesses. This was the charge given us upon your birth."

The other villagers nodded solemnly, all bobbing their heads at the same time. Ji-Lin had forgotten what it felt like to have everyone in a room focused on her. She wished they were just focused on Seika. She was the heir.

"Once, there was an emperor who had three sons. Biy, the oldest and the heir, was beloved by all. He was handsome and kind, with a generous soul and an open heart. Yu-Senbi, the middle son, was brave and wise. And Balez, the youngest, was a quiet scholar who wished to devote his life to recording the heroic tales of his two older brothers. During their father's reign, the two oldest brothers completed many acts of heroism, rooting out long-hidden koji and keeping our people safe. Many are the tales of their exploits on the back of the brave lioness Master Shai."

Alejan sighed happily at the mention of his hero, and Ji-Lin wished the villagers were telling happy tales where everyone was heroic and no one made any mistakes, instead of *this* tale. She shot a look at Seika, who was focused on the storyteller so intently that she barely blinked.

"After one particularly heroic feat, Prince Biy fell in love with a beautiful maiden with a spirit of adventure that rivaled his own. They were married, but during their honeymoon on the island of Jishin, tragedy struck. An earthquake shook the ground beneath their feet, shook the roof above their heads, and shook the rocks from the mountainsides. The rocks crushed the Palace of Memories on Jishin, destroying irreplaceable treasures and killing the heir's beloved."

A whisper of a sigh spread through the villagers.

"Racked with grief, Prince Biy became consumed with thoughts of vengeance. He convinced himself that there must be a way to stop the earthquakes — to kill that which had killed his love. As he sought a cause for the tremors, his wild thoughts led him to the dragon. She formed the islands; she must control the earthquakes, he believed."

Not true, Ji-Lin thought. The quakes came whenever they wanted and shook whatever they wanted. They weren't anyone's fault; they were just a part of island life. Her tutors had emphasized that when they told her this story.

"No one believed Prince Biy would ever let his grief interfere with his duty." The woman paused her story, bending over her harp to play several discordant chords as the innkeeper began serving the princesses: baked fish; grilled fish; poached, stuffed, and stewed fish.

Ji-Lin hated fish. She hated the smell, the taste, and the

slimy feel of it on her tongue, which was a problem, since she lived on an island. And it was more of a problem now, when she knew she was supposed to be polite to their hosts.

Beside her, Seika was eating a taste of every dish. "Delicious," she proclaimed.

The villagers murmured and nodded. They were pleased the princesses were pleased. The innkeeper was pleased the people were pleased the princesses were pleased. The cooks were pleased the innkeeper was pleased . . . and so on.

Surrounded by all these very pleased people, Ji-Lin squirmed in her chair. Seika had always been better at this, at being polite. Ji-Lin was better at *doing*. Couldn't Seika stay here and listen to this while Ji-Lin slipped out and made herself useful?

The woman continued. "At last the time came for Prince Biy to make the Emperor's Journey and renew the bargain with the dragon. Per tradition, he was accompanied by his younger brother Prince Yu-Senbi and a winged lion."

"Master Shai!" Alejan cried. His tail flicked from side to side as if he were an excited puppy, not a dignified winged lion.

"Yes," the storyteller agreed.

The innkeeper leaned across the princesses' table. "You aren't eating, Princess Ji-Lin. Is it not to your liking?" It was a loud whisper that carried across the inn. Everyone turned and stared at her.

Ji-Lin opened her mouth to ask for something other than

fish but then felt a sharp jab to her ankle — Seika had kicked her. Ji-Lin forced herself to smile and echo Seika. "It's delicious."

More happy murmurs from the crowd.

Ji-Lin felt as if her every movement was being watched and memorized. The villagers would be talking about this for days to come. *This isn't the kind of tale I want to be a part of: The day the princesses ate fish.*

"Please go on," Seika asked the storyteller.

When everyone turned to watch the storyteller, Ji-Lin took advantage of the momentary distraction and held her plate toward Alejan. The lion inhaled everything on it. She put the plate back on the table quickly, before the innkeeper saw.

The boy who had wanted them to hunt the monster giggled.

Ji-Lin met his eyes. She wished she could tell him they were going out to find the koji. *I'm sorry,* she wanted to say. But there was no way she could leave. The villagers had filled the room, and the caller leaned against the door. Everyone was focused on the storyteller, as if there weren't a monster out there just waiting for a hero to fight it.

She wondered if her sister felt the same way. She didn't look as if she did. She was still enrapt, listening to the story of their father and uncles. Didn't she know the worst part of the story was coming next?

"At dawn, the heir, Prince Biy, eschewed tradition and

insisted he enter the shrine alone . . . and then, instead of bargaining with the dragon"—she paused dramatically—"he challenged her."

And there it was—the reason Father hated this story. Ji-Lin felt her face blushing bright red, and she squirmed in her chair. Their own uncle had betrayed their people.

"We do not know what the prince said, but his words filled the dragon with fury. Enraged, the dragon caused the volcano to awaken." Leaning over the ancient harp again, the storyteller played a few more notes before she said softly, "Many died, including Prince Biy himself. Master Shai and Prince Yu-Senbi flew high to escape the fire and ash."

"They fled, but then they were brave!" Alejan said. "They went back!"

"Prince Yu-Senbi became the heir in that moment. Joined by his younger brother, the scholar Balez, they flew on Master Shai into the unquiet volcano. Before the sun set on Himit's Day, they braved its dangers and completed the Emperor's Journey. The bargain was renewed, the volcano quieted, and our people were saved." She plucked a chord that sounded like a goat's cry.

Seika had stopped eating and was staring at the storyteller with a look of horror. "I didn't know the dragon caused . . . Father always said that Prince Biy died in an accident."

"Yeah, an accident involving lava," Ji-Lin muttered. She'd heard other versions of the story while she was at the Temple of the Sun. One said that Prince Biy hadn't merely challenged the dragon; he'd attacked her. Another even said he'd hurled himself into the lava after failing to kill her. Many talked about the horrors of the eruption on the island of Kazan. The version she and Seika had been told as little children had left out a lot of the deaths.

"It was Prince Biy's death that allowed your father, Emperor Yu-Senbi, to complete the ritual in the proper way, thus saving us all," the storyteller said. "We tell this tale as a reminder of the strength of this ritual and the importance of your task. If you complete it, we will all be safe. If you do not, the bargain will be broken and the barrier will fall. The monsters will come again, and all will be doomed."

Seika looked pale, and Ji-Lin saw her hands trembling slightly, but she spoke in her clear princess voice. "We thank you for this tale, and promise you that we will not fail."

The people cheered.

Ji-Lin met Seika's eyes. And she silently made the same promise.

CHAPTER
SIX

MORNING CAME, WITH yellow light that poured through the inn's windows. Ignoring muscles sore from the unaccustomed effort of lion-riding, Seika bounded out of bed. A new day, a new place! She dressed, pulling out the travel garments that had been packed for her: a wrap dress and leggings, designed to be easy for her to put on without assistance. She did her hair in a simple twist on top of her head and hummed to herself as she pinned it in place. She was glad she'd been practicing how to do her hair on her own.

"Ugh, I forgot you're a morning person," Ji-Lin said.

"I like new days. They're fresh. No messes yet." No disappointments. No humiliations. A whole new set of things to get right! She added more pins to her hair.

Ji-Lin grunted and then catapulted herself out of bed. In the mirror, Seika saw her stretch by wrapping her foot around her head and then folding herself in half — *Ow!* Seika thought; she couldn't have done that, even without sore legs — and then Ji-Lin ducked into the small closet with the toilet. When she emerged, she was dressed and ready, while Seika was still wrestling with attaching her tiara. It kept sliding down her ear. She added more pins.

"I still think we should go after the koji," Ji-Lin announced.

Seika froze for a moment, her heart beating faster. Keeping her voice calm, she said, "We're supposed to continue the Journey." A pin slipped, and she winced as it poked her finger. "You heard the villagers — they believe in our quest."

"But they want to be safe, too," Ji-Lin said, looking alarmingly intense. *She's serious about this,* Seika thought as her sister continued. "What if there really is a koji out there, and it gets tired of sheep before the other lions and riders get here?" Ji-Lin waved her hands in the air to punctuate her words. "What if it decides it wants to try the taste of person? We're here. We could stop it. *I* could stop it."

"Or it could eat us. You don't even know what kind of koji it is." There were dozens of different varieties, each of them deadly. "Ji-Lin, it's much too dangerous. You have to see that." If she kept her voice reasonable, maybe Ji-Lin would let go of her crazy idea. Seika thought they'd settled this last night. She wished the caller or another adult were here to say no again.

"You're just scared."

"Terrified," Seika corrected her. She wasn't embarrassed to admit it. Or not very embarrassed. She'd read the histories and heard the tales. Koji were — by very definition — monsters.

"If it were a really dangerous kind, all the villagers would be hiding in the nearest koji shelter. It's most likely a medium-size monster. Large enough to be a danger to sheep and villagers but not to a trained warrior. Alejan and I can handle it."

"The villagers will send a messenger bird. That will be enough." At last she had the tiara secured. With so many pins, it wasn't going to move even in an earthquake. "If we delay, we jeopardize the ritual. We're supposed to be at the shrine on Himit's Day, which means we need to be in the next village tomorrow night."

Ji-Lin glared. "A koji is more important than being on time."

Seika didn't want to argue, not with her sister. Already the day didn't feel quite as sunny as it had a few minutes ago. But she didn't want Ji-Lin to run off on her own, waving her sword. "The Emperor's Journey is more important than a single koji. If the bargain isn't renewed, the barrier will fall. The islands will be exposed to the world!" She'd read *One Hundred Tales of the Hundred Islands* at least a dozen times, and she'd even studied the *Collected Works of the Winged Masters*, which had been written by lion claw dipped in ink and were very hard to read, and everything agreed with that. The Journey had to be undertaken every generation. Now it was their turn. And even if she didn't feel ready, obviously everyone else — Father, her tutors, the winged-lion masters — must have agreed that they were ready, or they wouldn't be here. "Weren't you listening to the Tale of the Three Brothers? Father stopped a disaster by performing the ritual. Following tradition is important! We have to complete the Journey and bargain with the dragon, the same way our ancestors did, for the sake of all those people out there." Taking a breath, she tried to change the subject. "I have always wondered why Uncle Biy decided to confront the dragon. What was the point? He had to know nothing would bring back his beloved."

Ji-Lin scowled out the window, as if she took sunrise as a personal insult. "Father must have been so furious. He was supposed to be a warrior, like me, not the emperor. And Uncle Balez was supposed to be a scholar. Can you imagine your whole life being changed by someone else's bad choices?"

"Can you imagine making such bad choices that you cause deaths?" Thinking about it, Seika felt as if someone were squeezing her stomach. Her cheerful mood had dissolved like sugar in the rain. She sank down on the foot of the bed. The Tale of the Three Brothers was a stark reminder that talking with the dragon could have serious consequences.

"What happened with Uncle Biy and the dragon has nothing to do with us," Ji-Lin said. "We're trying to complete a ritual. Uncle Biy was seeking revenge or something."

"But what if I make a mistake?"

"You'll do fine," Ji-Lin said.

"You don't know that."

"I know *you*. You always do everything right." Kneeling

next to their packs, Ji-Lin began shoving everything in, wrinkling the clothes. Seika debated pointing it out but decided not to. Ji-Lin was not a morning person.

"I try," Seika said.

"So do I."

Seika didn't know why Ji-Lin was suddenly so angry, though she had a guess, and that guess was out there eating sheep. She wished she could make Ji-Lin understand. "The ritual matters. Doing things right matters. And I don't want you to get hurt."

"I'm a warrior! I'm ready to fight! I can defeat a koji. I'm *supposed* to!"

"You're supposed to protect *me!*"

At that, Ji-Lin deflated as if she were a balloon that Seika had poked with a pin. She sat down hard on the bed next to Seika.

"Father should have warned us the Journey was coming so soon," Seika said. He'd told the acrobats and the dancers and the cooks, but not his daughters. If she'd known, she would have studied more. Practiced more. Asked more questions. Worried more. "Maybe he didn't want to scare us."

"I'm not scared," Ji-Lin said. "We can do this."

She sounded so certain. Seika wished she felt like that. "Do you remember when I wanted to pet a flying monkey, and you said you could catch one for me?"

Ji-Lin squeezed her eyes shut. "Oh yes."

"The monkey destroyed an entire banquet."

"We were four."

"It ate the grapes, tore apart the turkey, and threw bread rolls at Father." One had hit Father directly on the crown. There had been a silence, the most horrible silence Seika had ever heard, and then their father made a sound like a little snort — and then he'd laughed. Everyone joined in the laughter until it shook the stone walls, and Seika remembered blushing so hard that she'd thought her cheeks were going to melt off.

"He laughed."

"And we weren't allowed at any banquets for six months, until we learned to 'act our age,'" Seika said, quoting their tutor.

"We were *four*," Ji-Lin repeated. "We're a lot more experienced now."

Seika raised her eyebrows. "I've never been out of the palace. You haven't been beyond the imperial island."

"But I've trained! I'm ready. I can protect you."

Facing her, Seika seized her sister's hands. "Then please don't fly off and fight a monster! You can't protect me if you're dead!"

Ji-Lin opened her mouth, shut it, opened it, and shut it again. She wormed her hands out of Seika's. "You're right. Protecting you *is* most important. We'll continue the Journey and complete the ritual. I won't try to hunt the koji."

Seika sighed in relief. "Good."

They went downstairs, and the caller was waiting for them, along with Alejan (who had slept outside — he preferred to see the stars; they reminded him of his favorite stories, he said) and what looked to be half the town, and Seika wanted to run back upstairs, crawl under the covers, and try again tomorrow. She made herself smile sunnily at them. The crowd cheered.

The caller bowed. "Your Highnesses, we have prepared the traditional sendoff for you. If you would care to follow me . . ."

"Have you sent the messenger bird?" Ji-Lin asked.

"Do not concern yourself —"

"If you've sent it, I won't worry."

"Yes, Your Highness, we have sent it, though there were no sheep deaths last night. Our hope is that the koji, or whatever it was, has moved on. But the temple will send lions and riders to be sure. We thank you for your concern." The caller seemed sincere, and that was enough for Seika. She hoped Ji-Lin would let the matter drop.

Seika hadn't paid much attention to the town itself last night — she'd been too tired from the flight and too overwhelmed by the crowd — but she looked around as the caller led them through it now. All the houses were painted either white or blue and were built to lean against one another. Cracks split the plaster, a sign of recent tremors. Some of the cracks gaped large, like wounds. Others spread over the face of the houses, looking like veins. All the houses looked old, worn, but lived in. Like a soft, frayed blanket, the kind you wanted to stay wrapped up in all day.

Cats curled on windowsills and on roofs. A few of the cats had wings—she'd never seen so many. Some lived in the palace courtyards, stealing food from the kitchens, but winged housecats weren't allowed inside the palace. They caused too much trouble. She liked seeing them here —it felt like they belonged, and it looked like they were wanted.

The smell of roasted fish and hot pastries drifted out the windows and mixed with the tangy stench of old fish and rotten eggs. She hadn't thought about how different a place could smell. The palace smelled of jasmine and baked desserts. But this . . . She inhaled. It tasted different, and that was wonderful.

Pushing the morning's argument out of her mind, she concentrated on enjoying every second of this.

"Please forgive us," the caller said, "but we only had last night to practice the proper steps . . ." She clapped her hands, and a group of fishermen and fisherwomen hurried into the center of the street. A drum sounded, measuring out the beats, and the men and women began to dance across the cobblestones.

Seika knew what the dance was supposed to be: an expression of the villagers' shared hopes and wishes for a safe journey. It was supposed to show the unity of the people, supporting the princesses and wishing them well.

But there wasn't any unity in this dance. *They didn't have much time to practice,* she reminded herself. *They were caught by surprise.* Their faces were twisted in concentration, and all were staring at their feet. A few of them tripped over stray seashells. More villagers assembled in a line and began to dance, kicking their feet and linking their arms. Some used the wrong feet and kicked their neighbors by mistake.

Just because the villagers were dancing badly, though, didn't mean the ritual didn't count. Seika could tell how much this mattered to them. She could read it in their eyes and in their body language: they wanted the princesses to be happy, to like them, to want to protect them.

Seika winced as a fisherman thudded hard onto one knee and let out a word not usually said near princesses. The other dancers shushed him, and he marshaled on.

And Ji-Lin let out a snort.

Shooting her a look, Seika saw that Ji-Lin had clapped her hands over her mouth. She was trying not to laugh. Seeing her, one of the children — the boy who had first mentioned the monster — began to giggle.

It spread. First the children were laughing. And then the villagers. And Seika found a smile pulling at her lips. One of the dancers spun in front of her and held out a hand. Seika wasn't sure if she was supposed to take it — she didn't know the steps — but the dancer smiled right at her. Stepping forward, Seika joined the dance. Clasping hands with the villager, she kicked and spun.

As she passed Ji-Lin, Seika reached out and pulled her into the circle. And then they were all dancing together, skipping and swirling and laughing. Even Alejan danced with them, letting the littlest kids ride on him.

When the music ended, everyone clapped and cheered. Cheeks flushed, lips smiling, the villagers all looked at the princesses.

"We won't fail you!" Seika said in her loudest voice.

From the relief that shone in their eyes, this was the right thing to say.

Leaving after that was easy. The villagers thanked them, and all they had to do was wave and smile. Ji-Lin accepted gifts: food for the day's journey, fresh water, and ribbons to tie to Alejan's saddle. She loaded the packs onto Alejan, and Seika and Ji-Lin mounted and strapped themselves in.

And then they were flying, over the island and then over the sea.

◦◦◦

The ocean between the islands was pearly blue. Seika leaned to the side to see better, and Alejan curved toward the waves. A pod of dolphins leaped out of the water beside them, and sea foam sprayed into her face. Ahead was another island, its peaks a collection of rocks balanced on top of rocks, all different shades of gray. Within fissures between the rocks, brilliant yellow flowers grew in clusters, so that the precariously perched gray boulders looked painted with spots of sun. She'd seen paintings, but this . . . this was incredible!

Closer to the island, Seika saw figures standing on the rocks a hundred feet above the ocean. One man and two women, wearing thin white bands of cloth as their only clothes, stretched their arms over their heads, bent their knees, and then in unison leaped from the rocks. They dove down the side of the cliff, arms stretched straight.

"They're falling!" Seika cried.

"They're diving," Alejan corrected. "Ooh, ooh, this is the best part! Watch!"

Bodies straight as arrows, the three plunged into the blue water. Waves closed behind them. Alejan circled lower, and Seika and Ji-Lin watched the water, waiting for the divers to emerge, watching and waiting . . . and then one burst to the surface, followed by another, then another. One of the women punched a fist in the air, spraying water around her.

Amazing! Seika thought.

"Pearl divers," Alejan said. "They use the momentum from the fall to propel them to the bottom of the sea. Also, they think it's fun."

"They're crazy," Ji-Lin said, admiration clear in her voice.

"So says the girl who chooses to fly on the back of a large, majestic feline," Alejan said, pumping his wings for emphasis. "Admit it: you'd jump if your sister weren't here."

Ji-Lin didn't answer.

Seika pictured the gowns she had, embroidered with hundreds of pearls. She'd never thought much about the people who gathered them. "Each pearl is a laugh at danger." It was crazy, but also magnificent. Such fearlessness!

"Yes," Alejan said. "That's a poetic way to say it. You know, some of our finest emperors and empresses were poets. And Prince Balez, who rides Master Shai, has written several poems that I've memorized—"

"Please don't recite them," Ji-Lin interrupted. "He's our uncle, remember? We've heard his poetry. He recited some at a Winter Ritual once. We were six, I think. I fell asleep."

"It was beautiful!" Seika said. She'd read a lot of his poetry. Mostly he wrote about what had been lost and forgotten when their ancestors had fled from Zemyla. She thought of the story from Tsuri and how he'd wanted to be a scholar.

"I remember you read him your first poem."

Seika squinched up her face, remembering. It had been about a rock. A very nice rock. "*That* was not beautiful." She looked again at the cliffs beneath them. "Would you really jump if I weren't here?" Below, the pearl divers began climbing back up a path that was barely more than notches cut into the rock. The climb up looked nearly as treacherous as the plunge down. *Amazing,* she thought.

"I laugh at danger."

"Ooh, ooh, the poets should say that when they write

about you!" Alejan said. "And they'll say that I fearlessly roar in the face of danger!" He swelled his lungs as if he were about to let out a mighty roar.

"Don't!" Seika said quickly. "You'll startle the divers."

He exhaled a huff of air.

"You wouldn't dive?" Ji-Lin asked. "Just to see what it's like?"

Seika twisted around to see the divers again — from this distance, they looked like ants clambering up the rocks. She wished she dared do that. "I don't think the heir is supposed to dive off cliffs."

"So? And what if she were? Would you do it then? If it were a tradition? On her twelfth birthday, every princess is supposed to climb hundreds of feet into the air and plummet into the sea."

"It's not a tradition." *Instead, I just have to talk to a dragon.* Seika shuddered. She wished she felt as fearless as the divers. She wondered how they felt the first time they dove off that cliff. Were they scared or eager? Or both? Did they feel ready?

"Hey, it's okay," Ji-Lin said. She'd clearly felt Seika's shudder. "You don't have to do any plummeting into the sea. Sorry I asked. I was just joking."

It's not that, Seika thought. But she didn't want to talk about how she didn't feel ready to face the dragon. "I'm okay."

Flying on, they saw shrines on the tops of the towering rocks. Shepherds led flocks up and down narrow paths to plateaus covered in grass and flowers. The shepherds' houses were tucked into the cliffs themselves, carved into the rocks, with ladders that led to their doors. They were painted the same white and blue as the fishing village.

"I hope sending the bird was enough," Ji-Lin said after a while.

"The lions and riders will help them." Seika wondered if she should apologize for keeping Ji-Lin from hunting the monster. She didn't believe she was wrong, and her etiquette tutor, Master Pon, liked to warn against royal apologies: *Princesses take responsibility, not blame.* Still, Ji-Lin didn't seem happy.

"You'd better be right."

"For all we know, it might not have been a koji after all. The caller said it could have been a wolf with a taste for sheep. Or a hungry bear." She wasn't certain bears ate sheep. "If they'd been sure it was a dangerous koji, they would have fled to their koji shelter."

"Maybe." Ji-Lin didn't sound like she believed her.

"And besides, they said it left. No sheep deaths last night."

The lion spoke. "A koji shouldn't be there at all. It should be on the other side of the barrier." Alejan angled away from the island. "Look toward the south. You can see the shimmer of the barrier against the sky. Isn't it pretty? You know, Master Shai once flew the entire perimeter of the barrier without stopping for more than a few hours' sleep."

"I love that story," Ji-Lin said.

Seika studied the southern sky. She didn't see — Yes, she did! There it was! It looked like heat rising off stone in summer. The air wrinkled, and the solid line of the horizon wavered as she stared. Colors were caught in it, faint, like fish in a net. "It's beautiful." You couldn't see that from the palace.

"It's a promise," Alejan said, "to keep us safe from the world beyond. That's what Master Vanya always says."

"Ever wonder what's out there? Beyond, I mean?" Ji-Lin asked.

Seika hadn't, really. She'd spent hours imagining the world beyond the palace walls and beyond the mountains that cradled the imperial city. She'd dreamed of someday seeing all the islands. But the world beyond the islands . . . that seemed impossibly far.

"I bet they have amazing feasts," Alejan said. "The old stories are full of roast gazelle and antelope and great horned *augi* bulls . . . Supposedly they had multicolored spiral horns and tasted peppery. We never had those on the islands. And they made something called honey dragonberry bread that no one here knows how to make, even if we had any dragonberries. But the koji probably eat all their feasts and wreck all their celebrations."

They're probably scared all the time without a barrier to protect them, Seika thought. "We can't let our people live in fear. We have to complete the Journey."

"We will," Ji-Lin said. "Four more days, and that's counting today."

They flew parallel to the barrier for a while longer, over more islands, until the sun was low in the sky. Beneath them, on the island of Acara, shadows stretched, and the rocks were tinted burnt orange in the dying light. As they glided between the rock formations, Seika hoped they'd see the next village soon — Gyoson, she remembered it was called, on the island of Okina.

The Emperor's Journey was designed with clear stops for each night. Alejan knew the direction and the pace to fly. Seika's only job was to be a passenger. Still, she couldn't help worrying. If they missed the village, what would they do? Off the imperial island, villages were spread apart. Many islands were uninhabited.

"Gyoson is up ahead," Alejan said, "and it is strangely dark."

Seika felt Ji-Lin lean forward. The next island, Okina, was a cluster of low mountains. The village of Gyoson was nestled at the foot of one, beside a harbor. "Where are the lights?" Ji-Lin asked. "The fires? Someone should be cooking something. We should see smoke from the chimneys."

They should have seen lights from the houses and the streets. It was only dusk, but the villagers should have begun to light the lanterns. There were sunset rituals that Seika knew of, but those should have already happened ... "We can ask them when we arrive." If she was lucky, maybe this time there wouldn't be such a crowd. She didn't think she could face another mass of people, all of them looking at her expectantly, as if she were a figure out of a tale instead of a person. Not after flying all day.

They circled the village.

No one came out of the houses. No one waved. No one shouted and pointed. She didn't see any children. "There's no one here," Alejan said. "They're all gone."

"That can't be," Seika objected.

But as they flew lower, she realized he was right.

The town was empty.

CHAPTER
SEVEN

I
N THE ABANDONED town, Ji-Lin held still, listening for voices, footfalls, anything. But all she heard was the dull ring of the buoy bells and the wind as it rattled down the street.

Beside her, Seika raised her voice. "Hello? Is anyone —"

"Shh!" Quickly, Ji-Lin clapped her hand over her sister's mouth.

But she wasn't quick enough.

Ahead, in the gloom of the darkened street, a shadow shifted, waking.

Ji-Lin heard the heavy whoosh of wings as the shadow lifted into the air. A deeper darkness spread across the street — something with a wingspan as wide as a building flew overhead. It was enormous. Beyond enormous. "Hide," she whispered. She motioned to Alejan to retreat. He backed into an alley and huddled between barrels. Ji-Lin pulled her sister under an awning. They crouched, barely daring to breathe, but the huge winged creature flapped upward.

"There's something out there," Seika whispered.

"Yeah, I noticed." Ji-Lin peered through rips in the awning. The sky was dusty gray. Soon it would be dark. Her heart was beating so fast that it felt as if it wanted to jump out of her rib cage. "I guess that's the reason everyone left town. We were lucky it was asleep when we arrived."

Crouching in the shadows, Seika curled into a ball. "I shouldn't have shouted."

Ji-Lin's mouth was dry as sand, and her hands felt slick and sweaty. She wiped them, hoping Seika wouldn't notice. Ji-Lin was supposed to be the imperial warrior, the guardian of the heir, a future hero of the empire. But that thing had scared these villagers so badly that they'd all fled. A hundred or more people, up and gone.

"We can't stay here," Seika said in a tiny voice. "It'll come back."

"Then I'll fight it," Ji-Lin said immediately. Except that it had looked so very large. When she'd imagined fighting the koji back in Tsuri, she'd pictured a monster about the size of Alejan — something big enough to eat a few sheep but not big enough to eat a whole flock in one bite.

"You can't fight *that!* It's huge!"

Maybe it was a *bit* too large for just her and Alejan to fight. It was okay to admit that, wasn't it? "We could do it," Ji-Lin said carefully. "But it might be smarter to leave before it comes back." *I'm not being cowardly,* she told herself. *I'm being practical.* Keeping Seika safe was her primary responsibility, as she'd said that morning.

She wished she knew where the villagers of Gyoson had hidden themselves. There had to be a koji shelter nearby, but where? Entrances were always out of sight, for obvious reasons. If there were just someone here to tell them where to go, to tell her what to do . . . But there was no one. Even Alejan wasn't close enough to talk to. He was hidden in the alley.

She hadn't expected to feel this way when she encountered her first monster. She'd thought she was ready. It was a shock to realize that maybe she wasn't as ready as she'd believed. *If it weren't so big . . .*

Ji-Lin heard the whoosh again. Much closer. A shadow passed over the street, and she shrank back farther into the darkness. She held herself still, not breathing. She heard Seika next to her, her breath fast.

Then the shadow was gone.

"I'm sorry," Seika whispered.

Ji-Lin shot her a look and saw she was hugging herself tightly, staring up at the slivers of sky between rips in the awning. Her hair had slipped from the jeweled pins.

"This is my fault. I woke it."

"It'll be all right," Ji-Lin told her. "I've trained for this." *But training isn't the same as doing,* she thought. She wished Master Vanya were here. Or anyone.

"What do we do?" Seika asked.

Ji-Lin felt a flush of pride — her sister was asking her what to do! *She believes in me.* Chewing on her lower lip, Ji-Lin thought through their options. It was clear they couldn't stay here, and it was equally clear they couldn't fly away without being seen. It was sheer luck they'd made it this far safely. "We'll go on foot. Stay in the shadows and then find a place outside town to hide for the night." She tried to sound confident.

"Outside?" Seika's voice quavered.

"Maybe we'll find the villagers' koji shelter and spend the night with them."

Seika swallowed so hard that Ji-Lin thought it would echo. "That would be good."

"Follow me." Ji-Lin signaled to Alejan as well, and then she crept out from under the awning, keeping close to the sides of the buildings. Left, right, straight . . . Every footstep sounded extra loud. She listened for the sound of the wings. Around them, the houses were all dark and silent.

Her skin prickled. It wasn't natural. A town was supposed to have noise: Kids playing. Adults talking or cooking or cleaning or working. Dogs barking. She'd even have settled for a rat, but there was no noise except the wind. Finally, they passed the last house on the street. It was half collapsed, its roof caved in like an undercooked cake. She couldn't tell if it was due to damage from a tremor or from the winged intruder.

Ahead was a moonlit mountain. Keeping in the lead, Ji-Lin climbed a narrow, rocky path that zigzagged up, away from Gyoson. She watched for clues to the koji shelter — it would be well hidden, and it could just as easily be in the opposite direction.

"Maybe we should have hidden in the town?" Seika

whispered, looking down at the village. Ji-Lin glanced back too. Below, the dark town was quiet, nestled against the blue-black water of the harbor. The boats bobbed in the waves.

"Whatever's out there is in the town."

"It's just . . . I've never spent the night outside before."

"We'll find a place that's out of sight." Ji-Lin scanned the area around them. They were on a rocky slope, punctuated by scrub brush and gnarled trees. *Entirely too much in the open,* she thought. If the whatever-was-out-there lost interest in the town, it would see them in the moonlight. Maybe Seika was right and this wasn't the best idea.

Softly, Alejan whispered, "Look there. Refuge. When Emperor Himitsu himself first came to the islands, it is said that he hid in caves until the first fortress was built, on the volcano island. We're going to that very same fortress. So hiding is almost traditional."

Looking up, Ji-Lin saw an outcropping with a broad shadow beneath it—a possible cave. Perfect! They could wait in there until sunrise and then—

Beside her, Seika's skirt caught a bush, and she pitched forward. Leaping toward her, Ji-Lin caught her just as Seika grabbed Ji-Lin's arm.

"Thanks," Seika said.

"Are you all right?" Ji-Lin noticed that Seika was wearing dancing slippers, and her so-called travel dress was silk. Not practical sneaking-around-a-mountain clothes. Ji-Lin helped her straighten. *She belongs in a palace, not out here,* Ji-Lin thought. And a treacherous little part of her mind added, *You don't belong out here either.*

Testing her ankle, Seika said, "I'm fine."

Ji-Lin exhaled. "Good." Last thing they needed was a twisted ankle. Actually, the last thing they needed was to be found by that winged thing. An ankle could heal. She led Seika to the shadow, helping her over the rocks. Sword drawn, she peered beneath the outcropping. The wedge of darkness was almost as high as she was tall.

"Any bugs?" Seika asked.

Seriously? *That* was her concern? "You should be worried about whatever that giant flying thing was that scared away the villagers."

"Okay, any monsters?"

"I don't see any." Bending over, Ji-Lin walked into the shadows. As her eyes adjusted, she saw they were in a hollow-shaped curve of rocks that could have been a den for a bear or a large cat, but there was no trace of any animal now. "Nothing will be able to see us here." They'd be nicely tucked out of sight. "Good find, Alejan."

"Everyone should always travel with a very observant lion."

"You are very observant. And brave."

"Even though we're hiding?" He sounded anxious.

"Yes," Ji-Lin said firmly — and she hoped she was right. She'd never imagined hiding from anything, but there was Seika to keep safe . . . *I'm hiding for her sake, right?*

Entering the alcove, Seika sank to the ground. Alejan squeezed in beside her, filling the tiny cave with the musky smell of lion fur and the old-fish smell of his breath. Ji-Lin heard his stomach rumble as he settled in, trying to neatly fold his wings so they wouldn't bump either Seika or Ji-Lin. "Hungry?" she asked him.

His eyes seemed to glow in the shadows. The rest of him was shrouded in darkness. "Is that a trick question?"

"I know, I know. You're a growing lion." She dug into the packs. They'd eaten while they flew — the last village had given them meat rolls — but there must be at least one left . . . *Aha!* She pulled it out. It had become a bit mashed in the packs. Splitting it into thirds, she gave a piece to each of them.

Alejan inhaled his in a single swallow.

Seika bit in, and the juice dribbled onto her chin. She wiped it away and regarded her hand as if she wasn't sure what to do with it.

"Lick it off. I didn't pack napkins," Ji-Lin said.

Seika hesitated again and then licked her palm quickly, as if she was afraid a court lady would see her.

Ji-Lin laughed and then muffled her laugh into a snorting kind of giggle. "Do you think the bugs are going to criticize your manners?"

Seika swallowed a giggle too. "I'm sure bugs are very polite."

And just like that, hearing the laugh in her sister's voice,

Ji-Lin felt better. It was okay that they were hiding from a monster, because she was with her sister and Alejan. Tomorrow, she'd figure out what to do next, and everything would be fine.

They finished the meat roll and drank from the canteen. Ji-Lin gave Alejan most of it, pouring it into his mouth directly. She left a little for morning. "You two sleep," she said. "I'll stand guard."

"You're certain?" Alejan asked. "As your steadfast and true companion —"

"I can do it."

"You must be tired too," Seika said.

"I'll sleep tomorrow as we fly. I've done it before." She'd dozed occasionally while flying and had nearly fallen off Alejan, but she didn't mention that part. She would just strap herself firmly into the saddle.

Seika seemed to believe her, though, which was good enough.

Ji-Lin rooted through the pack. They should have emergency supplies, like blankets and bandages, even a tent, but in the dark, she could only find a woven jacket. "This could work as a blanket." She handed it to her sister. Seika wrapped it around herself and curled up against the pack as if it were a pillow. "You've never slept on the ground before?" Ji-Lin asked.

"I fell out of bed a few times, after you first left. That's not the same, though."

Ji-Lin had spent many nights out in the courtyard of the temple. Sometimes training exercises lasted for several days. Her bed in the temple wasn't much more comfortable anyway, just a canvas cot with a thin sheet. Students were expected to live without luxury. *Unlike Seika*, Ji-Lin thought. Seika got to live in the palace with its plush beds and endless banquets and beautiful gowns . . . *Go on, admit you're jealous.* But she wasn't going to say it out loud. "I didn't sleep well in the temple in the beginning," Ji-Lin admitted instead. "Got used to it, though." She'd cried a lot those first days, into her thin pillow, until she met Alejan.

"The servants began to put pillows on the floor on either side of the bed so I'd land on something soft if I rolled out," Seika said. "One time I woke to a full palace alarm. I'd fallen off the bed, then rolled off the pillows and underneath the bed. The guards couldn't find me and thought I'd been kidnapped. Father lectured me on the importance of not terrifying everyone in the palace. After that, I tied bells around my ankles so I'd wake up if I even shifted in my sleep. It worked. I learned to sleep still. Or at least, I learned how to sleep through bells."

Ji-Lin grinned, picturing Seika in her canopied bed amid all the lace blankets and many pillows, with bells around her ankles. The court ladies must have gossiped about that.

Softly, so softly that the words seemed swallowed by the darkness, Seika said, "I missed you so much." Or maybe Ji-Lin only imagined it. She could have formed the words out of the wind, or just heard them in her own head because they expressed how she herself felt.

She wanted to say it back, but she didn't want to look weak and mushy in front of Seika, when she was supposed to be her guard, strong and brave. Besides, Seika must know that Ji-Lin missed her. Of course Ji-Lin missed her sister. She was her *sister*. It went without saying, didn't it? Or maybe she should say it . . .

Before Ji-Lin could decide, the moment had passed. Seika was breathing evenly, slower than before. She'd drifted to sleep. *I'll say it tomorrow*, Ji-Lin thought. Silently, she placed her sword across her lap and stared out into the night, watching for monsters.

CHAPTER
EIGHT

SEIKA WOKE AND wished she hadn't. "Ow, ow, ow." She shifted, trying to wake muscles that had decided to knot during the night, and she bumped into a rock. Cracking her eyes open, she looked around the alcove.

In daylight, she saw they were in a shallow cave beneath an overhang of rocks, exactly as it had seemed in the night, which was a relief. She'd fallen asleep imagining bugs were crawling all over her and monsters were chewing on her feet, but that hadn't happened. The floor was ordinary, not-very-bug-infested dirt, and there was a circle of bushes around part of the opening, shielding the sisters and the lion from sight. Ji-Lin sat next to the opening, her sword on her lap, as if she hadn't moved in hours. Her eyes were fixed on the fishing village below them.

"Still deserted?" Seika asked.

"Except for the monster."

Seika felt as if she'd been dunked in the sea. She was suddenly *very* awake. Crawling, she joined Ji-Lin by the entrance. Wordlessly, Ji-Lin pointed. Seika followed her finger — and saw the koji.

The stories talked about many different kinds of koji. This one looked like a snake, except it was the size of a house and had five sets of wings on its sinewy back. Its scales were a brilliant fiery red with black zigzags across them. Seika felt sick. It was real. It was here. It was enormous. "Ji-Lin . . ."

"It's a *weneb.*" Ji-Lin's voice was clinical, and her eyes stayed fixed on the winged snake.

Seika latched on to the name — yes, a weneb. She'd read about them. "They grow to a hundred feet long. The females are larger than the males, and they will fly hundreds of miles until they find a place to lay their eggs. They'll create a nest by . . ." Seika looked more closely at the way it was curled between the buildings. "Ji-Lin, I think it's *nesting* here, in the village."

This could have been the same koji that had scared the people in the last village, except it had only been passing through there. Here, it had decided to stay, forcing an entire village to flee.

"I wonder if it ate the messenger bird," Ji-Lin mused, "the one that was supposed to tell the villagers in Tsuri we were coming."

Seika heard a soft sound behind her and jumped, but it was only Alejan padding toward them. He had to hunch down to fit next to them. "The bird could have been an appetizer before the sheep," he suggested.

A bite-size appetizer, she thought. The weneb's fangs were tucked into its mouth, but given the size of its head . . . it could have easily devoured the bird. "What do we do?" Seika asked.

"Option one: we fight it," Ji-Lin said.

What? No! Seika opened her mouth to object. They'd spent last night fleeing it —

Ji-Lin held up a hand, stopping her. "Option two: we take you back home to Shirro, to safety, and then come back with more lions and riders and *then* fight it."

Alejan stuck his large head between them to look out at the sleeping koji. "I like option two," he said. "I do *not* like snakes."

"I can't go back!" Seika cried. "We have to complete the Journey!" She thought of how the villagers had scrambled to perform for them, how eager and excited they'd been. *What we're doing matters to people,* she thought. *To our people. It's important!*

"A koji can't be allowed to nest here. If I can bring more lions and riders —"

"If we don't finish the Journey and the barrier falls, every village could have a weneb nesting in it." Seika took a deep breath. "There's a third choice: we sneak past it and go on."

"Past *that?*"

"It's asleep."

Ji-Lin frowned, and Seika could tell she was thinking about it. "What about the people of Gyoson? We can't just leave them homeless."

"They'll have help soon," Seika said. "The caller of Tsuri sent a message to the temple." She hoped the weneb hadn't eaten that messenger bird too — but it had moved on already, hadn't it? The villagers had said no sheep had been eaten last night.

Ji-Lin shook her head. "Even assuming the message got through, the lions and riders won't know the koji is here. They'll be looking in Tsuri."

"Then we send another message, from the next village. Let the temple know where the koji is. If it's truly nesting, then it won't go anywhere until after it's laid its eggs." She'd read enough about wenebs to know that. They'd nest, lay their eggs, and then fly away. Later, their eggs would hatch into baby wenebs, who would eat anyone who hadn't already fled. "Can't you see? This weneb is exactly why we *have* to complete the Journey!"

"It's not safe to continue with a koji out there. My responsibility is to keep you safe."

"We'll be just as safe flying on as we would be flying back," Seika argued.

"I can't guarantee our safety in the air in either direction this close to the village," Alejan said. "It could wake and see us. Of course, we could fight it in a heroic manner —"

"Yes, we could!" Ji-Lin chimed in.

"— and naturally, if there was someone in need of rescue, I would be the first to say we should attack, even though I hate snakes and it's a very large one and probably venomous . . . but given that no one is in danger, we cannot risk Princess Seika's safety. I recommend we cross the mountain on foot and then once we are out of sight, fly."

In a worried voice, Alejan added, "That would make a good story, wouldn't it? The sneaky escape?"

"I like that plan," Seika said.

Ji-Lin was scowling. "Fine. We sneak away on foot, fly to the next village, and then send another messenger bird." She spat out the words as if she didn't like the taste of them.

"The first sign of valor is knowing when to bravely run away," Alejan said.

"It's not running away," Seika said. "It's running *toward*."

Ji-Lin snorted. "Toward what?"

"Um . . . toward new adventures?" She wasn't sure if that was exactly right. "Toward our destiny!" Yes, that was better.

"Ooh, do you think someone will make a song out of our adventures?" Alejan asked.

"Not if no one lets me fight anything," Ji-Lin grumbled.

Seika wanted to shake her. Couldn't she see how unnecessarily dangerous it was? Look at the monster's teeth! Its claws! "I just don't want it to be a tragic song. Dead princesses might make for romantic tales, but you're my sister!"

Ji-Lin sighed loudly.

Below in the village, the weneb shifted in its sleep, knocking over a market stall. Seika's heart beat fast. She couldn't imagine fighting that thing, or watching Ji-Lin fight it. "Ji-Lin, as heir, I forbid it."

The order lingered in the air, and Seika thought about taking it back. She'd never spoken to her sister that way. But she meant it.

Without a word, Ji-Lin crept out of the cave.

Seika hurried after her, crawling through the bushes that encircled the cave toward the top of the rocks. She caught a glimpse of Ji-Lin's expression: pressed lips, flared nostrils, crinkled forehead . . . clearly angry. Seika felt a jab of guilt—she hadn't meant to make Ji-Lin unhappy. They used to agree about everything, right down to liking orange soup but not liking orange cake. *I'll make it up to her,* she promised. *Somehow.*

Ji-Lin pointed up the mountain, toward the trees. "Hurry. We're too visible."

Emerging from the bushes, Seika blinked in the dawn light and was shocked to see that it was a beautiful day. Surely a day with a monster in it should be dark and broody. But birds were chirping all around them. She saw songbirds swoop from branch to branch. So many birds! She hadn't imagined that waking up outside would be like waking up in the middle of an orchestra. Early-morning sun poured across the harbor, causing the water to glisten as if it were covered in crystals. Several boats rocked gently in the waves, waiting for sailors who weren't coming. A buoy tolled somewhere in the distance. And the monster slept fitfully.

Climbing higher, Seika felt every rock through the soles of her soft slippers. Brambles stuck to her skirt. Her mouth felt gummy, and her hair was matted against her head. She needed a hairbrush, soap, water, towels, and a spray of fig-blossom perfume. If the court ladies could see her now, they'd be appalled. But she didn't care.

It was enough that they were escaping.

It was enough that Ji-Lin had listened and wasn't foolishly fighting that monster.

It was enough that—

She saw the waterfall. Gasping, she stopped, transfixed.

"Seika?" Ji-Lin asked. "Are you okay?"

"It's beautiful," Seika breathed. The word didn't seem to go far enough. The waterfall was more beautiful than any art she'd seen in the palace. It tumbled from a gap in the rocks above them, cascading over mossy stones and between trees with paperlike pink flowers. Swimming through the falling water were little creatures—they looked like tiny children, no larger than her hand, with fins instead of arms. They were leaping into the water and swimming through it in figure eights. Sunlight gleamed on their wet, silvery scales, and Seika heard the sound of their laughter, mixed with the bubbling water. *Mer-minnows,* Seika thought. Kin to the waterfolk. Seika had read about them but never seen them. They only lived in the wild, away from cities and towns.

Seika, Ji-Lin, and Alejan climbed beside the waterfall, up into a forest. Looking back, Seika could barely see the village through the trees, which was good, because it meant the weneb wouldn't be able to see them.

She hoped the villagers were well hidden in their koji shelter.

As they climbed higher, her stomach rumbled. She wasn't used to skipping breakfast. Usually, when she woke, one of the girls or boys from the kitchen was only a bell ring away, to deliver toast or a bowl of sliced kimi fruit or even a few sweetened bananas, fried lightly with a drizzle of sauce. Yum. Her innards rumbled again as she thought about food.

Worth it to see mer-minnows, she reminded herself.

Ji-Lin didn't stop and didn't even slow. She kept trudging upward. Alejan loped behind her, occasionally looking over his shoulder at where the village was nestled against the sea. "It's moved," he reported.

"Where?" Ji-Lin asked.

"Still in the village, but it's awake. It's knocking down buildings, I think." They heard a faraway creak, and then a crash. "Yes, definitely knocking down buildings."

Making its nest, Seika thought. She hoped the warriors from the temple would come before the village was flattened.

"We should have fought it," Ji-Lin said.

Seika suppressed a sigh. *Not this again.* "I don't know how to fight." She knew how to dance the elaborate patterns of the masquerade, how to dissect a poem into its metaphors, how to eat a kimi (always with a spoon), and how to paint her face so she looked like a character from an old tale. But she'd never fought so much as a mouse.

"*I* should have fought it."

"It could have eaten you. And then come after me."

"I'm fast, especially on Alejan." But Ji-Lin didn't meet her sister's eyes.

"One time, I had an etiquette lesson, and I had to bow for three hours straight until I had it perfect. I was dizzy by the end of it, after bobbing up and down so many times. So if you want me to bow, I can do that. But I can't fight a giant snake monster."

"You bowed for three hours?"

"There are thirty-six different kinds of bows, each appropriate to a different ritual. Some depend on the time of day. Some depend on location. If you're in the throne room, it looks like this." Stopping, she executed a flawless bow, one that befit an emperor. "If you're greeting someone in a kitchen, a shorter bow is more appropriate. You need to be aware of the amount of space around you. One time, I was tired, and I did an imperial bow to the laundry. The seamstress was laughing so hard that she nearly sewed a sleeve shut!" Ji-Lin didn't laugh. She just looked at Seika as if expecting her to add more. "Well, it was funny at the time. She was the head seamstress. Sewing a sleeve shut . . . Never mind."

"I need breakfast," Alejan announced.

"Once we're safely out of sight, we'll see if we have anything left. Come on. It's not much farther," Ji-Lin coaxed. "Just over the ridge." They continued, climbing higher. The air seemed crisper up here. It smelled more like pine and less like sea.

"My point is: I was given different lessons than you were," Seika said, climbing alongside her. "I'm not strong like you are."

"You're strong enough to climb a mountain," Ji-Lin pointed out.

True, Seika thought. She hadn't known she was strong enough to hike this far or climb this high. She continued in silence — or not in silence. The world around them was singing and chirping and buzzing and rustling.

The bird songs were different up here. She heard them echo their melodies back and forth. A few were low calls that sounded like the bellow of a cow. A song snake was lying on a rock, crooning to itself up and down an octave. Climbing out of the trees, they reached the ridge . . . and saw the unicorn.

The unicorn was balanced on the ridgeline, very close. It was the size and shape of a mountain goat. Its pelt was thick, feathery fur, whiter than a cloud, and its spiraled horn was black as obsidian. It stood in profile, silhouetted against the blue sky, its long fur flowing in the wind. Its horn looked as if it were piercing the sun.

All three of them froze, staring at it.

The unicorn turned its furry neck and looked at them. Seika saw its nostrils flare once, and then it leaped away and ran along the narrow ridge, higher up the mountain, toward the bare rocks above. Sunlight glistened on its back, and its silver hooves gleamed.

"Wow," Ji-Lin breathed.

That was . . . Seika was breathless. She never thought she'd come so close to a wild unicorn. She'd seen the paintings, heard the tales . . . First mer-minnows, and now a unicorn. *If I'd stayed safe and fed in the palace, I'd never have seen any of this. I'd never have known the islands could be so beautiful. I'd never have known I could walk so far or climb so high.*

"What scared it?" Alejan asked.

"Oh, I don't know," Ji-Lin said. "Maybe the large lion stalking toward it?"

He fluffed his mane, offended. "I was not stalking."

Seika twisted to look back down at the village, mostly hidden by trees. "Do you think it saw the monster?" Ji-Lin and Alejan turned to look with her. Everything was silent and still as far as Seika could tell, but she could only see slices of houses through the forest. A few birds flitted from tree to tree. She heard rustling—but it sounded as if it was coming from above them.

"There's something up there," Ji-Lin said. "Over the ridge. That's what frightened the unicorn—do you hear it?"

"Another monster?" Seika asked, turning around. Ji-Lin was staring at the ridge as if she were a royal hunting dog who'd sensed a rabbit. Listening, Seika didn't hear anything. Not even birds.

Alejan sniffed the air. "People!" He trotted forward.

Seika and Ji-Lin hurried to follow. "Are you sure?" Seika asked. It could be the villagers! Or other islanders who lived nearby. Or bandits and murderers. "Wait, how do we know they're friendly?"

"We know the monster isn't," Ji-Lin said. "Come on. Almost there!"

As they climbed higher, Seika stumbled on the rocks, and Ji-Lin helped her. Seika had to lift her skirts. Her toes felt pounded as she bashed them against the stones. Several loose rocks tumbled down.

"Quickly," Ji-Lin said. "We're too exposed here."

Scrambling, Seika climbed. Her back itched, and she couldn't stop thinking that any second, that koji was going to pluck her off the mountain with its sharp claws . . . But then they reached the top.

On the other side of the ridge, a man and a woman — the people Alejan had smelled — climbed up to them and helped them over the top of the ridge while talking in overlapping whispers. "Your Highnesses, quickly, please, careful, hush, are you hurt? Are you well? We didn't know you had arrived. And to spend the night outside, with a koji near! You are so brave. The Emperor's Journey . . . We received the emperor's messenger bird and were so worried about you." And then they were safely over, hidden from the sight of the weneb.

Panting, Seika ducked. She lay against the rocks and decided she never wanted to move again. Her skin felt filthy, her throat was dry as sand, and her stomach was achingly empty. The two strangers pressed canteens of water into Seika's and Ji-Lin's hands.

Seika drank and drank, and so did Ji-Lin and Alejan. After her throat felt less raw, Seika asked, "Are you from Gyoson? Where are your people?"

"In the koji shelter, underground," the woman said. She was dressed head to toe in brown and green, to blend in with the mountainside. Her hair was pinned back slick against her scalp, and she had a dagger at her waist.

"We came out to scout," the man said, "to see if the weneb has moved on." He had a bow strapped to his back, and his hair was tied in a ponytail. A spyglass hung on a chain from his neck.

"It hasn't," Ji-Lin reported. "Did everyone make it to safety in time?"

"Yes, Your Highness," the man said. "One of the lads spotted the weneb while fishing in the harbor and sounded the alarm. Everyone made it to the caves before the foul beast came to shore."

"Have you sent messenger birds to the temple?" Seika asked.

"Right away. We used the same bird that brought word of your coming. We included a warning to you to steer clear —though I can see you didn't receive it in time," the woman said. "Please accept our apologies that we weren't able to perform the traditional greetings upon your arrival. Your Highnesses greatly honor us with your presence, but you must not linger. The koji is in the village now, but it may fly again soon. This is your best opportunity to flee to safety, before it rises again."

The man dug into his pack and produced several meat rolls. Seika and Ji-Lin devoured one each, while Alejan gobbled three. Ji-Lin tucked the rest into their bags. "Go while you can," the man said. "The farther you can fly, the safer you will be."

"Quickly!" The woman practically shooed them onto Alejan's back.

Ji-Lin climbed on, and Seika strapped herself in behind her. "Thank you," Seika said to the man and woman. "Your kindness will be remembered." She hoped she sounded gracious and regal and that they couldn't hear the fear in her voice.

Crawling back up to the ridge, the man peered through his spyglass at the town.

"I hate leaving with a koji in your home," Ji-Lin said. "We could wait. Stay and fight with the lions and riders when they come . . ." She half unsheathed her sword.

"You're our princesses," the woman said. "You're our hope for the future, for our children and our children's children. If we know you're out there, completing the Journey, we can weather anything."

Alejan stretched his wings.

From the top of the ridge, the man whisper-called, "Go now!"

Leaning forward, Ji-Lin urged, "Fly, Alejan!"

Without another word, Alejan lunged forward, off the mountainside. Seika felt her stomach drop as they plummeted. Skimming the tops of the trees, they flew on, in the shadow of the mountains, away from the village and its monster.

CHAPTER
NINE

As Alejan skimmed the waves, Ji-Lin leaned over his side and dipped her hand into the water. It splashed up her arm; the cold drops felt like tiny bites. The sun flashed on the waves, as if there were a thousand mirrors on the surface of the sea. She saw the reflection of the clouds and the shadow of Alejan's wings, and she grinned.

We did it!

She felt as if they'd done the Unmei Run in record time. She wanted to sing at the top of her lungs, or better still, have someone sing a song about them, about their escape.

I could have fought it, of course, she reassured herself. She'd only run because her sister had asked, and Seika was the heir. It wasn't because the koji was so large. Or snakelike.

"Do you think we're safe now?" Seika called in her ear.

"Yes!" She patted Alejan's neck. "He's the fastest lion of all."

"How did it get past the barrier?" Alejan asked. "It shouldn't have been able to see the islands, much less reach them!"

It couldn't have crossed the barrier. Nothing could cross the barrier. Or even see it — from the outside, the barrier made the islands both invisible and inaccessible. Hidden from all. No, the weneb must have grown in secret on one of the uninhabited islands, only coming out now because it needed to nest ... which meant there had to be a daddy snake-monster somewhere. Suddenly, Ji-Lin felt a bit less excited. "Stay alert, Alejan. Just in case."

"I'm always alert. For example, watch out!" Dipping down, he burst through the top of a wave. Spray spattered them. Laughing, he flew higher.

Together, Ji-Lin and Seika cried, "Alejan!" And then Seika was laughing, a sound so happy and free that Ji-Lin couldn't help laughing too.

He soared up toward the clouds. Midday sun soaked into their backs, drying them quickly. Only a few puffy clouds dotted the sky. Behind them, Okina Island had shrunk to a green smear. Ahead were more islands.

There were dozens more — the so-called Hundred Islands of Himitsu — mostly uninhabited and mostly tiny. Many were just lumps of green that poked out of the waves. The water was clear between them, and Ji-Lin could see dolphins leaping and schools of bright-colored fish swimming around coral reefs.

"Lunch!" Alejan proclaimed, and dove low again, scooping a silver fish out of the waves with his paw. He devoured it as he flew, and Ji-Lin's stomach rumbled.

A thought occurred to her ... The sun was directly overhead. The uninhabited islands lay before them. "Alejan, how much time did we lose climbing this morning?" It had been slower going than she'd thought. They hadn't crossed the ridge until midmorning. They had to be seriously off schedule.

"Don't worry. We'll make it to the next village by nightfall."

She wasn't so sure about that.

"And if not, my night vision is excellent."

Ji-Lin felt Seika tense behind her. She knew if she turned she'd see Seika's face screwed up in her worried expression. She wore that expression a lot. When they were little, Seika never used to look worried. Except when Ji-Lin suggested they climb to the top of the spires. Or slide down the banisters. Or try to outswim the waterfolk. Or . . . "We can't fly at night!" Seika cried. "Not if there could be more koji."

"There aren't any more koji," Ji-Lin said, though she wasn't sure if she was lying. Where there was one, there could be more. She thought of her earlier idea about the daddy snake-monster. It was actually likely there was at least one more koji hidden somewhere on the islands. "But Seika's right. We shouldn't take unnecessary risks. Can you fly faster?"

"I am speed. Like Master Shai when she flew the length of the barrier." Alejan gave a mighty flap of his wings. She heard the whoosh of wind. Rising, he caught a current, and they flew on.

The islands below were patches of green forest and tan sand. She saw waterfolk swimming near their shores and birds winging over their trees. Ahead, she saw a flock of cloud fish. They were grouped together, their white scales blending so they looked like a cloud, except they moved against the wind. "Seika, look."

She felt Seika shift and then heard her gasp. "Oh, they're beautiful!"

The fish swarmed together, their scales reflecting the sun — they weren't just white. They were white composed of a rainbow of colors. When the sun hit them, they were jewels. As one, they plunged into a real cloud. The puffy white closed around them as if swallowing them. Ji-Lin watched for them to reappear, but they didn't.

Ji-Lin, Seika, and Alejan flew on in companionable silence, until Seika spoke again, "Ji-Lin, I hate to say this . . . but I'm thirsty. And hungry."

Seika was likely not used to going without. Ji-Lin thought of the vast banquets she remembered from life at the palace. All they had to do was ask for something, and it would be delivered with a flourish. That had ended for her when she left for training. "In the temple, some days we'd start exercises before dawn and keep on until we were so hungry we were dizzy. The masters said it focused the mind."

Alejan snorted. "Sure. Focused it on *food*."

"I'm sorry, but do we have any more water?" Seika sounded so meek, so unprincessy, that Ji-Lin immediately felt guilty — it wasn't Seika's fault she'd stayed in the palace, cushioned and coddled. Leaning over Alejan's packs, she unhooked a canteen of water and passed it to Seika.

Seika drank.

And drank.

And . . . "Stop," Ji-Lin said, taking the canteen from her. When Seika flinched at her tone, she added more apologetically, "We don't know when we'll have more." She didn't mean to get annoyed with her sister. It was just . . . this wasn't like the tales. Seika was relying on her, and Ji-Lin wasn't sure she even knew what she was doing. She'd never planned to encounter a real koji and flee, and she'd never expected to run out of supplies.

"The people of Heiwa will help us," Seika said confidently. "It's their honor and their duty." But she didn't ask for the water back.

Ji-Lin took one cautious sip. It was barely enough to moisten her tongue, and drinking it only made her thirstier. She took another sip. Seika was right that they'd be able to get more at the next village, but just in case . . . She put the canteen away and reached into the packs, looking for more food. She was hungry too.

They'd eaten the last meat roll.

That wasn't good.

By late afternoon, Ji-Lin was even hungrier, and she knew Seika must be too. Worse, they were still over the tiny uninhabited islands. "Alejan, how far is it to Heiwa?"

"Not far."

"Truly?"

"Mmm . . . No. Not truly. It's possible I was overly optimistic."

Seika leaned forward. "What do you mean? Ji-Lin, what does he mean?" Her voice sounded shrill.

Ji-Lin wondered if Emperor Himitsu's sister had felt this way when she flew with her brother across the islands for the first time, as if she was on the verge of a massive mistake. Had Uncle Balez felt like he was faking it when he'd flown with their father? Ji-Lin looked ahead at the islands. "Don't worry," she told her sister. "It will be fine."

They flew on.

It's not going to be fine, Ji-Lin thought.

⁓

Seika had noticed that when people said "Don't worry" it usually meant the opposite. She looked at the sun. Low, its light was splayed out on the waves. Soon it would touch the horizon. Once it did, it would melt quickly into the sea. She didn't want to be in the air when that happened. "You said we could make it."

She didn't mean to sound so accusatory.

"We'll make it," Ji-Lin said. "Alejan's fast."

The lion spoke. "I am also tired, despite my heroic strength. Carrying two plus packs is possibly more than I expected. I am sorry, Princesses. The tales never mention the heroes getting tired."

"What do we do?" Seika hated how her voice got shrill. Taking a deep breath, she tried to calm herself. She imagined she was talking to a tutor. "I'm sorry. I know you're doing your best. I delayed us. I'm not accustomed to climbing."

"Don't blame yourself," Alejan said. "Blame the koji. It was unexpected."

Absolutely nothing in the Emperor's Journey was supposed to be unexpected. It had been performed every generation for two hundred years, and every inch of it was mapped out and prescribed. Each stop was precisely one day's flight from the prior one, ending in their arrival on Himit's Day, the same day Emperor Himitsu had bargained with the dragon two hundred years earlier. But there was nothing in the stories that said the dragon watched their approach — good thing, too, after the disaster at Gyoson. The tradition could be bent a little further, couldn't it? Under the circumstances? If it helped them get back on track, and meant a soft pillow and warm blanket tonight? "Maybe there's another village?" Seika said. "A closer one?"

"Not on these islands. Look." Ji-Lin pointed. Below, the islands were no more than patches of beach, collections of rocks, and clumps of tiny forests. Only a few were even large enough to land on. None had villages. "We'll have to find one to camp on. Alejan, can you keep an eye out for a good site? If we're going to stop, it's better to stop soon so we have time to set up before dark. Last night it was too dark for a proper camp, and the koji was too close. But tonight, don't worry, Seika."

Seika tried to think of something positive to say but failed. Camping! Outside again, all night! Her stomach growled. She was hungry and thirsty, and she'd been looking forward to a night in a proper bed. She blinked quickly as her eyes heated up with tears.

Don't be ridiculous, she told herself. *Princesses don't cry.* Especially not over a little thing like the lack of a soft bed. Especially when she'd been lucky enough to see such wonders as a unicorn, mer-minnows, and cloud fish.

It was just that she was so hoping that after flying all day, they'd be back to doing what they were supposed to do. This was *not* what they were supposed to do. The dragon might not mind much if they veered from their route, but Seika minded. A lot. She'd wanted to do it all exactly right. Even if they went to a different village, that had to be . . . less untraditional . . . than an island campsite.

Alejan flew toward the biggest of the nearby islands. Like the others, it looked uninhabited, but at least this one was large enough that it could have held a village. It was very rocky, though, with cliffs and plateaus and craggy peaks. A few trees were clumped here and there, but the island wasn't flat enough for a farm.

Gliding between the rock formations, they looked for a place to land. Seika saw several that looked fine to her but kept quiet — she knew nothing about camping. How to curtsy properly, yes. How to dance in formal costumes, yes. She wished she could be more helpful.

Alejan spotted their campsite: a plateau with a river that sliced through it and tumbled off in a massive waterfall. He circled it before settling beside the river. It was nicer than any of the other landing spots Seika had seen, and she was glad she'd kept her mouth shut.

Seika slid down, careful this time to keep hold of Alejan's saddle until she was sure her knees weren't going to give out. She let go only when they quit wobbling.

Ji-Lin jumped off and began unstrapping the packs, as well as removing the winged lion's saddle. Alejan stretched full out, arched his back, and then rolled in the grass.

"Now we need shelter, water, and food." Ji-Lin ticked each item off on her fingers, but she didn't seem to be talking to Seika.

"I will hunt for dinner," Alejan offered. "I'm a mighty hunter, like Master Shai when she—"

"Great," Ji-Lin cut him off. "I'll have everything ready when you get back."

Seika watched as Ji-Lin unpacked a roll of fabric and several bamboo sticks. She laid them out on the ground and stared at them.

Then she moved around them and stared at them some more.

"Can I help?" Seika asked.

"No, I got this." Ji-Lin paused, as if realizing that sounded unfriendly, and added, "But if you want to help, you can see if there's anything to eat that doesn't need to be cooked. Berries or fruit or nuts. Check the trees and bushes."

Scouring the plateau, Seika looked for anything vaguely edible. The grass was soft and full of white bell-like flowers she'd never seen before. They smelled like honey mixed with cinnamon. In the west, the sun was low enough to kiss the horizon. Amber light pooled in the sea. At the edge of the plateau, she stopped and stared at it. She could still see the barrier, or imagine she saw it, twinkling in the sunset. A few seabirds flew over the water, black silhouettes in the setting sun, and she heard crickets chirping around her, a steady chorus beside the sound of the waterfall. She'd dreamed about seeing a place like this someday. Every blade of grass was beautiful.

She just wished she weren't so hungry.

She looked around again. Maybe the flowers were edible? She'd read that the islands boasted many edible plants, including flowers. The palace chefs often added blossoms to salads. Kneeling, she plucked one. She sniffed it. It smelled nice. Carefully, Seika nibbled on the petals. Swallowing, she waited to see if she felt sick.

She was still waiting when the world went black.

CHAPTER
TEN

J I-LIN SAW SEIKA collapse. One second, she'd been standing by the cliff, looking all picturesque and princessy, framed by the rosy red of the sunset. Ji-Lin had been sure she was composing poems instead of looking for food. And then the next second, she'd crumpled like a marionette whose strings had been cut.

"Seika!" Dropping the bamboo poles, she ran across the grass. *Oh no, oh no, please be okay! Please be fine. Sit up and say it's just a joke, a bad, bad joke. Don't be . . .* She skidded on her knees, stopping at Seika's side.

Oh, thank Himitsu, she's breathing!

Her chest rose and fell. Even. Steady. Strong breaths.

Then what . . . Ji-Lin saw Seika's hand clutching a bunch of irina flowers. Sleep flowers. Putting her face in her hands, Ji-Lin rocked back and reminded herself to breathe and to not scream. "Of all the stupid . . . She didn't know. How could she know? She's never left the palace. She knows a dozen ways to bow. She doesn't know not to eat flowers that put you to sleep."

Plucking a few of the flowers, Ji-Lin broke open the stems. She scraped the insides onto her finger and shoved the tip of it into Seika's mouth. "Come on, wakey-wakey. Swallow, Seika."

Seika's throat moved.

And then her eyelids fluttered open.

Awake.

"You could have fallen off the cliff," Ji-Lin told her. "If you'd collapsed at the edge, you could have tumbled off and hit your head or fallen into the sea. I wouldn't have gotten to you in time. That was *stupid*."

"I'm not stupid," Seika said automatically. She pushed herself up to sitting. "Whoa, everything's spinning. Ji-Lin, what happened? Why am I on the ground?"

Ji-Lin waved a bunch of irina flowers in her face. "You ate sleep flowers. You're lucky you aren't a bug. That's how they catch their prey. Bugs eat the petals. Bugs fall asleep. Flowers eat the bugs."

Seika sprang up to her feet. "They're carnivorous flowers?"

"The petals put you to sleep; the stems wake you up." Ji-Lin tossed the flowers away. "Didn't your tutors teach you anything? Oh, I forgot, you have excellent table manners." Seika should have known better! She could have died! "Just . . . come back to camp. Away from the cliffs. Away from the pretty flowers, before you hurt yourself."

Before she said anything else ugly, she pivoted and stomped back toward the tent. Or what should have been a tent. Right now, it was a flat piece of fabric and a bunch of bamboo stakes. Someone clever had put a tent in the pack in case of emergency, but no one had thought to include instructions or teach Ji-Lin how to assemble it. She squatted next to the bamboo and glared at it. It would have been better if she had extra food in the packs. She'd happily trade this useless tent for a handful of nuts. One of the winged lions must have overseen the packing — they must have assumed the princesses could hunt for their food, like a lion.

"Maybe . . . maybe I can help?" Seika asked.

"You've done enough helping."

"But I —"

"Just don't eat anything poisonous for the next ten minutes. I have to think." Obviously, the fabric went overhead, and the poles held it up, but she couldn't tell how exactly they connected. Out of the corner of her eye, she saw Seika sitting as still as a statue. Her face was as expressionless as their father's. "What?"

"I said nothing."

"You were thinking. Loudly." Ji-Lin crossed her arms and glared at Seika.

"I'm sorry I scared you."

She sounded so very sorry that Ji-Lin felt like a kite without wind, fluttering to the ground. She dropped her arms. It was impossible to be angry with Seika when she sounded so meek. Ji-Lin felt like she'd been kicking a kitten. "Oh. Well, you did. I thought you were dead."

In a light voice, Seika said, "At least I know you don't want me to die."

She was making a *joke?* About *this?* Ji-Lin threw her arms in the air. "Of course I don't want you to die!" She let out a short scream and then stomped away. She paced on the edge of the plateau. A few stars were poking through the blue. The sun was only a streak of red on the horizon, and the sea was a deep red in front of it, as if the sun had melted into the sea.

A sunbird was flying low over the water, sparks from its wings sizzling in the waves. The sparks ate along the feathers, until the bird's feathers turned to char. The bird shook itself, and the burnt feathers fell as dust into the water. Ji-Lin watched as the bird began to plummet—and then new feathers sprouted impossibly fast, reaching full length just as the sunbird hit the water. An instant later, the phoenix-like firebird burst out of the water, with brand-new plumage and a fish in its mouth. Sparks once again began to play on the tips of its feathers.

She saw Alejan just beyond the sunbird. He flew closer. He too was fishing in the waves. She watched him dip low and smack his paw into the water.

She watched him fish until she felt calmer. And then she walked back to camp. The tent was up—lopsided, but up—and Seika was standing beside it, a bamboo pole in one hand and her tiara in the other. She had a smudge of dirt on one cheek.

"It's not exactly right—" Seika began.

"It's perfect," Ji-Lin said. She didn't know why she felt like crying. But she blinked quickly to clear her eyes and pretended to study the tent construction until the feeling passed.

Anxiously, Seika watched Ji-Lin examine the tent. Her sister let out little *hmm*s and snorts and other noises. She looked at the leftover bamboo pole that Seika held and then shoved it in one of the sides, diagonally, until the tent stood straight.

"It's a nice tent," Seika said.

"We should dig a latrine too, somewhere behind it," Ji-Lin said.

Seika wanted to agree—anything to keep Ji-Lin from getting angry again—but she had no idea what that was. "A . . . what?"

"A place to, you know, pee."

"That's . . ." She failed to think of a word that fit what she thought. ". . . a practical idea." Plumbing in the palace was a marvelous mystery, and she liked it that way. But she followed Ji-Lin's lead, picking up a flat rock and using it to dig a hole away from the tent. She wondered what they'd use for wiping paper.

As they finished, Alejan landed. He opened his massive jaws and spat out three fat fish. "Behold, the mighty hunter has returned!" He pranced in a circle around the still-flopping fish and then posed next to his catch. Behind him, the sun had set completely, leaving the sky a burnt orange on the horizon and a deep blue overhead. Silhouetted in front of the orange, he almost glowed.

Seika got the sense she was supposed to clap. So she did. He looked pleased.

Ji-Lin rolled her eyes. "They're very nice fish, but we can't eat them without cooking them." She looked at the fish with distaste. "I hate fish, but it's better than starving. Thank you, Alejan."

Seika recognized them, from a book, of course — she wasn't allowed to handle raw fish in the palace, or any other uncooked meat. She'd never even wielded a kitchen knife. "These are silverfish," she said. "Do you know how to make a fire?" She wondered how one got the fish meat out of the fish itself. She knew you weren't supposed to eat the scales.

She wished the fish would stop flopping.

"I . . . think I know. You rub a stick against a flat piece of wood." Ji-Lin drew her sword. "Let me just first . . ." She walked toward the three flopping fish, and Seika shut her eyes. She heard a wet sound and wished she could unhear it, even though she knew it was cruel to let the fish just suffocate in the air and even though they planned to eat them anyway. She missed the palace kitchen, where all the food was made pretty before she ever saw it.

"I can find wood," Seika offered. Not looking at the fish,

she held up a hand to stop Ji-Lin from saying anything. "Don't worry. I won't eat any flowers."

Searching around the camp, she picked up branches and twigs. After she had an armful, she carried them back and dumped them in a circle of rocks Ji-Lin had made. Thankfully, Ji-Lin was done cleaning the fish. Alejan was happily nibbling the heads.

"Not like that," Ji-Lin told Seika. "You need to create a pyramid of sticks, add in tinder . . ." Seika felt herself begin to smile as Ji-Lin began rearranging the sticks, laying the larger branches to the side and creating a structure within. Glaring at her, Ji-Lin said, "Are you laughing at me?"

She blanked her smile. "No. It's just . . ." She'd never thought she'd see her twin acting so much like an elderly tutor. She decided not to say that. "How do you know all this?"

Licking his lips, Alejan plopped down next to them. "She doesn't. She's bluffing. She's never spent the night outside the temple. That's for advanced students."

Ji-Lin glared at him. "I've had *training*."

"Go on, then." He crossed his paws and laid his chin on them. "Light a fire."

"You're supposed to be on my side," Ji-Lin growled at him, but she sat down next to the fire circle, picked up a stick and a fatter piece of wood, and began to twist the stick against the wood.

And nothing happened. Ji-Lin glared at the stick, then

at the fire pit. Seika wondered if she should say something encouraging.

Ji-Lin twisted faster, using the palms of her hands, going back and forth.

Still, nothing.

Ji-Lin stopped, blew on her hands, which Seika saw were starting to look red, and tried again. This time she held the piece of wood steady with her feet as she twisted the stick against it. The stick was beginning to wear a divot into the wood.

A tendril of smoke rose.

"You're doing it!" Seika said.

The smoke died.

Ji-Lin kept trying, but nothing more than a whiff of smoke rose from the wood. At last, she collapsed backward. "I can't do it. I'm sorry." She studied her hands, which were filthy and red and raw.

Seika fetched a canteen and gave it to Ji-Lin. Her sister took a drink but her eyes didn't leave the fireless fire pit. She was glaring at it as if she expected it to light just from her anger.

It was growing darker. Soon they wouldn't be able to see anything except the moon and stars. Already the moon was a pale disc in the sky, and a few dozen stars were visible, like jewels scattered on a bed sheet. The only other light came from the sparks of the sunbird fishing in the sea. She watched as its feathers charred. *Amazing*, she thought, waiting to see the magical bird regrow its feathers.

Seika had an idea.

"We need a feather," she said.

"What would —" Ji-Lin began.

Seika pointed toward the sea, at the fiery sunbird.

"Oh! Yes! Alejan —"

Alejan didn't move. "Say that I am the mightiest hunter that ever lived."

Ji-Lin gave him a look. *"Alejan."*

"You're the mightiest hunter that ever lived," Seika said.

"Why, yes, I am. Thank you for noticing." Spreading his wings, Alejan rose, ran to the edge of the plateau, and took off. Seika and Ji-Lin both ran after him, stopping at the edge and watching. He came in high, above the firebird, flying in the reflection of the moon.

The sunbird flew straight, sparks lighting the dark water below. It didn't seem to notice the lion. Seika held her breath as Alejan suddenly dove fast and silent.

The bird let out a cry that echoed over the waves. Frightened, it shed two flaming feathers. Swooping under the bird, Alejan caught the feathers on his mane — and his mane began to smoke. He flew toward them. Sparks jumped off the feathers and nestled in his fur.

Alejan landed hard and shook his head. The fiery feathers flew off his mane and landed next to Seika. Smoke continued to curl around his fur, and Alejan dropped to the grass, rolling like a dog. Using sticks to scoop them up, Seika dumped the feathers onto the fire pit as Ji-Lin anxiously watched Alejan.

The fire lit.

It spread across the wood, bright and dancing.

Alejan quit rolling — all the sparks were out on his mane now — and collapsed next to the fire.

Ji-Lin patted him. "I'm sorry, Alejan. We should have thought that through and found a better way for you to carry the flames."

Seika reflected on the flower she'd eaten. She hadn't thought that through either, but she'd been trying to do the right thing.

"I'll forgive you," Alejan said, "if you'll share the fish."

"Of course." Ji-Lin checked through his mane. Seika could see that tufts were charred, the tips shriveled back, but the bulk was fine. He didn't seem hurt. The feathers hadn't burnt him, just singed his fur a little.

The three of them settled around the fire. Ji-Lin roasted the fish on a stick, and they ate it hot. Seika thought it tasted as sweet as anything in the palace. Her stomach full, she lay back in the grass and looked up at the stars. Ji-Lin leaned against Alejan's side.

"You can't see this many stars from the palace," Seika said. "Even from the highest spire, half the sky is blocked by the mountains, and the lanterns from the city wash out so much." She'd never known there were so many. They looked like grains of salt spilled across a black table. She tried, and failed, to count them.

"You can see them from the temple," Ji-Lin said. "For my first week, I cried myself to sleep every night, until Alejan came into my room, informed me that my sobbing was keeping him awake, and insisted I come outside with him and look at the stars while he told me a story."

Seika knew she should feel bad that Ji-Lin had cried so much, but she remembered how she'd felt when her twin had been taken away — as if someone had cut off her arm. It was strangely nice to hear that she wasn't the only one who had been sad.

"She stopped her sobbing after she heard my story," Alejan said. "As you may have noticed, I'm not all glorious brawn. I also happen to enjoy retelling tales. In fact . . . But maybe this isn't the time."

"It's okay, Alejan, go ahead," Ji-Lin said with a smile.

"If you insist . . ." Clearly pleased, he repositioned himself, lifting his head and stretching his paws so that he looked like one of the statues on the Bridge of Promises. "I have come to tell you a tale," he began.

In unison, the sisters gave the traditional response: "We have come to hear it."

"The stars were born on a summer's day . . ." His voice was low. It swept across the camp, and Seika closed her eyes to listen better.

"I've never understood that beginning," Ji-Lin complained. Seika's eyes snapped open, and she giggled at Alejan's miffed expression, which included a fluffed-up mane. Ji-Lin always used to interrupt their tutors, and they'd worn identical offended expressions, minus the mane. "How can it be summer before the stars?"

"You said I could tell a story; now don't interrupt," Alejan scolded. "The stars were born on a summer's day, and the sea wept salt tears that the unblemished blackness of night was now speckled with light. From each of her tears, a creature was born to swim inside her, crawl onto land, or fly into the sky: fish, animals, birds, humans. And Ji-Lin, do *not* say that the sea can't cry because it's already salt water."

"I wouldn't dream of saying that," Ji-Lin said demurely.

Seika smiled, positive Ji-Lin had been about to say exactly that. She used to drive their tutors crazy with her practicality. She poked at every metaphor, questioned every exaggeration, and rolled her eyes every time her tutors tried to pretend they knew the answers when they didn't. Maybe Ji-Lin hadn't changed that much, despite all her special training.

"The stars looked down on these new creatures and were not impressed. 'Your creations are weak and soft,' the stars said. 'They will die in your waters and on your shores while we look on, eternal.' The sea was angry at that insult, rolling and rising until the voices of her children cried out and she stilled, sparing their lives. The sea told the stars, 'Before they die, they will multiply, as you cannot,' and so the sea's children did, spreading through the world."

The fire crackled. Sparks flew toward the sky, dimming against the true stars and then vanishing. *This is nice*, Seika thought. Comfortable and warm, she felt her eyelids droop.

"The stars saw the truth of the sea's words and were angry in turn. 'We *can* multiply,' they said, 'if we die.' 'Then die,' the sea told them, 'and leave my body pure of your light, for I miss the darkness, and I tire of your endless talk.'

"Angry at the sea's taunting, one of the stars blazed so brightly that he exploded into a thousand pieces. 'See,' the other stars said, 'one of us has multiplied.' These pieces fell into the sea and on the land — and from these star pieces were born the koji. Born with the strength and long life of the stars, the koji were a scourge on the land and in the sea, killing indiscriminately."

Seika thought of the koji they'd seen today. She hadn't been ready to see her first monster. She'd be seeing it in her dreams, she knew. *We have to complete the Journey*, she thought. *Those things can't be allowed back on the islands.*

"Seeing her children slaughtered, the sea's heart ached. She tried to destroy the koji but could not. She found, however, that she could change some of them. Capturing several koji, she brought them deep within the world and remade them. From their celestial-born bodies, she created glorious new creatures, made of earth and sky and sea and stardust combined together, and released them into the world as winged lions."

"Very glorious," Ji-Lin murmured.

"Indeed. The winged lions came to land and discovered that the sea's children were scattered. The birds and animals lived in fear, and the humans hid in caves, afraid and alone, with barely enough to eat, since hunting brought the koji. The lions protected these humans, coaxed them out of the caves, and guarded them while they tilled the earth and built their cities. The humans, in turn, tamed the wild dogs, cats, horses, and others, and protected them. Soon they all existed in harmony, humans and lions and the other children of the sea together."

"I love this story," Seika said. "You tell it beautifully." She'd never heard it told by one of the lions before. Hearing the tale from him outside under the stars, at the top of one of the islands, changed it. The story felt larger, more magical.

"Humans and lions were meant to live in harmony," Alejan said. "Many centuries ago, one of the emperors of Zemyla tried to erase the old stories and make the winged lions his slaves instead of his equals, but he could not destroy all the tales. When the scholar Himitsu shared them with the lions and proposed they unite against their oppressor . . . Well, you heard *that* tale grander than I could ever tell it, complete with acrobats and firedancers. Our glorious first emperor Himitsu restored the harmony between humans and lions, here on the islands of Himitsu. Humans built the Temple of the Sun for the lions, and we pledged to help the humans fight the koji that remained after the barrier was raised."

"You know what the best part of that story is?" Ji-Lin said.

"The lions?" Alejan guessed.

"That we're a part of it now," Ji-Lin said. "We're on the Journey. And when we reach the dragon, we'll be protecting our people from the koji, like Emperor Himitsu did. Like the sea did. We'll be heroes."

Thinking of the koji they'd seen, Seika shuddered. "I was scared today," she admitted.

"I'd never seen a real koji before either," Ji-Lin said. "It was larger than I'd imagined." It sounded as if she was admitting something too. Both of them were silent for a few moments.

"I wonder what it was like, when the koji first came," Seika said, looking up at the stars again. "People must have been so afraid." She tried to imagine it, life before the winged lions. She'd always known the lions and their riders were there to protect them. She'd never had to be afraid.

"People must still be afraid, beyond the barrier," Alejan said. He shuddered, and his mane shook. Sparks leaped from the fire and popped in the air. "Imagine if the barrier fell."

"We won't let it — that's the whole point of what we're doing," Ji-Lin said, and yawned. "Ugh, I feel as though I've been pushed through a strainer."

"Sleep," Alejan told her. "I will guard you."

"But you need sleep too," Ji-Lin protested. "You flew all the way here."

"I will wake you in two hours, and you can guard me. Then you wake me, and I will guard you again. It might not be as glamorous as in the tales, but I think the old heroes would approve." He rose, shifting Ji-Lin off, and padded in a circle around them, as if claiming their camp as his own. He settled a few yards from the tent, his back to them. The sisters crawled inside the tent while Alejan stood guard.

Seika dreamed of monsters.

CHAPTER
ELEVEN

J I-LIN WOKE IN the darkness to the feeling of being tossed into the air. Beside her, Seika screamed and clutched Ji-Lin's arm. Beneath them, the ground heaved, as if it wanted to chuck them off the island. It rolled back and forth, and she couldn't do anything but lie flat.

Outside, Alejan was roaring. Seika curled into a ball, and so did Ji-Lin, each holding tight to the other's arm. She heard the fabric of the tent whoosh as it buckled around them. The bamboo poles creaked, and then the earth stilled. Everything quieted.

"Is it over?" Seika asked.

"I don't know." Ji-Lin's voice felt rusty, as if she hadn't used it in a long time. She'd felt tremors before, but always she'd believed she was safe. She'd been surrounded by other people and known where she was. But here, alone with her sister in the darkness, on an unknown island . . .

From beyond the tent, Alejan called, "Ji-Lin? Are you all right? Seika?"

"We're fine!" Ji-Lin called, then asked Seika, "Are we fine?"

"I think so." Seika released her grip on Ji-Lin's arm, and Ji-Lin noticed her arm was throbbing a little. She'd have bruises there in the morning. Seika was stronger than she seemed, and also had pointier nails. "What time do you think it is?" Seika asked.

"Late. Early. I don't know."

Lying there in the darkness, Ji-Lin tried to guess the time based on how tired she felt. Her heart was still beating too fast to tell. She wanted to jump out of the tent with her sword and fight something, but there was nothing to fight. The enemy was the earth itself.

The next tremor, a light aftershock, came quickly. It felt like a wave beneath them, raising them up. They heard loose stones falling, rattling as they tumbled down from the plateau. What if a boulder fell on them? She couldn't fight that. She couldn't even see it.

The waterfall of stones slowed, then stopped.

Silence again.

Slowly, the chirping of crickets began again. Ji-Lin heard a few night birds and animals rustling outside. She heard Alejan pacing around the tent, his breath snorting as he sniffed at everything.

"I miss walls," Seika said.

"At least there aren't any to fall on us," Ji-Lin said. "We've had a few bad tremors at the temple, but people whisper that worse are coming. Sometimes I hear the masters talk about it."

"We've had some that cracked bridges. In the poorer parts of the city, some buildings have fallen, but only ones that weren't sturdy to begin with," Seika said. "The palace guards are always sent out to help. I was never allowed to go. Do you think they felt this one in the capital?"

"Probably. I have no idea."

Seika was silent for a moment, then said, "I can't fall back to sleep. I keep waiting for the next one. I wish we'd made it to the next village. We *have* to get back on track. We aren't supposed to be out here on our own."

Ji-Lin agreed. None of the heroes in the tales ever lay in the darkness, waiting for the earth to shake again beneath them. They were always flying or fighting. "What did you do in the palace during a tremor?"

"Hid in the bath, if it was close enough." The baths were stone, very solid. "Or an archway, if we weren't close enough. Everyone really likes to gather in the eastern arch, because it's closest to the Music Academy. The musicians play for everyone after the tremors stop. What did you do in the temple?"

"Went to the closest courtyard. A lot of the buildings are stuck to the side of the mountain. Once, one broke off with a loose chunk of the mountain and slid down hundreds of feet. You can't fall off a cliff if you're in a courtyard."

A second aftershock hit.

The earth rose and fell beneath them, as if it were yawning, and then the tremor ended. They listened to the sound of stones rolling downhill, and then pebbles, and then sand, and then silence again.

"Maybe . . ." Seika said, "we could talk about something other than quakes?"

"Yeah." But Ji-Lin couldn't think of a single thing to talk about. She wished they could jump on Alejan's back and fly onward. Helpless in the dark, she didn't feel like a hero on the Emperor's Journey. *As soon as it's light,* she thought, *we'll fly.*

"Do you remember Master Pon, the etiquette tutor?" Seika asked. "He sneaks into the kitchen after banquets, when he thinks no one is watching, and eats leftover cake icing, straight from the bowl."

Ji-Lin snorted. "Not Master Pon." He was the fussiest of their tutors, with a mustache that he kept slicked into curls and pristine white robes that never seemed to have a smudge of dirt.

"Even saw him lick out a tub of buttercream once. Bits of it got stuck in his mustache."

Imagining this, Ji-Lin snorted again, this time a giggle escaping with the snort. "Did he know you'd seen him?"

"Possibly. He did assign me fifty pages to read in *The History of Court Manners* the next day, the chapter about utensils."

"Someone wrote fifty pages about knives?"

"And spoons. Don't forget the spoons."

Seika said it so seriously that Ji-Lin laughed out loud. She heard Alejan pace closer to the tent. "Are you two okay? Ji-Lin, you're laughing. Is that good or bad? You weren't hit on the head with a rock, were you?"

"We're both fine," Seika called to him. "How is everything out there?"

"I think there's a mouse hiding where I'm sleeping."

For some reason, that struck Ji-Lin as immensely funny. She laughed louder, and soon Seika was laughing again too. Eventually, they fell asleep. If there were more aftershocks, they didn't feel them.

⌁

At dawn, Seika crawled out of the tent. She stood and stared. All around their tent were rocks, littered there in the night. It looked as if a massive hand had picked up the plateau and shaken it, then set it back down again.

Ji-Lin was already outside and alert, as if she'd been awake for a while — Alejan must have woken her to stand guard. "No additional excitement," she reported.

"We were lucky," Seika said. If one of those boulders had rolled onto them . . .

"Very lucky," Ji-Lin agreed.

Seika realized she was shaking. She took a deep breath. "Let's find the next village, okay?" The sooner they were back on track, the happier she'd be.

Ji-Lin nodded vigorously. "Definitely. I've had enough of this place."

Packing up, they mounted Alejan. In a few short minutes, they were airborne. Seika saw the island shrink beneath them. It had seemed so idyllic last night, when she was full of fresh fish and listening to Alejan's story.

"Don't worry," Ji-Lin said. "The rest of the Journey will be much easier."

Seika winced. "You're practically daring the islands to smush us."

"Don't be superstitious," Ji-Lin said. "Everything will be fine."

"Stop it," Seika said.

Ji-Lin was grinning. "Nothing bad will happen."

"*Ji-Lin.*"

"Only rainbows and sunshine and puppies."

Alejan spoke up. "No puppies. I don't like dogs. Especially those yapping little ankle-biters that courtiers think are so cute."

"Yes!" Seika jumped on the change of subjects. "I know plenty of those dogs. Some of the court ladies like to carry them in elaborate purses to dinner. Once, one jumped out of its purse and chased a flying cat all over the banquet hall, knocking over three bowls of soup and landing in the center of a pyramid of bread. After that, Father banned them from meals." She grinned, remembering. It had been chaos — the dog yapping, the cat screeching, the court ladies screaming. She wished Ji-Lin could have seen it.

They flew quietly for a few minutes.

"I've heard the earthquakes are getting worse," Ji-Lin said.

Seika had heard her tutors say the same thing. Two hundred years ago, when Emperor Himitsu and his people came to the islands, the land was newborn and stable. Since then, the tremors had been increasing in both strength and frequency—she'd heard her tutors talking about it when they didn't think she was listening. Some said there had always been quakes and always would be; others insisted they'd started only a few generations ago and were worse every year. "Father always says not to worry. Of course, he didn't expect us to be sleeping outside on an unstable island . . ." No one could have expected that. The ritual journey had been performed in exactly the same way for two hundred years.

Alejan rumbled beneath them. "The tales don't talk about the little trials amid the greater quest — the tiredness, the hunger, the fear . . . The storytellers don't talk about the heroes being afraid. They say, 'They journeyed, and then they were there.' They talk about battles faced, not battles avoided."

"Maybe the heroes had their problems too," Ji-Lin said, "but the problems just didn't get included in their stories. You don't know how they felt about their adventures. Just because we were scared doesn't mean we can't be heroes.

Maybe when the storytellers tell our tale, they'll leave out these bits too, and everyone will think we were ready and brave and steadfast every second of the journey."

Seika thought of how peaceful it had been yesterday evening while Alejan told his tale beneath the stars. She thought of how amazing the sunbird had been, with its fiery feathers, and how magical the cloud fish had looked and how incredible the unicorn had been . . . "We've had wonderful moments too. Don't forget that."

"Like flying on a magnificent lion?" Alejan suggested.

Seika laughed. "Exactly."

CHAPTER
TWELVE

Leaning against Alejan's mane, Ji-Lin looked down on a snarl of thick forest. She heard the cry of the golden monkeys. So few humans had ever walked on any of these islands.

"I must rest my wings," Alejan announced.

"We have to keep going!" Seika said. "We were supposed to reach Heiwa last night!"

"A quick rest? It's been hours since we set off," he pleaded. "Even Master Shai rested on the occasional island when she flew around the entire barrier. I promise we'll still make it to the shrine by Himit's Day."

"All right," Seika relented. "A few minutes' rest."

If Ji-Lin remembered her maps correctly, the island beneath them was large enough for a name: it was Jishin. "This is the island from the Tale of the Three Brothers!"

"Jishin?" Seika asked. Ji-Lin felt her shift as she leaned over to peer down at the island. Ruins from an old palace poked up from the center of the forest.

"Yes!" Alejan said. "It was here that the quake killed Prince Biy's beloved. Stories, all around us! We tread on the path of history!"

Not a happy history, Ji-Lin thought.

"Do you think we'll be safe stopping here?" Seika asked.

"I promise we'll continue soon," Alejan said. "I only need a moment or two."

Gliding down, he landed on a beach, running a few steps through the sand before stopping. Ji-Lin unbuckled, helped Seika with her straps, and then slid down onto the beach. Her feet sank into the warm sand.

The sand was filled with stones that sparkled in the sun, flecks of ruby-red and emerald-green. Twisted trees grew out of the sand, marking the start of the forest. Ji-Lin stared into the dark shadows between the trees. Shrubs clogged the forest floor, and the trees grew so close that branches were woven together. Butterflies and insects with wings as large as her palm flitted between the plants. She heard the rustle of unseen forest animals. The cries of the monkeys were louder, though the monkeys themselves were hidden by the leaves.

"I wish we had time to explore," Seika said.

It was so exactly what Ji-Lin had been wishing that she grinned. "Later? When it's over?" she suggested. "Maybe we could sneak out."

"I tried to sneak out to see you," Seika said.

Ji-Lin tore her eyes from the tangle of forest to look at Seika's face. She was in profile, gazing at the forest as if she wanted to drink it all in. "*You* tried to sneak out?" That was the most un-Seika-like thing she'd ever heard. Seika *always* followed the rules. She was always the good girl. She was always the first princess, the better princess.

"For our birthday. Almost made it."

"The lions would have been furious." Ji-Lin was certain that Master Vanya would have scooped Seika up like an unruly kitten and carried her straight back. "You're the heir!"

Seika's shoulders slumped. "I know. And I promised not to ever abandon a ritual again. That's what Father was most angry about — that I tried to leave during the Spring Ritual."

She looked so sad that Ji-Lin impulsively hugged her. "Once this ritual is done, I'll officially be your guard. So long as you're traveling with me, you will be protected, and we can go anywhere on the islands." Ji-Lin didn't know if that was true, but it sounded true, which was close enough.

Seika brightened so much that it made Ji-Lin feel as though she'd just saved her sister from a horrible fiery doom. "You're right! We could explore it all." Looking again at the forest, Seika promised it. "We'll explore everywhere. This won't be my only adventure."

They let Alejan rest for a few minutes more, and when he felt ready, they climbed on his back again. Ji-Lin only looked back at the island of Jishin once — maybe twice — before it became a distant blur. Leaning against Alejan's mane, she began to doze.

"Ji-Lin!" Alejan's roar woke her.

Jerking up to sitting, she patted his neck. "Alejan, calm

down. What's wrong? Are you—" Ji-Lin began, and then stopped as she saw what he had seen.

"That's impossible," Seika breathed.

Below, in the distance, a strange-looking ship cut through the waves. It had three masts and was as sleek as a gondola but larger than the largest fishing boat that Ji-Lin had ever seen. Its sails were white, not red, and it flew three-colored banners from the tops of its masts. "What *is* that?" Ji-Lin asked.

"I've seen it, or ships like it, in books," Seika said. "Old books."

Ji-Lin hadn't studied ships, but she'd seen plenty from above the imperial harbor. None looked like this. "You have?"

"I think . . . it's a pirate ship."

"That's impossible," Ji-Lin said, echoing her. The islands of Himitsu had no pirates. Smugglers, yes. She knew there were plenty of small-scale thieves who darted in and out of coves. They weren't a lion and rider's responsibility, though the warriors were supposed to report any they saw. But pirates? The kind from stories, who traveled in ships from port to port, sinking other ships after stealing their cargo? "We don't have pirates."

"We have them now," Alejan growled. "And worse. Look!"

Seika gasped, and Ji-Lin looked at the ship in time to see an enormous tentacle wrap itself around one of the masts and snap it like a twig.

Sea monster. Koji.

"It's attacking them!" Seika cried.

That was obvious. Ji-Lin couldn't hear the screams of the pirates, but she could imagine them as figures ran across the deck, trying to find a way to fight the behemoth.

A boom shook the air.

"Earthquake?" Seika asked.

It didn't sound like it was from the island. It sounded as if it had come across the sea. From the koji? Or from the ship? She itched to unsheathe her sword and *do* something. "We have to help them!"

"I . . ." Seika twisted in the saddle, and Ji-Lin looked back too.

They were too far from the last island to take Seika to safety. By the time they flew to shore, the battle would be long over. "If you say 'don't,' I won't." It hurt to say that — everything in her was screaming to fight — but this wasn't about just her. "I can't promise it will be safe."

Across the water, they saw the sea monster slap the ship's deck with a tentacle. The ship rocked violently, and water flooded across the deck. The pirates clung to the side. Ji-Lin couldn't see their faces from this distance, but the pirates had to be terrified.

"We have to help them," Seika said. "It's our duty, right? We protect our people, whether by bargaining with the dragon or fighting the koji. So . . . let's do it."

"Are you certain, Princess Seika?" Alejan rumbled. "In the Battle of Doskaki, when Empress Maiyi ordered the clearing of a den of cave koji, she did not ride into battle . . ."

"I don't *want* to fight. But . . . we can't just *watch.*" Seika was wringing her hands.

That was good enough for Ji-Lin. Here, at last, was a chance to do what she'd trained to do. "Fly, Alejan! Fast as the wind!"

Alejan flapped his wings hard and shot forward as a second boom blasted through the air — it had come from the ship. A weapon of some kind?

Ahead of them, another tentacle burst out of the waves and wrapped around the prow. The ship rocked forward, and waves crashed on either side of the hull. As they flew closer, Ji-Lin saw the pirates racing over the deck and hacking at the tentacle with swords and axes. "Circle the ship!" she called to Alejan.

One of the pirates spotted them, pointed, and shouted, but then the monster squeezed with its tentacle, and the ship creaked and groaned. All attention went back to hacking at the tentacle.

The first tentacle wound itself around a mast and pulled, cracking it.

"It's underneath the ship!" Seika shouted.

The water was roiling around the ship, and Ji-Lin saw that Seika was right: the body of the monster was submerged beneath the hull. It was huge, easily twice the size of the ship itself. She saw the massive shadow as it shifted to extend yet another tentacle.

The pirates kept hacking at the tentacles.

That's not going to work, Ji-Lin thought. There were too many tentacles, and they were too strong. The monster was going to rip the ship apart before the pirates could hack them all off. She saw a pirate light the end of a black iron tube with a torch, and then another boom split the air. One tentacle recoiled, struck by the strange weapon, but only an instant later, the tentacle was back, bashing the deck.

They had to hit the monster where it was vulnerable, but its heart and eyes and any other suitable targets were under the water. If they aimed that weapon correctly . . . "We have to draw it up out of the water so the pirates can strike its heart!"

"You're right!" Seika said. "But how?"

Urging Alejan lower, she skimmed the deck, flying near the pirates. "Be ready to hit its heart!" she shouted to them. To Seika, she said, "Hold on, and hold your breath!"

"What are you doing?" Seika cried.

Ji-Lin leveled her sword and held tight to the hilt. "Hang on, Seika!" She hoped this was a good idea. *Be unexpected,* she thought. "Take us down, Alejan!"

"I hate when you're inventive," he complained, but he dove fast and straight toward the rolling shadow in the sea. He skimmed the hull as Seika screamed, and then they hit the water, diving into the waves.

Rising in the saddle as the water rushed around her, Ji-Lin jabbed forward and sliced, and she felt the impact as her blade hit the soft squish of the sea monster's body. She yanked on Alejan's mane, and the lion switched direction, propelling himself up and bursting out of the water. Ji-Lin gasped in air. Heavy with water, Alejan's wings pushed him one great arc forward onto the deck of the ship. He collapsed onto it, and Ji-Lin leaped off his back, her sword ready.

Screaming a shrill sound that made her ears ache, the monster rose out of the water, searching for its attacker. Its face was only a mouth, with four lips that widened to show rows of sharklike teeth within.

"Hit it now!" one of the pirates cried.

Boom!

The sound shook the ship, and Ji-Lin saw smoke from a black cylinder — the pirates had fired their weapon. The monster jerked backward as its body exploded in red and yellow slime that sprayed across the ship.

The tentacles loosened.

Shouting, the pirates pushed the tentacles off the deck. Ji-Lin ran to help, and so did Alejan, leaning his full weight against the tentacle until the monster slid into the sea.

The dying monster flailed once more, spraying the deck with water. Ji-Lin looked back to see Seika clinging to an unbroken mast. "Hold on!" she shouted to her sister. Slogging through the water, she reached her and wrapped one arm around Seika's waist and the other around the mast. They clung together as the ship rocked.

The pirates hacked the final tentacle free, and it slipped off the ship and into the ocean — and then the pirates cheered in shouts and whoops. One of them clapped Ji-Lin on the back. "Good work! You did — Whoa, you're just a kid!" He called to the others, "Hey, it's a kid! Two kids and their cat! Oh, lord of the sea, it's a winged lion! They have a winged lion! Get the captain!" Others took up the cry: "Where's the captain? Anyone seen the captain?" Then: "Is everyone safe? Anyone overboard? Did we lose anyone?"

Ji-Lin knelt beside Alejan. "Are you all right?"

Quietly, he said, "I'll need to dry my wings before I can fly again."

The pirates continued to celebrate around them, marveling at Alejan and gawking at the princesses, as some counted their crew and others checked the hull for leaks.

"How long?" Ji-Lin whispered to Alejan.

"An hour. Maybe two."

"Let's hope they're friendly pirates," Ji-Lin said.

CHAPTER
THIRTEEN

ALL OVER THE ship, the crew was busy trying to repair the damage from the sea monster. Sails were ripped and one mast was snapped in half. The whole ship smelled like sulfur as the sailors melted down black rocks and smeared the hot goop onto the holes in the hull. Seika felt a headache between her eyebrows from the stench and hoped Alejan's wings dried soon.

After being left to wait awkwardly, Seika and Ji-Lin were ushered into the captain's quarters, a low-ceiling cabin filled with maps and spyglasses. The captain sat at a desk that was covered in charts. Peeking at them, Seika didn't recognize the shoreline — it curved and curled like no island she knew. *How strange*, she thought. She'd studied plenty of maps in the palace library, and none looked like this. Her history tutor used to wax on in a voice of near despair about all the maps of the world they'd lost over the years . . . Still, it seemed unlikely that this pirate captain would have them.

The captain sported a beard that reminded Seika of a swallow's nest. She'd seen them in the palace spires, tucked into the rafters, where the cleaners couldn't easily reach them. She and Ji-Lin used to climb up and count the eggs and check on them until they hatched. Once, they'd found an egg that had fallen and broken. Ji-Lin had cleaned it out and given it to Seika as a present. She still had it, tucked into her jewelry drawer, in the back where the ladies-in-waiting couldn't find it and toss it out. The captain's beard could have housed several eggs, as well as a few birds. He stroked his beard as he considered them. "Exactly what am I supposed to do with you?"

"You aren't supposed to do anything with us, except thank us," Ji-Lin snapped.

Nodding in agreement, Seika tried to hold her borrowed blanket around her shoulders with as much dignity as the emperor held his robes. She'd changed into drier clothes, but the sailors had lent her a blanket. She was still cold from the dunk in the ocean.

The pirate captain drummed his fingers on his desk. Seika decided she didn't like him. He was looking at them as if they had caused problems, instead of coming to his ship's rescue. "I thought we were goners when that scylla grabbed us. It had been hunting us for several days. We'd had good wind for a while and were able to outrun it, but then the wind died and so did our luck."

"Several days?" Ji-Lin sounded startled, and Seika knew why: if the scylla had been in the sea around Himitsu for several days, the lions and riders would have spotted it. No, this meant that the ship and the sea monster had come from outside. Beyond the barrier.

But that was impossible. She dismissed the idea as

nonsense. He must have been sailing around the islands. It was a many-day trip around all of them. Her eyes drifted back to the strange maps . . .

"And then out of the blue come two children and their kitty cat."

Ooh, Ji-Lin is not *going to like that*, Seika thought.

"He's not a 'kitty cat,'" Ji-Lin said, nearly spitting the words. "He's an imperial guardian, celestial born, beloved of both the stars and sea!" Glancing out the porthole at the deck, Seika saw Alejan resting by the broken mast. Several of the pirates milled around him, and she noticed they still had their axes and knives in their hands from battling the sea monster.

He snorted. "Winged lions haven't been 'imperial guards' for over a hundred years. Tell the truth: where did you come by that thing, and how did you tame it?"

Seika saw Ji-Lin's hands curl into fists. She looked about three seconds away from losing her temper. Before Ji-Lin could reply, Seika jumped in. Using her most royal voice, she demanded, "The question is: how did that sea koji cross the barrier and enter our waters?" She tried to picture herself acting as imperiously as her father. As the emperor's heir, Seika should be asking the questions, not this pirate.

"What barrier?" the captain asked.

Seika exchanged glances with Ji-Lin. "The magic barrier that protects Himitsu," Ji-Lin said.

Then she added, "You aren't from Himitsu, are you?"

The change in the captain's face was remarkable. His mouth opened like a fish, his eyes widened until they looked like they'd pop from their sockets, and his cheeks reddened and then whitened. He exhaled in a gust that rustled the maps on his desk. "We found it." He slapped the desk with his meaty fist. "We found it! We'd hoped, when we ran the coordinates, but there are so many uncharted areas. And all the scientists said the barrier would fall years ago, when the egg hatched, but no one could find it . . . But here you are, and you have a tamed winged lion . . . You said Himitsu? The fugitive called this place after himself, huh?"

Seika raised her eyebrows. *Fugitive* wasn't a term usually used to describe their illustrious ancestor, the architect of the islanders' freedom and future. And no scientist expected the barrier to fall.

"Are you pirates?" Ji-Lin asked bluntly.

Seika winced. They should be trying to stay on the captain's good side, at least until Alejan was ready to fly. She didn't want to swim for shore, especially since she didn't know what else had passed through the barrier with the sea monster.

"Pirates? What makes you think — No, child, of course not. No wonder you look so tense. We're explorers!" He spread his arms wide, as if to embrace the entire ship. "We seek out new lands — and lost ones. These islands have been lost for so long that many believe they're merely legend. Sweet bedtime stories. But you tell me the Hidden Islands are real?"

Ji-Lin glanced at Seika, and Seika knew that it was time for her to sound her most princessy. "I am Princess Seika d'Orina Amatimara Himit-Re, firstborn daughter of Emperor Yu-Senbi, many times descendant of Emperor Himitsu, he who delivered us to freedom and peaceful beauty, and this is Princess Ji-Lin a'Tori Eonessa Himit-Re, second-born daughter —"

The captain snorted. "You expect me to believe you're princesses?"

He was certainly rude enough to be a pirate, even if he wasn't one. Seika didn't think she'd ever had anyone talk to her like this before. She drew herself up tall. "We are who we are, whether you believe us or not, and as soon as our lion's wings are dry, we will be on our way. We're on an important quest and can't be delayed."

Slapping his knee, the captain laughed. "Oh my, that's rich. Two princesses on a quest! I remember when I was your age, I used to play conqueror. I'd lead my battalion of toy soldiers up the hill and capture the dog pen."

"She's telling you the truth. We're on an important journey." Ji-Lin was running her fingers over the hilt of her sword. Seika saw that her arm muscles were tense and her knees loosely bent. She hoped Ji-Lin had noticed how outnumbered they were. There was a major difference between how the sailors looked at them and how the villagers had acted — the villagers had treated them with honor. The pirates — *sailors,* she corrected herself — treated them like

. . . like . . . well, like she and Ji-Lin were untrustworthy little children.

"Of course you are." Still amused, he shook his head. "We shall see, though. As soon as we have fixed our ship, we will sail to speak with your emperor. If you're truly princesses, you can help us arrange an audience with him. Until then, you have the freedom of the deck." He waved his hand as if dismissing them, or shooing away pesky flies. Studying his maps, he didn't look up again as they retreated out the door.

As they exited the captain's cabin and returned to the deck, Seika whispered, "He's not going to let us leave, not voluntarily." She knew lords like this captain, used to getting their own way.

"He doesn't have wings," Ji-Lin whispered back. "As soon as Alejan's feathers dry, we can be away from here. Just a little while more. He dries fast."

"Whoa, you have a pet lion!" a young voice cried. "Can I pet him?"

Seika turned to see a boy, scrawny thin, about their age, perched on a broken ladder that led to the ship's wheel. He had an oversize hat on his head from which tufts of black hair stuck out, so frizzed that they looked like they defied gravity.

"He is *not* a pet," Ji-Lin said in nearly a growl. If she were a cat, her fur would be bristling. "And no, you can't pet him, unless he allows it."

"I don't mind," Alejan said, lowering his head.

Ji-Lin shifted her glare to Alejan.

The boy plunged his hands into the lion's wet mane and scratched behind his ears. "Dad doesn't like nonhuman creatures, on account of the fact they're usually trying to eat us. You're lucky Dad didn't attack him."

"I'd like to see him try," Ji-Lin muttered. She switched her death glare to the sailors who milled around them. Shrugging off the blanket they'd given her, she wrapped her hand around her sword hilt.

Seika noticed that the sailors weren't looking at the winged lion with friendly expressions. She read mistrust, even outright hostility. She wondered how they'd be acting if Alejan hadn't just helped them fight a sea monster. *Dry,* she thought at his wings. She turned to the boy. "Where's your home?" she asked.

"Western Zemyla."

Zemyla! But that . . .

Ji-Lin tightened her hand around her sword. "Seika . . ." She knew what Ji-Lin wanted to say: a ship from Zemyla, the land their ancestors had fled, was here.

"Impossible," Seika breathed.

Or not impossible. If the scylla was here, why not a ship too?

She thought of what the captain had said about wanting an audience with the emperor. If it occurred to the captain to use them against Father . . . She'd never been held hostage before, and she didn't want to be. Zemylan history was full of kidnapping attempts and royal hostages, and she really didn't want that to be her chapter in the Himitsu history books.

The boy was still talking. "Guess I can't really call it home, though, because we never lived in one house very long. Dad likes the sea. It's his home. I wish we had a real house, on dry land. I get seasick. Especially when we get attacked by giant sea monsters. Not that it really matters, because I'm dying anyway." He delivered all this so quickly that Seika felt like she'd been caught up in a whirlwind.

She grasped on to the last thing he said: "What do you mean you're 'dying'?"

The boy shoved up his sleeve to show his bare arm, which was mottled with red and gray splotches. "It started as a red dot, but it's been spreading fast. Last week it was the size of a field mouse. Now it's more like a fat rat. I'll probably be dead in a day."

She didn't know what to say or do. He said it so matter-of-factly. She half wanted to hug him and half wanted to run away. "I'm so sorry."

"You're very calm for someone who's dying tomorrow," Ji-Lin said. It was clear from her voice that she didn't believe him. But why would he lie about that?

He shrugged. "Yeah, the doctor said it's happening, but I just . . . I mean, I'm alive now, so how can I be dead in a day? From a dumb bite? I try really, really hard not to think about it. Right now, I'm just glad I wasn't eaten by a scylla. You were amazing! I saw you up on the lion. Your sword raised!" He mimed hacking at the air. "And when you dove into the sea . . . I thought you were goners for sure!"

The cabin door opened, and the captain strode out. He began barking orders at the sailors — fix that, move this, carry that, sew the sails, add more pitch to the hull . . . "Report!" he roared.

One of the sailors scurried up to him and began listing the issues. "Two days at least until we're ready to sail."

Scowling, the captain stomped across the deck. "Make it faster! We have a chance at history here, people! Look alive!" He then crossed to the princesses and the boy. "Kirro, what are you doing out of bed? You're supposed to be resting."

"A sea monster woke me up," the boy, Kirro, said.

"Get back and rest some more. This excitement isn't good for you. You know what the doctor said about your heart."

Kirro nodded. "Harder it pumps, faster the sickness spreads, until — pop — my heart is squeezed until it stops." On the word pop, he opened his hands and then squeezed them into fists. His tone was light, but Seika was used to looking for what people didn't say. Lords and ladies always said one thing and meant another. He might have pretended he was fine, but she saw the sadness that quivered in his eyes and pulled on the corners of his lips. He truly was sick. And scared. Deep-down, bone-quiveringly scared, and trying his hardest to hide it. Her heart went out to him. No one should have to be that scared.

The captain paled, and his voice softened. He rested his hand lightly on the boy's shoulder. "Rest, please."

"Yes, Father." Shooting a lopsided smile at Seika, the boy scampered down a hatch into the hull. She wanted to call him back, say she was sorry, ask if she could help . . .

The captain heaved a sigh and looked so sad that Seika began to revise her opinion of him. Maybe he wasn't so unlikable after all. He did care about Kirro. He was just being stupid about the princesses. In her experience, people were often correct about some things and dumb about others, especially those adults who thought they had to be right all the time. "He said it was a bite," Seika said. "What bit him?" She'd seen marks like that, in illustrations in the records, but she couldn't remember which book or what the explanation was. Her tutors would be disappointed in her — a practical chance to apply knowledge, and she couldn't recall more than the image.

"It was a scuttle beetle. Caught us by surprise on an island we thought was safe. We'd stopped for fresh water and a rest. A chance to get solid earth under our feet again. I told Kirro to go to shore — he'd been begging. He doesn't fare well on the waves. Makes him sick, so I thought it would be good for him . . . Never regretted a decision so much. The doctor says . . . We don't know how much time he has left. Could be weeks. But could be hours."

Now that she knew the name, she could picture the page in the text. Waterhorse spit counteracted the poison of a beetle bite. It couldn't heal the damaged skin, but it kept it from getting worse. He shouldn't be dying! She'd never known anyone to die from a scuttle beetle bite. "Did you ask a waterhorse to spit on the bite mark?"

The captain frowned. "What do you mean?"

"It heals scuttle beetle bites."

Beside her, Ji-Lin nodded. "There's a story about a water-horse who saved a soldier —"

"Yes, that's right!" Seika knew that story too. It was in a book of children's tales. "The soldier was alone, separated from the rest of the imperial guards —"

"A scout," Ji-Lin added. "They were searching for a place to build the imperial palace, and the scout put his hand into a nest of scuttle beetles. Howling in pain, he ran for the nearest river and plunged his hand into the water. The water-horse heard his screams —"

"He was trying to sleep, you see," Seika said. "It's really a funny story. 'You are a rude man,' the waterhorse said, and spat all over the soldier. And the man was cured!" Yes, that was it! Waterhorse spit cured scuttle beetle bites. Everyone knew that.

The captain's bushy brows were low over his eyes as he scowled at them. "This is my son's life we're talking about. I don't find it funny."

Seika shrank back, then reminded herself she was a princess and he was an intruder. A rude intruder. "It's not a lie. I swear on the honor of our father's throne. Ask your doctor."

He scowled at them for a moment, muttered under his breath about thrones, and then spun around and barked to one of the sailors, "Get the doctor!"

Seconds later, a woman bustled up onto the deck. She wore an ankle-length coat that was covered in pockets and purses, and she carried a wooden box, which she set down with a thump. Her hair was braided in a style Seika had never seen. "Where's the patient?"

The captain waved his hand at the princesses. "These two claim that waterhorse spit will cure my boy. Are they telling the truth, and if so, why haven't you cured him?"

The doctor studied them. "The records claim that it was a viable cure, but we don't have access to any waterhorse spit. Waterhorses were hunted out of existence in Zemyla thirty years ago."

Glaring at the princesses, the captain pivoted and shouted to the nearby sailors. "Secure them in the hold! They'll be useful when we find their emperor, *if* they aren't telling another story about that." Several sailors advanced on the princesses.

Useful . . . So the hostage idea *had* occurred to him. "It's not just a story!" Seika said. She felt her face flush and her hands start to shake.

"Don't raise his hopes," the doctor scolded. "Impossible remedies are no better than —"

"It is not impossible." Standing, Alejan flexed his wings. He spread the feathers and ruffled them. "Not here."

Six sailors readied their swords and axes. Ji-Lin drew her sword and stepped in front of the lion, between him and the sailors. *Don't fight,* Seika thought at them all. *Please don't fight!*

Deliberately, the lion yawned, displaying his teeth, and said, "The Hundred Islands of Himitsu have plenty of waterhorses. Just like we also have winged lions. All you need to do is find one, and he'll be cured."

The doctor gasped. "The Hidden Islands!" She spun to glare at the captain. "You didn't tell me we're *here!* If it's true, and if they really still have waterhorses, this changes everything!"

The captain held up a hand, and the sailors halted. Ji-Lin glared at them, sword extended, turning slowly in a circle to see them all.

"I've read theories—" the doctor began; then she interrupted herself. "Captain, you hired me for my expertise not only in medicine but in isolated ecosystems. The presence of the lion confirms my hypothesis that even in only two hundred years, there can be significant differences, due to hunting and climate—"

"To the point, Doctor," the captain said. "Are you saying you believe these children? They have delusions of grandeur. They claim they're princesses."

The doctor studied them, circling both Seika and Ji-Lin, examining their clothes and their hair, peering into their eyes as if cataloging every shade of iris color. "They are children of wealth. You can tell by the quality of the stitching. And look here—" She pointed to the embroidery on Ji-Lin's sleeve. "It's clear this is a uniform. See the variation on the Zemylan imperial symbol?"

Enough of this, Seika thought. *We're wasting time.* They needed to get back to the Journey! They were supposed to be at the shrine tomorrow! "I am Princess Seika d'Orina Amatimara Himit-Re, and I swear on my father's throne that every word we have spoken is the truth. These are the islands of Himitsu, and there are waterhorses that can cure the captain's son. And now we must continue on our quest. It is of the utmost importance."

"I know it is difficult for you to trust when you feel so much fear," the doctor said to the captain, "but you must consider that they may be telling the truth."

"They're children!" the captain protested. "Scared children who are telling us what we want to hear."

Alejan shifted, his wings fluttering. He stretched his claws.

His wings are dry, Seika realized. If they could get on his back without being skewered . . . Seika had a burst of inspiration—she could help the boy *and* avoid being held hostage. "As a show of good faith on behalf of the people of Himitsu, let us take the boy to be healed before we continue our quest."

Ji-Lin elbowed her. "Seika? What are you doing?"

Seika ignored her. "It would be our honor and privilege."

One of the court ladies liked to say that. Seika always thought it sounded very dignified.

"He's my son," the captain growled. "I'm not letting you take him anywhere."

He wasn't going to respond to court manners, Seika saw. She switched tactics. "He's dying," she said bluntly. "If you don't let us take him temporarily, then death will take him permanently." She saw the captain pale. "I promise on my honor, on my people's honor, that we will do what we can to help your son."

"Captain, with all due respect, I must insist you seriously consider accepting this offer," the doctor said. "It is highly probable that these girls do have access to a cure. I have long speculated about the presence of flora and fauna on the Hidden Islands that have gone extinct on the mainland. Your boy is beyond my skills . . . Please, let them try to save Kirro."

The captain seemed as if he couldn't decide who to glare at — the doctor, the princesses, or the entire world. "Then we sail to where this waterhorse lives. I'm not trusting two delusional children and their pet monster with my only son! And the waterhorse itself — it could be dangerous. There's a reason they were hunted."

The doctor put her hands on her hips. "You don't have time to wait for your ship to be fixed. He could have days to live, but it could be only hours. Don't be foolish. This is an opportunity! Your son doesn't have to die!"

"Let us help," Seika said.

In her ear, Ji-Lin whispered, "Are you crazy? Let him find his own waterhorse. He's not really that sick — you saw him. He's fine. The doctor must be exaggerating."

He wasn't fine. Seika could tell from the doctor's eyes, the concern that wrinkled the corners. If they didn't help him, he could die. And they'd still be stuck here, prisoners on this ship. This was their best option: a compromise, diplomacy — exactly what she'd been trained for.

Kirro's voice drifted through the hull. "Father? I want to go." His head popped up as he climbed back onto the deck. "I don't want to die." All the fear that he'd hidden before was plain in his voice and on his face. His hands were shaking, his cheeks were pale, and his eyes were bright with tears. "The winged lion is their friend, so they can't be all bad. And they saved us from the sea monster. I saw them dive into the water to draw it out. They didn't have to do that. They didn't have to come help us at all."

"You aren't going with them alone," the captain said. "I will —"

"I cannot carry more than the three children," Alejan interrupted. "I may look as strong as any lion warrior, but I . . ." His voice dropped to a mumble, as if he didn't want to admit it. "I have limits."

Seika crossed her arms and tried her best imperious voice, hoping it was good enough. "We're offering to help you. It's up to you to decide if you trust us."

The captain opened and shut his mouth and then heaved his shoulders forward with such a heavy sigh that he seemed to deflate. "Bring him back safe, or you'll wish we *were* pirates."

"We will," Seika said. "We promise."

CHAPTER
FOURTEEN

T HE BOY, JI-LIN decided, was going to be a problem. He would not stop shrieking in her ear every time Alejan changed altitude. "Whoo-hoo!" He punched his fist into the air as if he wanted to punch a cloud, and Ji-Lin ducked to the side to avoid being hit. As Alejan dipped down, Kirro hollered, "Eeeeee!" They skimmed the surface of the sea. Waves flashed beneath them, catching the sun. Leaning over in the saddle, Kirro tried to touch the surface.

Ji-Lin twisted around to glare at him. "Honestly, don't you have any common sense? Alejan, fly straight. Don't encourage him." Ugh, she couldn't believe Seika had brought this boy along. He didn't seem sick at all, no matter what the doctor said.

Thinking of the bite spreading across his arm, she felt a twinge of doubt.

"You are no fun," Kirro told her.

"And you are acting like . . . like a *child*." She delivered the last word in the most scathing voice she could manage, the voice of one of the masters. Didn't Seika realize they were helping the enemy? He was from Zemyla! Okay, so maybe the Zemylans hadn't been enemies in two hundred years, but still . . . She didn't want him with them. Especially after his father basically said he'd planned to use them as hostages.

The boy snorted. "You're the one pretending to be a princess on some all-important quest. How old are you? Ten? Eleven?" He poked her shoulder.

Ji-Lin knocked his finger away. "Twelve."

"I'm thirteen, or I will be soon, and my dad says he won't even let me steer the ship until I'm fifteen. Admit it: you snuck away to have an adventure. It's okay. I admire that." He threw his arms into the air. "Seriously, you need to try this. Raise your arms! We can't fall. We're belted in."

Behind Kirro, Seika was laughing. Glancing back, Ji-Lin saw she was waving her arms in the air too. *Traitor,* Ji-Lin thought. She shouldn't be listening to this boy, this Zemylan. He didn't understand. He thought Alejan was a *pet* and that they were out here for fun. Flying was a privilege. It required seriousness, and respect for the wind and the sky and for the earth and its pull. It called for trust in the strength of Alejan's wings and knowledge of air currents. Also, she did *not* sneak away to have an adventure!

Granted, Seika *had* tried that, but it hadn't worked.

"Don't you think this is amazing?" Kirro asked, shouting over the wind. "Come on, admit it. It's amazing! Beyond amazing! Stupendously amazing!"

"It *is* amazing!" Seika agreed.

Fine. Yes. Of course it was. At least he appreciated that.

Ji-Lin remembered the first time she'd been hoisted onto Alejan's back. She'd met him the night before, when she'd been crying and he'd brought her out to see the stars. On her way to breakfast, she was called into the courtyard and found Alejan and Master Vanya waiting for her. *He requested you,* Master Vanya told her. *Let's try out this pairing and see how it works.* And then one of the older students came up behind her and, before she had a chance to protest or ask questions, tossed her into the saddle and buckled the straps. *Trust me,* Alejan had told her. *The sky will heal you. And if it doesn't, I'll catch you a really juicy antelope. Antelopes always cheer me up.* And he'd leaped into the air. She'd screamed for the first two minutes and then looked down and realized she could see the imperial city, caught in the valley, with its ribbons of canals. After the flight ended, she didn't cry again. She'd left her tears in the clouds.

Leaning to the side, Kirro spread his arms as if he wanted to catch the wind. Ji-Lin felt the weight in the saddle shift — Seika was leaning over too. "We can't *play,*" Ji-Lin said. "We have responsibilities." Seika should have been the one saying this. "Right, Seika?"

"Forget them," Kirro said. "Just for a few minutes."

"I can't. And I don't know how you can forget you're dying." She still didn't believe he was really dying.

The saddle shifted as he sat upright again. "I want to forget."

"Ji-Lin, that wasn't nice," Seika scolded.

Ji-Lin felt herself blush. She hadn't meant to be cruel. It was just that they were supposed to be in this together, she and Seika and Alejan, not the three of them plus a sailor boy from Zemyla. It was *good* just her, Seika, and Alejan. She thought of how good it had been camping, before the quake, listening to Alejan's story. Even hiding in the cave from the weneb had had its slice of fun — they'd giggled about bugs. And they'd flown together, comfortably, for hours. "He's an enemy," Ji-Lin muttered.

"Two hundred years ago, yes," Seika said. "But now? Besides, we're doing exactly what we're supposed to do: going to the next village. We'll be back on track very soon!"

Alejan rumbled beneath them. "She's correct. The next village is Heiwa-su, on the island of Heiwa, which is our prescribed route."

"And then we'll be on the Journey again, like nothing ever went wrong," Seika said. "We can make up the time, if we fly fast enough, and still be at the shrine by Himit's Day. Isn't that wonderful? Doesn't it make you feel like celebrating?"

Well, yes, it was good. But Ji-Lin still wasn't happy about the Zemylan ship or the sea monster. And she wasn't happy having an extra person on what was supposed to be their special journey. Especially a person who kept insulting her. "The Journey is supposed to be the heir, the sibling, and the lion."

Seika shifted uncomfortably, rocking the saddle. "I know, but . . . It's a compromise. Don't you see, Ji-Lin? The captain wouldn't have let us leave otherwise."

Ji-Lin shook her head. She'd never have guessed that *Seika* would be the one compromising on tradition.

"How do we find a waterhorse?" Kirro asked.

"Ask Seika," Ji-Lin said. "She's the expert." She couldn't stop herself from adding: "I'm just the one out for an adventure." Exactly how did this boy think they'd snuck away, anyway? Seika had tried to escape the palace for just one day and failed. The two of them could never have snuck away even for lunch, much less a cross-island adventure. Ji-Lin told herself she didn't care what he thought. He was a stranger. Not even an islander.

"Most villages have a few waterhorses near them," Seika said.

"Whoa, isn't that unsafe?" Kirro asked. "I mean, they're dangerous, right? Especially to children. That's what the legends say. That's why they were hunted."

"They are not dangerous," Alejan said. "I've met a few. Kind of aloof." Ji-Lin wished Alejan would stop being so friendly too. The boy was an interloper. Wasn't anyone else bothered by his being here?

"They keep the water pure for drinking," Seika said, "so people like to encourage them to stay near towns and villages."

"Huh. How do you 'encourage' them?"

"I read they like apples. And they're supposed to like stories. The books say you can lure a waterhorse to you if you tell a story they haven't heard."

"These same books say waterhorse spit can cure me? And you believe them?"

Ji-Lin heard the doubt and fear creep into his voice, and she suddenly realized he'd been pushing that fear down with all his annoying antics and shrieking. She knew what it was like to push down fear. *Maybe he really is dying,* she thought. For a brief moment, she felt guilty for being so irritated with him.

A very brief moment.

"Yes," Seika said. "I know that part is true. It's confirmed in enough accounts. Sometimes, though . . . well, sometimes the books exaggerate to make a better story, and you can't always tell what's true and what's not."

"There are a lot of tales about waterhorses," Alejan volunteered. "They're made of water. I know a poem about a waterhorse that fell in love with a rainbow."

"That can't be true," Kirro said. "I mean, I'm sure there's a poem, but a horse made of water? How does it eat? Can you see its stomach sloshing around?"

Ji-Lin wanted to growl. Here they were, helping him, in defiance of tradition, and he was arguing. All her new sympathy evaporated. "Are you calling us liars?"

"Hey, I didn't say that. You're putting words in my mouth! It's like you want to not like me. Are you always this grumpy?"

"Only sometimes," Seika said.

Ji-Lin turned again to glare at her.

"It's true," Seika said. "You aren't always grumpy."

"You're not helping," Ji-Lin said to her. To Kirro, she said, "How about no more talking? We'll take you to the water-horse, and you can see for yourself." And then they'd return him to his ship and be done with him. They'd continue the Journey with no more interruptions. With luck, they'd still make it to the volcano island before the end of tomorrow.

They were approaching the island of Heiwa. According to the maps she'd studied with Master Fen, the island was supposed to be shaped like a claw. As Alejan flew toward it, Ji-Lin saw that the maps hadn't lied: the center was a crater that looked like a cupped hand with "fingers" of land that stretched out from it. Inlets ran between the fingers, and rivers were everywhere, crisscrossing like lines on its palm. Grapevines, fig trees, and olive trees made varying shades of green.

Alejan flew low, and Ji-Lin saw that this island, unlike the others, was inhabited.

In one vineyard, she saw workers between the vines. In an olive orchard, a woman was riding a six-antlered elk. Beside a farmhouse, instead of a sheep corral was a nest that housed a griffin. The griffin was napping in the sunlight. Its eagle head rested on its lion paws.

"It's so peaceful and, well, empty," Kirro said. "Zemyla, at least the part where I was born, is packed with people. City after city, up and down the coast. That was one reason Dad took to the sea. I liked the cities, though. Towers that stretch to the sky! Markets packed with every kind of treat you can imagine! And the races — oh, you haven't lived until you've seen a *veevee* race!"

"What's a veevee?" Alejan asked.

"Kind of like a rabbit. But it can breathe fire. Very exciting races."

Ji-Lin tried to imagine what that was like. Here, the villages were spread apart and mostly small. The only city was the capital on Shirro. She'd like to see a place full of cities . . . Except: "That can't be true," Ji-Lin said. "You aren't protected from the koji. How could that many people survive the monsters?"

He shrugged. "We fight them. Or hide from them. We've learned to live with them, I guess. We've got a lot of tricks up our sleeves. Dad said it used to be easier, before the lions quit protecting us, but we manage."

Not all the lions had come to the islands with Himitsu. The ones who had stayed behind had claimed loyalty to the Zemylan emperor. From what Kirro had just said, and from the ship captain's reaction to Alejan, she guessed the lions hadn't stayed loyal permanently. "So they finally threw off their oppressors?"

"I don't know about that. But the empire could really use them back. And the knowledge you have that we lost. About the waterhorses. And how to survive within a dragon's barrier . . ."

Ji-Lin twisted around in the saddle to stare at him. "Is that why your ship came here? You're a spy?"

"No! We're explorers! We came because we're curious! Besides, you guys are supposed to be legends — we weren't expecting to actually find the legendary Hidden Islands. Well, the doctor was really hoping we would, but that's because she wants to write a book about this place. I bet she'll include a whole chapter on waterhorses."

"It is good to be curious," the lion said. "It is what separates your kind from the golden monkeys." He considered that for a moment. "Well, curiosity and basic hygiene. Monkeys, when agitated, like to throw their . . . waste."

"Oh yeah." Kirro nodded vigorously. "Once, my father and I went to this jungle island, and it was only inhabited by monkeys. It was supposed to have a golden temple somewhere on it, and —"

Seika cut him off. "Is this going to be a story about" — she coughed — "waste?"

"Um, yes?"

"Can we skip it? Please?"

"Oh," Kirro said. "All right." He was quiet for a moment. "I also have a story about throwing up. I was —"

"No," Seika and Ji-Lin said in unison.

They flew on. Below, the fields and orchards looked like

stained glass, their various shades of green outlined by blue-black water. They shimmered in the sun. As the wind shifted direction, Alejan soared with it. Leaning forward, Ji-Lin pointed. "There! See it?" Up ahead, a collection of houses lay between two rivers, with fields beyond them. Violet-colored trees were clustered around the river. One house, the largest, rose above the trees.

From far away, it looked like the first village they had visited: all the houses were white and blue, with seashell-coated streets between them. But up close, Ji-Lin could see there was damage: one of the flimsier-looking houses was leaning to the side. A shed had toppled. Rubble lay in a heap all around it, and people with wheelbarrows were carting away the mess.

The earthquake had hit here, too.

Alejan circled the village. Everything was a mess. It looked as if an irate toddler had picked up the village and dumped it upside down. People were working together, clearing and cleaning and hauling away piles of debris.

"Whoa, what happened?" Kirro asked.

"There was a tremor last night," Seika said. "We have lots of them. I hope no one was hurt." Ji-Lin hoped so too. It looked as if this village had been shaken pretty hard.

"The seas were choppy close to the islands," Kirro said. "A couple killer waves. We rode it out, but there was a lot of water in the hull. The crew was scooping it out for hours, until the sea monster arrived to make things extra exciting."

"Land there." Ji-Lin pointed at a clear space in the center of the village.

As Alejan landed, a woman dropped the basket she was carrying and ran to the tallest house. Pounding on the door, she shouted, "Caller! Caller, they're here! They made it!" Out in the field, the men and women began to shout and cheer. "They're here! They've come!"

"Weird," Kirro said. "Unless this is not weird? Is this normal?"

"It's better than normal!" Seika crowed. "They are expecting us! The messenger bird must have arrived. At last, something's going right!" She hopped to the ground much more gracefully than the first time she'd climbed off Alejan's back.

As she dismounted too, Ji-Lin felt a few of the knots in her shoulders loosen. Seika was right — this was a good sign. All they had to do was take care of the boy, and then they could return to the Journey, only half a day behind. Maybe Seika had been right to bargain with the captain. Maybe they'd reach the volcano island as they were supposed to. Maybe, if they hurried, they'd complete the Journey by Himit's Day.

Three little kids who had been playing in the dirt dropped their toys and ran to Alejan, cooing at him and petting him. Climbing off Alejan, Kirro said, "Hello. We're looking for a waterhorse. Do you have a waterhorse near your village? Are waterhorses real?"

One of the little girls stared at him and then stuck her

thumb in her mouth. A slightly older boy giggled as he poked at the singed bits of Alejan's mane. All of them wore bright colors, yellows and purples, and they were all barefoot, their toes stained black with the damp, rich soil from the fields.

"Careful," Kirro warned. "He's a lion."

"I don't eat children," Alejan said, offended, "though, come to think of it, I am a bit peckish. I hope they have meat rolls."

"The damage doesn't look *that* bad," Ji-Lin said. She wondered what would have happened if the tremor had been just a little stronger. It wasn't such a leap to imagine a quake that could knock all these buildings down. She thought of how the masters whispered about the quakes getting steadily worse, and she shivered. The ones she'd felt had been bad enough.

Beside her, Seika was smiling broadly, as if she'd been given the best present ever, and she waved at the people in the fields. They bowed back and hurried toward her. "We really did it! We're supposed to be here! Everything will be okay."

The door of the tallest house swung open and a hulking shape filled the doorway — *Koji!* Ji-Lin's mind shrieked. She reached for her sword. But then the shape strode out, and the sun hit it, and she saw that it was just a man. An enormous man. Rings decorated his arms, clamped tight around his muscles, and his chest had been painted with the symbols for peace and harmony. He also wore the pendants of a caller, as well as several other necklace chains. She released her sword's hilt. His voice boomed across the fields. "Your Highnesses, welcome to Heiwa-su, on the lovely island of Heiwa." Rings and chains tinkling, he swept his body into a low bow.

"Whoa," Kirro breathed. "You're really princesses?" He was looking at them with so much barely suppressed excitement that he was nearly vibrating. His eyes were wide, and he twisted his neck as if he wanted to see everything all at once.

"We've had a difficult journey," Seika said to the caller, "and we are very happy to be here." The people were beginning to gather, coming in from the fields. A few had brought out instruments and were setting them up to play.

The man clasped his hands in front of him and bowed again. "It has been difficult for everyone lately, as you can see. But we too are very happy you are here."

"Was anyone hurt?" Ji-Lin asked.

"Only shaken," he said, sweeping his arms to gesture at the tiny village. "We were lucky this time. Our villages are not built to withstand anything stronger . . . but that is not your concern. Your quest is noble and must be completed regardless of our troubles. You must speak with the Dragon of Himitsu and continue the tradition of safety established by our forefathers."

Kirro was staring at all of them with his mouth hanging open. He waved his hands in the air as if he wanted to clear it of fog. "Wait, you want them to talk to a *dragon?* Do you know what a dragon can do?"

"She keeps us safe," Seika said to him. "Years ago, the Dragon of Himitsu erected the barrier to protect both herself and our people from the cruel tyrant who ruled Zemyla. Every generation, the next heir journeys across the islands to thank the dragon for her continued protection."

"You can't talk to a dragon," Kirro said. "She'll eat you."

Seika frowned, her forehead crinkling prettily. "You don't know what you're talking about." *Ha!* Ji-Lin thought. *Even Seika notices he's irritating.* "You didn't even know about waterhorse spit. Speaking of which . . ." Seika propelled Kirro forward by his elbow. "We brought him here in hopes of finding a waterhorse." She pushed up his sleeve to show the caller. "He was bitten by a scuttle beetle, and we — that is, *I* — promised we'd help him."

Looming over them, the large man leaned closer to Kirro's arm. Kirro started to shrink back, but Ji-Lin gripped his arm tightly. The caller snorted, and his nostrils flared. The hairs on Kirro's arm blew in the air from his exhalation. "One more day and you will die."

Ji-Lin stared at him. *Whoa, he really is sick.* Kirro hadn't been exaggerating. The captain had been right. She couldn't imagine being so close to death and so calm. She began to revise her opinion of the boy.

Kirro swallowed hard. "I was hoping our ship's doctor was wrong."

Ji-Lin wondered if she owed him an apology. If she'd had her way, he could be dead.

"Your doctor was not," the caller said. "I have some skill in medicine. It's necessary, being so far from the capital and its doctors."

If Seika hadn't offered to help . . . If they hadn't found the village . . . If Ji-Lin had left him behind like she'd wanted to . . . She hadn't believed it was so serious. He didn't look sick. He didn't act sick. But the caller had no reason to lie. *We did the right thing bringing him here,* she thought, *even if he's a stranger, even if he's from Zemyla, even if he's irritating.*

The man straightened. At full height, he cast a shadow so broad it seemed he blocked all sun. "You must be healed. After the ritual stories and dances, we will tend to —"

Seika interrupted. "I'm sorry, but there isn't time. We need to heal him now, and then we must return him to his ship and continue the Journey."

Ji-Lin stared at her. She'd thought *nothing* would ever compel Seika to voluntarily skip a ritual. On the other hand, they should have been here in Heiwa-su last night. They had no time to lose. Making it to the volcano in time was more important than the little rituals along the way — or at least, she hoped that was true. They'd already skipped over several.

The caller looked surprised as well, but he didn't argue

with the heir. "Yes, of course, Your Highness. We will make haste to speed you on your way. Himit's Day comes, and you must finish your quest, for the sake of the islands we all love."

"I promise we will," Seika said. Ji-Lin wondered how many promises they'd made since they began this Journey — and whether they'd be able to keep them all.

CHAPTER
FIFTEEN

C LOSER TO THE river, Ji-Lin caught a glimpse of one of the six-antlered elk through the purple trees. Its antlers ran all the way down its neck, each antler sporting several prongs. The elk carried pouches on either side of its stomach, and a woman wrapped in scarves walked next to it, taking seedlings out of the pouches and planting them in the ground. When she saw the princesses by the water, she left the elk and hurried to watch.

She looked worried, Ji-Lin thought. All of them did. And they didn't even know about the koji that had slipped through the barrier. *Earthquakes and monsters,* she mused. Their islands were supposed to be a safe haven. That was the promise of Emperor Himitsu, when he fled from Zemyla. When had their home become so dangerous? *We have to finish the Journey.*

The villagers fanned out behind them, a silent audience.

Stopping at the edge of the river, the caller knelt, scooped water into his cupped hands, and drank. "Fresh," he announced. "The waterhorse is near." Beckoning to one of the little boys, he said, "Run to my house and fetch an apple. You" — he pointed to Kirro — "must tell a story. If he is pleased, he will heal you."

Kirro gulped. "And if he's not?"

"You will die a painful death when the beetle rot reaches your heart."

"Oh. Um, I can tell the story I was told about Prince Himitsu and the Hidden Islands. I think it might explain why my father was so surprised to see you." Kirro climbed onto a rock next to the river. Seika sat behind him, and Ji-Lin stayed with Alejan on the riverbank. The water burbled over the stones and deepened in the center. Craning his neck, Kirro peered into the river. "Uh, do I start? I don't see a horse."

"Begin," the caller commanded. "He will come. Stories draw us all."

Kirro's eyes darted around as if he was looking for a direction to run, but he stayed on the rock. "Okay, um, two hundred years ago, the emperor of Zemyla had a brother named Prince Himitsu, who —"

"He wasn't his brother," Seika corrected him. "And he wasn't a prince. He was a scholar and a servant. 'A humble man who rose to greatness,' according to *The Dawn of Himitsu, a History*."

"You said to tell a story," Kirro said. "This is the one I know. It's not my fault it's different from yours. It's the story my dad told me to distract me from all the fish parts I was throwing up because my stomach doesn't like being at sea and *really* doesn't like rotten fish, but I know you don't want a story about throwing up, so can I talk about Himitsu?"

The caller laid a hand on Seika's shoulder. She blushed. "Sorry — the old stories are ... I've read a lot of them." *Understatement of the year,* Ji-Lin thought. Seika had memorized most of the traditional tales before she was even old enough to read, and then she'd read every one she was allowed to read in the palace library. "Go on," Seika said.

Kirro took a deep breath. "The emperor had a younger brother named Himitsu who wanted to be king. Really, really wanted to be king. The emperor's advisors warned him: your brother is going to betray you, and he said, no, he's my brother, I trust him. And they said, no, really, we think you should execute him or something because he's plotting to kill you. And he said no, I won't hurt my brother!"

"That is indeed different from ours," Alejan noted.

Ji-Lin felt her mouth hanging open. Himitsu wasn't ambitious; he was oppressed! Beside her, Seika was looking at Kirro as if he were a formerly friendly puppy who had inexplicably snapped at her.

"Himitsu, the emperor's brother, befriended a lion who was in prison for cowardice —"

Alejan ruffled his mane. "Excuse me? Winged lions are *never* cowards."

The water began to churn. Ji-Lin leaned forward, but all she saw were bubbles stirring, as if the river were beginning to boil. She wondered what a waterhorse would think of a story full of lies. She could tell what Seika felt about it.

Whatever her sister had thought of the sailor boy before, she clearly wasn't happy with him now. She felt a twinge of pity for Kirro. He didn't know he was digging himself into a hole.

"He was a deserter who was supposed to be guarding the city gate but fled instead. Lots of people died. It was a famous battle. Blood running like water in the streets. There are a lot of poems and songs about it. Before that, winged lions were imperial guardians. After that . . . no one trusted them, least of all the emperor."

There was definitely something in the water. Ji-Lin crept closer on her hands and knees. The head and neck of a horse emerged from the ripples. His mane was flowing water, and the water that formed his head sloshed and shimmered.

With a yelp, Kirro pulled his feet back from the edge. He then continued, in a quavering voice. "The emperor's brother and the traitorous lion hatched a plan. Himitsu set fire to the prison, freeing the lion, and then spread the fire to the palace. The lion was supposed to scoop up the emperor and drop him into the middle of the flames, killing him, but the emperor hid inside a box so the fire couldn't hurt him, and the lion couldn't find him."

Ji-Lin guessed the waterhorse didn't mind hearing such a string of lies. She did, though. The stories . . . who she was and who she was supposed to be was based on them. Lying about them was *wrong*. "If this is true, why didn't the box burn?" Ji-Lin challenged.

"It was a stone box."

"It still would have heated up. Why didn't he cook inside it?"

"It was a magic box? I don't know. It was two hundred years ago, and I wasn't there. The point is that the plan failed, and the emperor and his guards chased his brother and the lion, along with all their conspirators, all the way to the sea. The emperor should have killed him then, but he still couldn't, because he was his brother. So he banished him. Exiled him, his people, and the treacherous lions from Zemyla."

Ji-Lin pressed her lips together. It took all her willpower not to shout that this was the biggest bunch of . . . of . . . *waste* she'd ever heard. Himitsu was a hero! Their savior! He'd escaped a cruel tyrant and led hundreds of people to freedom. And winged lions were heroes, not traitors! She, Seika, and Alejan were all directly descended from heroes.

"The emperor hoped that his brother would find another land and live the rest of his days in peace and happiness, and he could have, but Prince Himitsu's own distrust of his brother was his undoing." He'd dropped into a storytelling voice, complete with dramatic whispers. "Fearing the wrath of the emperor, Himitsu and the other traitors sneakily followed a dragon koji to her nest—a string of newly formed islands off the coast of Zemyla—and hid themselves. Everyone knows that when a dragon lays an egg, she surrounds herself with a magical barrier to protect her egg until it hatches. The traitors timed it just right. As soon as they snuck on shore, the islands vanished, hidden by the dragon." He wiggled his fingers in the air for emphasis.

Seika's voice was so polite that it was chilled. "You think the barrier is to protect a dragon egg, not us?"

Ji-Lin snorted. "Ridiculous."

"The emperor believed the dragon discovered the traitors and ate them, since that's what dragons do with anyone and anything found within their barriers. He mourned them. Even created a holiday to honor their deaths. On it, we all eat pastries with chicken eggs baked in the middle." Obviously pleased with himself, Kirro beamed at all of them. "And that is the story of Prince Himitsu and the Hidden Islands." His smile wavered. "Don't look at me that way. It can't all be true, because you're here, which wouldn't be possible if your ancestors had been eaten. It's just a story!"

The waterhorse spoke, his voice like droplets hitting stone. "Stories are never just stories. They are as essential to life as water."

All the color had drained from Kirro's face. Clearly, he hadn't expected the waterhorse to talk. Ji-Lin almost laughed at him — he deserved that shock.

"Stories are how we understand who we are and who we wish to be. Heroes. Traitors. Both at once. We define ourselves by the stories we tell. We shape ourselves by the stories we hear." The waterhorse rose from the river, the river itself forming his body. Water pooled within him and then dripped down his sides, cascading in streams that formed his head, neck, torso, and legs. His tail was a spray of foam, as was his mane. His eyes were whirlpools. "You wish a boon for your story?"

Swallowing hard, Kirro nodded and held out his arm. *At last he's finally at a loss for words,* Ji-Lin thought. Seika was glaring at him with blazing eyes.

Unexpectedly, Ji-Lin felt sorry for him. He hadn't yet realized how badly he'd messed up, alienating the only one who really liked him. She thought of how she'd feel if she ever alienated Seika.

The waterhorse lowered his face to Kirro's arm and opened his mouth. Water poured out. It encased Kirro's arm, clinging to his skin for a moment before sloughing off.

The caller tossed an apple to the waterhorse. He caught it in a mouth of foam. Turning away, the waterhorse galloped through the shallows. Water sprayed off his mane and scattered beneath his hooves, leaving a dry riverbed behind him.

Twisting his arm backward and forward, Kirro asked, "Am I healed?"

The caller reached over, steadied Kirro's arm, and then flicked the gray scales from the boy's skin. He rubbed the remaining water across the red until it faded to pink. "You will bear the mark always, but it will never worsen."

"That was incredible." Kirro stared again at the retreating

waterhorse. The waterhorse was galloping across the rice fields, leaving a trail of water in his wake, a snaking line across the green.

"Yes," Ji-Lin agreed. "It was." As annoying as the story itself had been, seeing the waterhorse had been amazing.

Kirro tested his arm, bending and stretching it. "I'm not dying." He said the words as if trying them out like a new set of clothes. Ji-Lin couldn't see any trace of the gray rot. The miracle of it was almost enough to erase the insult of his story. *It's just a story,* Ji-Lin thought, *no matter what the waterhorse said.* And he was healed. They'd done what they said they'd do, and now they could return him to his father and go on with what they were supposed to be doing.

"I am curious," the caller said. "Why is this boy with you and not his own people? They should not have distracted you with his fate. You're on the Journey, and your time is precious."

"His people didn't know about waterhorses," Seika explained.

"Oh, they knew," Alejan said darkly. "They just killed them all." He, Ji-Lin could tell, was still offended by Kirro's story. She knew how proud he was of his heritage—he believed he was descended from a line of heroes, and that that would be his future too. She believed she was as well. She didn't like what Kirro's story implied about her own ancestors either. But it was only a story, a meaningless set of lies.

"We thought they were dangerous!" Kirro protested. "They were said to lure innocent children to ride them and then drag them under to their watery deaths!" He waved his arms over his head, as if that would emphasize how dangerous waterhorses were.

"I am ashamed that any islander would embrace such ignorance and teach their children to believe such lies." Considering the boy, the caller walked in a circle around him. "Where are you from, child?"

"Uh . . . a ship?" He shrank back, as if suddenly realizing how unhappy everyone around him was. His eyes darted right and left, as though he wanted to bolt, except there was no place to run. Ji-Lin thought of how she'd felt on the ship, when the doctor and the captain were studying and judging them. She fidgeted, uncomfortable with the way this was going. Couldn't they simply take him home, then fly to the shrine?

"He's from Zemyla," Seika said. Her arms were crossed and her eyes stormy. She said the word *Zemyla* as if it were the greatest insult she could think of.

Poor little sailor boy, Ji-Lin thought. He'd managed to *really* irritate Seika. He couldn't have known how much she loved the old tales and traditions.

The caller recoiled. "You bring danger to our islands!" he said to Kirro. "You are the harbinger! You are the scout. You come to see if we are ripe for invasion." He then advanced on Kirro. His hands were curled into massive fists.

"What? No!" Kirro backed up so quickly that he tripped over rocks and clumps of grass. He fell hard and then scrambled up again. "We're explorers! We look for new trade routes and new items to trade and new ideas that will help our people against the koji." He bumped into Alejan. The lion ruffled his wings, and the boy jumped forward. He spun in a circle as if suddenly realizing he was trapped. Ji-Lin felt even sorrier for him. It wasn't his fault he'd been taught that awful story. And it wasn't his fault his father's ship had come through the barrier.

"Their ship looked like illustrations I've seen of pirate ships," Seika said. She continued to glare at Kirro. "And it had a weapon that shook the air and killed a sea monster."

"We're not pirates! Smugglers, maybe, but only when money is short. And the weapon is called a cannon. It's for defense against scyllas and valravens." He looked as if he wanted to sink into the ground. "You promised to return me when I was healed!"

The caller loomed over Kirro. "And what will you tell your people when you return to them? How will you portray the many-times-great-grandchildren of your would-be emperor-killer?"

Kirro shrank down until he was kneeling. "I'll tell them the t-truth."

Ji-Lin looked from Kirro to the caller and back again — couldn't the caller see he was scaring him? He was just a boy who didn't want to die, and he'd only done what they'd told him to do: tell a story.

"What is the truth in your eyes, Zemylan boy?" the caller bellowed. "Will you call our kindness weakness and say we are ripe for the plundering? Will you speak of our comfort and wealth as though they were prizes to be won? Of our peace as though it were a folly to be laughed at and scorned?"

"No!"

"You may look the innocent child, but you're a viper in our midst, ready to sting us. You should be locked away so you cannot spread your poison. Tossed into darkness and forgotten until all danger has passed."

Kirro pivoted to face the princesses. "You said you'd return me. You promised! 'Bring him back safe,' my dad said." Ji-Lin felt herself blush — they had said they'd take care of him. Letting this man bully him was not taking care of him.

Seika seemed to deflate. "We *did* promise."

"Be grateful they saved your life, little enemy," the caller growled. "These are our princesses, the living embodiment of our freedom, honor, and hope for the future."

Kirro scrunched his face. "They aren't 'embodiments'; they're kids like me. Like me! I'm just a kid! I'm not the embodiment of your enemies. I'm just me, Kirro, ship's boy. I'm not a danger. And I want to go home."

"Can you promise there is no danger to our princesses if they return to your ship? Can you promise they will be allowed to remain free and unharmed?" The caller's voice thundered so loudly that the other villagers, who had all been watching from a discreet distance, jumped. Ji-Lin knew how Kirro felt — the caller's voice was as loud as a master's roar. She knew what it was like to be roared at like that.

"His father wanted to use us as hostages," Seika said.

"He didn't!" Kirro yelped. "He wouldn't! Well, maybe he would, but he wouldn't hurt you. He just wants to talk to the emperor, and once he does, he'll let you go." Ji-Lin thought of how she'd felt when the captain didn't believe them.

The caller gripped his arm. "Then by your own words, the princesses cannot return to your ship. I said it: enemies!" Echoing him, Alejan growled.

Trying to twist away, Kirro yelped. Tears pricked his eyes. *I still don't like him, but this isn't right.* "Let him go," Ji-Lin ordered.

Everyone turned to look at her.

Bowing, the caller released Kirro. "Forgive me, Your Highness. I am only concerned for your safety and for the completion of your Journey. You must be at the shrine on the volcano island on Himit's Day. That's tomorrow!"

Ji-Lin looked at Kirro. He massaged his newly healed arm as his eyes flickered from the caller to the princesses to the villagers. She didn't want to feel sorry for him, but she couldn't help it. He was right: he was a kid, like they were, not an embodiment. Just a kid.

"We can leave him here," Seika said. "You can send word to the boy's ship. When the ship is fixed, they can come claim him. Do you have messenger birds?"

"I can't stay here!" Kirro yelped. "They hate me!"

He was right. If he stayed, they'd imprison him—the caller had already threatened it. And what would happen when the Zemylan ship came to claim him and discovered Kirro being treated as a prisoner? She looked at the caller's muscles and his still-red face and thought of the Zemylans' strange weapon. If the caller and the captain argued . . .

The caller shook his head, and his necklaces clapped together like tiny bells. "A Zemylan ship, here? Your Highness, I beg you to reconsider! We are but a tiny village, with no defenses. If they should choose to attack . . ." That was not so different from what Ji-Lin had been thinking, but what else could they do? They couldn't risk further delay.

"They say they're explorers," Ji-Lin began.

"Please, Princesses, take me with you!" Kirro said.

All of them stared at him. It occurred to Ji-Lin that this was the first time he'd called them princesses. He'd accepted who they were.

"Let me come with you to the dragon," he pleaded, "and then you can return me after."

"You *want* to stay with us?" Ji-Lin asked. She didn't like

this idea — and from their expressions, Seika and Alejan clearly hated it — but they couldn't abandon him here, not if the caller refused to allow him to stay outside a cell. There was something so sad and pathetic about the way he was looking at them.

"I don't think we should —" Seika began.

"He's our responsibility," Ji-Lin interrupted. "You decided that, remember?" She still didn't like it, but they had promised to take care of him. They couldn't leave him to be imprisoned.

Seika glared at her, then at Kirro, then at the caller. At last, she sighed. "I know. You're right. I promised. Very well, we bring him."

To the caller, Ji-Lin said, "Will you send a bird to his people and let them know he's healed and to sail to the volcano island? They can reclaim him there."

The caller bowed. "Yes, Your Highness. And thank you. Prince Balez and Master Shai will be better equipped to welcome, or repel, his people as needed."

To Kirro, Seika said, "You can't come with us all the way to the dragon. We're bending tradition enough as it is. The final ritual must be me, my sister, and Alejan."

He bobbed his head. "I won't interfere."

"It could be dangerous," Ji-Lin warned. So far, they'd encountered koji and weathered a tremor. She couldn't predict what else would happen. "Are you sure you'd rather come with us than stay here?"

Kirro waved his arms in the air. "Yes! You healed me with a horse made out of a river. You're friends with a winged lion. Absolutely, I want to stay with you and see what other miracles I can."

More bravery, or truth? Ji-Lin wondered. Or did he just not want to be imprisoned? She exchanged glances with Seika. Sighing, Seika gave a small nod. "Okay, it's settled," Ji-Lin said. "You can come with us. But please, try not to be so annoying."

CHAPTER
SIXTEEN

THEY FLEW FAST and low over the fields and orchards and then the marshlands that fed into the sea. Flocks of birds startled from the rushes and took to the air, until the sky was so thick with birds that they swept like a cloud over the island, casting shadows beneath them. Soon Alejan had crossed the island, and they were again over open water. Seika watched the waves below and wondered if they hid more sea monsters.

"You're serious about going to talk to a dragon?" Kirro asked. "You know they're monstrous lizards who roast people for lunch, right? Especially people who go anywhere near their hoards of gold and jewels."

"She's the Dragon of Himitsu," Seika said, trying not to sound irritated. He had to have noticed how badly he'd upset them, yet he'd returned to cheerfulness almost instantaneously, as if he hadn't just insulted their heritage and all their beliefs. "She doesn't roast people; she summons lava."

"Oh, okay. That's so much better."

"You're thinking of northern land dragons. She's not an oversize lizard, and she doesn't have a hoard of gold and jewels. She's not that kind of dragon. Years ago, she created the islands," Seika continued. "All the islands of Himitsu are volcanic. It was the dragon who caused the earth to explode in fiery rocks and rise out of the ocean, and it was the dragon who caused the volcano to calm again so the lava could cool into land."

"How do you know?" Kirro asked.

"I've studied our history," Seika said, "which is better than you, repeating ignorant lies." The emperor of Zemyla must have spread those lies to hide his ancestors' cruelty. She told herself she shouldn't blame the sailor boy. It wasn't his fault he was ignorant, though it was his fault for repeating such things. She could blame him for that. And she didn't have to like him anymore. *I only liked him because I wanted my own friend,* Seika thought. *Ji-Lin already has Alejan.* It had been nice to have her own travel companion. Until he'd proved to be rude.

"I only know what I've been told."

"You've been told lies."

"Hey, you only know what you've been told too!"

He was right, and that thought made her squirm in the saddle. Seika didn't want to be having this conversation anymore. She wished they could have left Kirro back on Heiwa. But she didn't break promises.

She'd never wanted so badly to break one. Back on the island, she had been seconds away from leaving the boy and his lies behind. Instead, Ji-Lin had pushed for them to do the right thing, even though she didn't seem to like Kirro at all.

What's wrong with me? Seika wondered. First she'd bent

tradition by bringing Kirro with them, and then she'd been tempted to go back on her solemnly given word.

Catching a shift in currents, Alejan soared higher above the sea. The sun was already touching the horizon, and Seika stared at it, searching for the flicker — there, the barrier.

That's what's wrong, she thought. *Not me.*

The boy and his ship shouldn't have been able to cross it. The sea monster shouldn't have been in their waters. "Nothing is turning out the way it was supposed to," Seika said.

"Indeed," Alejan said. "We are half a day off our schedule. We should have been in Heiwa last night, not today. I thought I could make up the time, but . . . we won't make the next village by nightfall."

Ahead, she saw black sand beaches. Strange trees grew from the sand, shaped like ladders that climbed into nothing. She didn't have the maps of the islands memorized the way Alejan and Seika did, but she believed him. "What do we do?"

"We either fly in the dark, or we camp on a beach," Ji-Lin said. "Both are dangerous. Given our rotten luck so far, we could just as easily run into another koji while we camp as while we fly."

Seika considered it. If camping wasn't guaranteed to be safer, then they should just fly on. Every mile they flew brought them a mile closer to completing the Journey. "We should keep flying," she decided, "so long as Alejan is able."

"I'll fly until I can't fly any farther," Alejan said. To emphasize his point, he flapped harder, and they shot through the air. Wind blasted Seika's face. "Straight through to the volcano island. If we don't stop, we can make it by dawn of Himit's Day."

"Don't push yourself too hard," Ji-Lin cautioned.

He slowed, but only slightly. The wind still streamed around them. Seika brushed her hair off her cheeks.

"I'm sorry," Kirro said meekly.

"Are we doing the right thing by bringing the boy?" Alejan asked. "Is this what Master Shai would have done?"

"Yes!" Kirro chirped, then: "Who's Master Shai?"

"We couldn't have left him there," Ji-Lin said. "You saw how angry the caller was. What if he'd stayed that angry when Kirro's father came for him? They could have fought. Our people could have been hurt."

To Kirro, Alejan said, "Master Shai is a Guardian of the Shrine. She and Prince Balez ensure that no one disturbs the dragon. Master Shai is one of the greatest heroes that the Hundred Islands have ever seen." As they flew, he told them the story of how the great lioness had saved a village from a lava flow.

The sun set, the moon replaced it, and stars speckled the sky. Below, the sea was dark, and ahead, the islands were shadows, a string of gray beads on the black water. This wasn't the way Seika had imagined her first journey across the islands. It was supposed to be triumphant. It had started that way, with drums and dancing, but now . . . it felt so wrong. First the weneb, then the Zemylan ship, then the boy and his story . . .

"How do you even know she's alive?" Kirro asked. "Your Dragon of Himitsu. Say she really created the islands two hundred years ago. Shouldn't she have died by now?"

That was a horrifying thought. Seika wished Kirro hadn't said it.

"And even if she's not dead, shouldn't her egg have hatched? Dragon eggs take a long time to hatch, but two hundred years? Dad says it should have hatched fifty years ago, at least. He said there was a big push to find the islands when he was a kid, but it failed. Maybe the egg's a dud. Maybe it died in the shell."

Alejan rumbled. "The barrier exists; therefore, she does."

"And our stories don't even mention an egg," Seika put in. "It doesn't exist."

"How do you know?" he asked. "What do your stories say?"

In his storyteller voice, Alejan said, "The great dragon was injured in a mighty battle and unable to defend herself, and so the first emperor, Emperor Himitsu, struck a bargain to defend her from any koji that remained on the islands if she would let him, his people, and the winged lions live here in peace."

Kirro snorted. "She stayed injured for two hundred years?"

"Some wounds don't heal," Ji-Lin pointed out. "Maybe she can't defend herself. There are always two Guardians of the Shrine — a warrior and a lion — at all times, who are there to guard her and make sure no one but the heir ever disturbs her."

"But you don't *know*," he countered. "She could be vicious, and the 'Guardians' are there to keep her from eating everyone. Maybe they sacrifice princesses to her to make her happy."

Seika again wished he weren't here — Ji-Lin had been right, back on the Zemylan ship. He didn't belong with them. It should have been simple: fly to the island, renew the bargain, and complete the ritual, but he had to complicate it with his stories and questions. Seika didn't want complicated, not when everything was already messed-up enough. "She won't eat me," Seika said firmly. "There's no egg. And she's not dead. Now, please — and I ask this with all politeness — please shut up."

She thought she heard Ji-Lin swallow a laugh.

They flew in silence toward the black shore, shrouded in night. The moon glinted off the water and then was swallowed by clouds. Seika thought back to how quickly they'd been sent on their quest. She hadn't felt ready — and everything that had happened since only proved they weren't.

"A storm brews," Alejan said.

"Yes, it does." Even though there had been many wonderful moments, there were too many things that felt wrong.

"I never expected any of this to happen." Seika studied the back of Ji-Lin's head and wondered if she felt the same. Of course not. Ji-Lin was always so certain and confident.

"I am not speaking poetically," Alejan said. "Clouds are building, and there is a . . . sense in the air. Can you feel it?"

"We need to turn around," Ji-Lin said. "We can't risk flying in a thunderstorm."

"But we're already miles from the last island," Kirro objected. He glanced behind them, and Seika heard the whoosh of wind and then a cry, birdlike, carried on the night air. "Um, can you fly faster?"

"I am already at my limit." Alejan's wing strokes had slowed. They dipped low, toward the darkened sea. "We will not evade the storm."

Kirro again looked back. "Maybe go past your limit? The storm isn't the only thing we need to evade."

Seika turned too, as did Ji-Lin. It took her brain a few seconds to sort out what she was seeing, and when she did, she gasped. "Koji!" There were three of them, with bat wings and wolf heads. They writhed as they flew.

"Faster!" Ji-Lin shouted.

Alejan pumped his wings, grunting from the effort, and they shot through the air. Seika, Ji-Lin, and Kirro held on as they flew low over the water, toward the nearest island.

"What are they?" Ji-Lin asked.

Seika tried to remember illustrations and descriptions from the scrolls —

"*Valravens!*" Kirro cried.

"You know what they are?" Ji-Lin asked. "How do you fight them?"

"We shoot them with a cannon!"

"We don't have cannons,'" Ji-Lin said grimly. Seika thought of the cannon on the ship — Kirro had said they used them against scyllas and valravens — but her people didn't have anything like that. It must have been a Zemylan invention. *If koji are going to keep coming like this, we need one,* she thought as Ji-Lin shouted, "Alejan, we need more speed!"

Seika shot another look back at the valravens. Closer, she could see that their snakelike bodies were covered in black raven feathers, and their white wings looked like those of enormous bats. Catching the wind, the three valravens spread into a V formation. "They're gaining on us!" she cried.

"Down!" Ji-Lin ordered Alejan. She leaned forward, and Seika and Kirro leaned with her. Alejan dove toward the ocean, pulled up, and skimmed the waves. Behind them, the valravens dove as well, calling to one another.

Waves crashed beneath them, and Seika felt the spray on her face. "Look for a cave!" Seika called. The island up ahead, the island of Dokutsu, was supposed to be riddled with them. There should be hundreds. As they neared the island, Seika looked back to see that the valravens were even closer. So close she could see the glow of the leader's eyes. "Alejan!"

With a mighty wing beat, he flew toward the clouds.

"Hold on!" Flying nearly vertically, he entered them. Everything blurred to gray. Seika couldn't even see his wings. She felt rain on her face and arms. Behind her, she heard the cries of the valravens.

Thunder rumbled.

"Get out of the clouds, Alejan," Ji-Lin urged. "Lightning!"

"I am born of the earth and the stars," Alejan said. "The sky will not harm me." He pounded his wings harder. "Just a few . . . seconds . . . more . . ." Half of the sky lit up, the clouds brightening, and thunder boomed around them, shaking her all the way down to her bones, as if it were echoing inside her. Alejan aimed for where the light was brightest. And then another bolt formed ahead, snaking through the cloud down to the sea.

Looking back, Seika saw a valraven's wolflike jaws only a few feet behind them. Spittle dripped as its gums curled back in a snarl.

Another bolt of lightning — this time, behind them.

Seika heard one of the valravens scream as another clap of thunder sounded so close her teeth rattled.

Abruptly, Alejan dove out of the clouds toward the ocean, and then skimmed along the black sand. Lightning lit up the beach. "There!" Kirro pointed past them at a darker patch in the rocky shore, briefly lit. Veering toward it, Alejan flew into the cave. He collapsed just inside the entrance.

All of them sat on his back, not moving, listening.

Rain fell hard outside, hitting the sand and the sea. They heard caws, then another clap of thunder. The cries of the valravens receded. Finally, there was only rain.

"Must rest," Alejan said as the three of them tumbled gently from his back.

"Sleep, my friend," Ji-Lin said, her voice floating out of the darkness. "You flew bravely today. You'd make your ancestors proud."

"My ancestor was not a deserter," Alejan mumbled. "He was brave. Like I am."

"He was, and you are," Ji-Lin said. "Very brave. Now sleep."

Soon the lion's breathing slowed to a steady purr. Seika wrapped her arms around herself and leaned against the wall of the cave.

In the darkness, Kirro spoke up. "Listen, I'm sorry about the story. If I'd known it would make you all so mad, I'd have told the one about the sea monster who fell in love with a rock, or about the griffin who only ate vegetables. I just . . . I thought the waterhorse would want an important story. I swear I wasn't trying to insult you."

Seika knew she should forgive him. It was silly to stay angry. It was only a story. But he was right: the story was important. "Himitsu founded our islands and created a safe haven. He gave us peace. Everything we are is because of him."

"It was two hundred years ago. How do you even know he was real?"

"He was," Seika said.

"All right. Not going to argue with you about this. But —"

"You can't say you aren't going to argue, then say 'but,'" Ji-Lin said. "You apologized, and we accept your apology. Leave it at that."

He fell silent.

Seika closed her eyes. All her muscles felt tense, as if they were still fleeing from the valravens through the storm. She listened to the rain hit the sands and rocks.

"You know, I'm really a likable guy, once you get to know me."

"Kirro, be quiet," Ji-Lin said.

"You're determined to think the worst of me, just because I'm from Zemyla. It's not my fault where I was born. And you know what? Even though you're from an island of traitors — *not* my words, just how you're known — and even though you're kind of stuck-up and full of yourselves, I like you. You're interesting."

Seika didn't know how to respond to that, but she heard Ji-Lin snort.

"There's a saying: 'May your life be interesting,'" Kirro said. "It's supposed to be a curse . . ." Seika remembered seeing that saying in one of the older scrolls. It had been set off alone on a page, as if it were too significant to be near other words. ". . . but I'd rather be interesting than dead."

"Keep talking and you *will* be dead," Ji-Lin threatened. Seika didn't think she meant it. Not entirely.

"Right. Sleep. Sorry. Can you try to like me a little better when you wake up?"

"Depends on whether you get less annoying," Ji-Lin said.

"I'll try," he said, sounding utterly sincere, and then he stopped talking. After a while, his breathing became even, and so did Ji-Lin's. Seika lay awake, thinking about the boy and the koji and the dragon and the barrier that was supposed to keep them safe.

Somehow, she slept while the storm continued to rage.

⌒

By dawn, the rain had stopped. Seika woke with fuzz in her face. In her sleep, she'd used the winged lion as a pillow. She spat out bits of fur as she sat up. "Sorry, I —"

"Shh." Ji-Lin was crouched by the mouth of the cave, hidden behind a rock. Outside, the sea and sky looked gray and empty, but the black sand beach . . . less so. "They're there," she said quietly. "Two of them. I think the third was hit by lightning."

Creeping forward, Seika peeked through the rocks, and Ji-Lin pointed to the shapes by the water. The two koji were stretched on the black sand. Their white bat wings were splayed out, drying in the dawn. "Do they know we're here?" Seika asked.

"No. Maybe. Probably. Does it matter? We can't get past

them anyway." Ji-Lin crept back into the cave, and Seika followed her. "Father should have sent someone else, an experienced rider."

Seika had never heard Ji-Lin talk like that. It was almost as unsettling as seeing the valravens relaxed on the beach. "The Emperor's Journey is supposed to be —"

"We are a long way from 'supposed to be.'" Ji-Lin sucked in air. "With koji on the islands, we'll be lucky to make it to the volcano at all, much less home again."

Seika didn't know what to say. Ji-Lin always seemed so confident. The idea that she was doubting herself . . . doubting *them* . . . questioning the tradition they'd always believed in . . . "We *have* to make it." As she said the words, the reason why began to crystallize.

"Why?" Kirro asked. "We're safe in this cave. Can't we stay here until the valravens get bored and go away? I don't want to be their breakfast."

"We have to complete the Journey before the end of the day," Ji-Lin said. "If we don't, the barrier will fall and the islands will be overrun with even more valravens and scyllas and wenebs and a hundred other monsters, each probably worse than the one before."

Seika took a deep breath and said, "The barrier is already failing."

As soon as she said it, it felt real. She knew in a deep-in-her-bones kind of way that it was true. It explained the koji and the Zemylan ship. It even explained why they'd been sent on the Emperor's Journey *now*. The magical barrier that had kept them safe for two hundred years was weakening, allowing in their age-old enemies. "We weren't sent on the Emperor's Journey because we were ready," Seika said. "We were sent because we're needed. The barrier is failing, and we are supposed to ask the dragon to fix it and keep it strong. *I* am supposed to." As hard as she tried to stay calm, Seika heard her voice become more and more shrill. "Father didn't trust us enough to tell us the truth. He didn't think we were ready to know anything important. But he had to send us anyway, because if he didn't . . ."

Ji-Lin reached over and took her hand. Seika's fingers closed around hers.

"I'm right, aren't I?" She should have realized it sooner. But the thought had crept up on her, one impossibility after another, until the truth was right there, staring her in the face.

Alejan stood and shook his mane. "If you are correct, then we have to fly! Every moment we delay, more monsters will come."

"Um, monsters outside right now, remember?" Kirro said.

Ji-Lin's other hand closed around her sword's hilt. "We'll have to fight them."

That was a terrible idea. Seika knew Ji-Lin had trained

to fight, but she'd also seen those monsters' teeth. The four of them had barely escaped last night, and that was with the help of the lightning. "There are two!"

"I know that," Ji-Lin said. "Do you have a better idea?"

Seika looked away from the opening toward the darkness. There were supposed to be tons of caves all over this island, according to the books she'd read. "Are either of you afraid of the dark?"

Kirro raised his hand. "Yes. I mean, no. Not the dark. Just the things in it. Especially things with teeth. And bats. I don't like bats. Guano stinks really bad. This one time, my father landed the ship on an island with, like, a thousand bats. Everything stank for weeks."

Seika reminded herself she'd been through the tunnels under the palace. She could do this. Standing up, she walked away from the mouth of the cave. Hands in front of her, she kept walking until the shadows closed around her.

"Seika? Are you all right?" Ji-Lin's voice was soft but worried.

"I think it . . . it's a tunnel. I don't know how far it goes." She returned to them. "But if we stay close and are careful, we can try it. Maybe there's another exit."

Ji-Lin looked back out at the valravens. "And if there isn't, we come back and fight."

"You two have terrible ideas," Kirro said. "You know that, right? Talking to dragons, wandering through strange caves . . ."

". . . bringing along annoying boys," Ji-Lin finished.

"Ooh, nice," Kirro said, but he stood and dusted off his pants. "But coming along was my idea."

"Hah. Only after an entire village didn't want you," Ji-Lin pointed out.

"Please stop," Seika said. Arguing wasn't going to help. She stared into the darkness and thought again of the tunnels beneath the palace. She wasn't afraid of the dark.

"I will go first," Alejan proclaimed. "It is not as dark for me. Hold on to my fur." He padded forward, and as he passed, Kirro grabbed his tail. Ji-Lin took his hand, and Seika took hers. They headed into the blackness. "Aren't you glad you brought a cat along?"

"Always," Ji-Lin said.

He purred, as if he were a housecat instead of a lion.

"For the record, I don't like caves, with or without bats," Kirro said. "I didn't know I don't like caves, but I really don't like caves. But I like valravens even less."

Seika tried to pretend that this was no different from being beneath the palace. She'd braved rats there. This cave could also have bats and spiders. Or it could have monsters. There were monsters in places that shouldn't have monsters. She wondered if any place was safe anymore. *Not with the barrier failing,* she thought.

Why was it failing?

She thought about Kirro's story and about all his questions. The dragon had lived for two hundred years. Seika didn't know what was old for a dragon. Maybe the dragon was sick. Maybe she was dead. Maybe she was gone.

"Can we sing or something?" Kirro asked. "It might make this less, you know, ominous and awful."

"I don't sing," Ji-Lin said.

She used to, Seika remembered. Loudly and off-pitch. It used to drive the court ladies crazy when she bellowed out ballads, mangling the words. "Remember this one?" Seika sang the melody softly:

> *"When twisted gray the morning, the riders*
> *   started out.*
> *The wind was strong, the sea was deep, there was*
> *   danger about.*
> *When dark and cold the afternoon, the sailors*
> *   raised their sail.*
> *The sea was rough, the wind was fierce, the water-*
> *   folk did wail . . ."*

It was the tale of the Tragedy of the Deep, when the largest kraken ever seen attacked a ship off the coast of Zemyla, centuries before Himitsu was born. Six warriors and twenty sailors lost their lives.

Ji-Lin joined in, taking the lower harmony.

And then Alejan, his voice deep beneath theirs.

"Hey, I know that one," Kirro said. "Even know the same words. Everyone dies, right?"

"It's sung on the darkest day of the year at the Temple of the Sun, to remind riders and lions of the risk we all may be asked to take in defense of the innocent," Alejan said. "The kraken was defeated, though at great cost."

"We're better at it now," Kirro said. "All our ships carry cannons."

"As I remember it, you still needed our help," Ji-Lin said.

"And I did say thanks, didn't I? If not . . . thanks."

"You're welcome."

They sang together softly as they walked through the darkness, until they saw a speck of light ahead. It was a splash of amber at first, but it grew into a glow. They quieted, shuffling toward the light in silence, until they could see the walls of the tunnel.

The cave floor rose, and Seika thought the path looked worn. She saw a child's shoe wedged between two rocks, and then a shard of pottery. "People were here," Seika said quietly. She picked up the shoe. Its leather was still soft, and it wasn't covered in dust. "Recently."

After many minutes of walking, the tunnel widened. Sconces shed amber light all around them. Cots lined the walls, and piles of crates filled the center of a vast hall. One crate was busted open, and a set of shelves had fallen over. Dishes were broken on the floor, and a jar of rice had spilled —all caused, Seika guessed, by the latest tremor. But the walls seemed sturdy. And more importantly, it felt safe. "It's a koji shelter!" she said.

"Then there must be a village nearby," Ji-Lin said.

"There must be *food*," Alejan said.

Looking around, Kirro said, "This is much nicer than that dark tunnel. Can we stay here? Whoa, are those diamonds?" He pointed toward the ceiling. Seika looked up and saw glittering stones inlaid in the black ceiling, in the shape of stars, to make it look as if they were walking beneath the night sky.

Alejan was already trotting toward some of the shelves, helping himself to a string of dried fish. The others dug into the stores. There was water. And food! Seika ate until her sides hurt.

A scrape echoed through the hall.

"Was that you?" Kirro asked.

"Someone is here," Alejan said.

"You heard it too?" Kirro asked.

Alejan sniffed the air. "I smell them."

"That's freaky," Kirro said. "Unless they need baths. Then it's just disgusting."

A scrape, then a thud. *Scrape, thud. Scrape, thud.* Quickly, Ji-Lin replaced the lids on the jars they'd been eating from. They crouched together behind a collection of crates.

Peeking out, Seika saw a woman step out of a patch of darkness—through a door they hadn't seen before. She wore a blue silk dress covered in flecks of gold and had her silver hair piled on top of her head and filled with jewels. One of her legs was made of silver. She walked toward where they were hidden, her silver leg dragging with a scrape and a thud. She wore a caller's pendant. "Come out," the woman said. "I know you're there."

They looked at one another.

"She doesn't sound friendly," Kirro whispered. "Maybe we should go back."

Seika knew she should let Ji-Lin step out first — she was her guard. But this woman was one of their people. And Seika was the heir. "I'll talk to her."

"Wait — she could be dangerous," Kirro said. "Not all people are nice."

"It's traditional for the islanders to help us on the Journey," Seika said. "Besides, I trust our people. They want us to succeed. They *need* us to succeed."

Seika emerged from behind the crate, and whatever she was going to say fled from her mind. The woman was beautiful. She rivaled the portraits of their mother. Her face looked as if it had been carved and polished by a master artist and then painted. She even frowned beautifully, her lips in a perfect rainbow shape. Seika felt grubby and flawed in front of her. Worse, she couldn't think of what to say.

Ji-Lin hissed, "Seika!"

Now was the time to speak, not to be shy! Seika reminded herself she was a princess. She'd had lessons on poise and proper manners. She'd survived a weneb, a Zemylan ship, and a flock of valravens. But before she could gather her nerves, she realized the woman was not alone. She turned her head. People were in the shadows, skulking at the edges of the light. Dozens of them, maybe even a hundred, watched them from all around their hiding place. "I am Princess Seika d'Orina Amatimara Himit-Re, and we are on the Emperor's Journey. My companions and I seek your help."

Grumbling, Ji-Lin stepped out from behind the crate, as did Alejan and Kirro.

The woman bowed deeply. "Your Highnesses!"

"See?" Seika said to Ji-Lin. "They're friendly." She knew her people. She had to trust that — the way they trusted her. *I won't let our people down.*

"We received the emperor's messenger bird and expected you in Doskaki before nightfall — but then the monsters came. We feared the worst." The caller had a tear in her eye. It crept down her cheek. "I speak for all of us when I say we are so happy to see you safe and unharmed, and we swear we will protect you to the best of our ability, until the lions and riders come to rid us of this scourge."

"We haven't come for protection," Seika said as firmly as she could. "Today is Himit's Day. We must reach the volcano island and complete the Journey as quickly as possible."

She heard the gasps from the shadows.

"Oh no, you cannot leave! Please, Your Highnesses! There are valravens on the island." Wringing her hands, the beautiful caller bowed again. "Forgive me, but your safety is important to all of us."

"The safety of our people is what's important," Seika said. She knew she'd never sounded so much like her father's heir, but then she'd never been so convinced she was right. After Uncle Biy's disastrous meeting with the dragon, Father had completed the ritual and it had fixed everything. Once she completed the ritual, everything would be fixed again. *That's why Father sent us,* she thought. "Our quest cannot be delayed. We must escape the valravens."

"There are two, and they fly fast," Alejan said.

"If the valravens could be distracted," Ji-Lin said thoughtfully, "we could slip past them." She met Seika's eyes as she added, "It's not running away; it's running toward."

"You are asking me to place you, our princesses, in danger!" The caller looked distressed. "You cannot ask me to do that."

"We *are* asking you," Seika said. She raised her voice so all the hidden, watching people could hear. This was her responsibility, and she was *not* going to let anyone, no matter how well-intentioned, prevent her from doing what she knew was right.

CHAPTER
SEVENTEEN

O N THE OTHER side of Seika, Kirro raised his hand. "I might have a suggestion."

Everyone turned to look at him.

"You do?" Ji-Lin asked. She didn't mean to sound quite so incredulous. "Sorry. Go ahead. What's your idea, Kirro?"

He was blushing bright red. "The towns in ... well, where I come from ... we have a trick for trapping valravens. It doesn't always work, but it should hold them at least temporarily, and then you could clobber them or whatever. But you need nets."

Huh, he's actually useful, Ji-Lin thought. "It's a fishing village. They have nets."

The caller nodded in agreement. "Continue, please."

Kirro explained: The trick was to lure the valravens into a canyon and then trap them in nets. Loud noises were used to draw them, and then you had to distract them with barrels full of fish — or they also loved octopi, he said — while you threw the nets on them. The bait was key. He knew many stories of failed attempts when the valravens just snacked on the villagers instead. But if all worked as planned, then while the monsters were being held, Alejan could fly to safety, straight up into the clouds. They'd escape, and the islanders could destroy the koji.

Ji-Lin didn't like the plan. It put the villagers in danger while the princesses ran away. *I would rather fight*, she thought. But it didn't matter what she wanted. What mattered was getting Seika to the dragon as quickly as possible. They were running out of time.

The caller showed them a map of the island, and Ji-Lin pored over it with her. The caves had two exits: the one on the beach, and one that opened onto a rocky canyon not far from the village. Led by the caller, several of the villagers would make noise on the canyon floor: bash pots, sing loudly, throw rocks, anything to draw the two koji. Other villagers would be silently waiting, hidden at the top of the canyon walls. When the valravens flew into the canyon, the villagers would drop weighted nets on the koji from above, capturing the valravens before they could harm anyone. Meanwhile, the princesses would fly out the beach exit.

"How strong are your nets?" Kirro asked.

"Our nets are not rope," one of the fishermen said. "We mine the metal the princess's sword is forged from. They will hold."

"The nets should tangle their wings so they can't fly or fight," Kirro said. "But if you want to make extra sure, you could stick the valravens with harpoons. That's what we used to do, before we had the cannons."

"Please be careful," Seika said. "We don't want anyone hurt."

"We will take every precaution," the caller reassured her. "Wait at the mouth of the cave by the shore and listen for our signal."

Seika bowed to the villagers. "Thank you, all of you."

The caller bowed back, and so did the villagers. "Good luck, Your Highnesses." She also bowed to Kirro. "And thank you. We will speak of you in our tales."

Ji-Lin wished that didn't sound so ominous.

This will work, she thought. *I hope.*

Leaving the caller and villagers, they headed back through the caves to get into position by the beach exit. A few villagers escorted them, carrying lanterns to light the way. As they reached the cave opening, Ji-Lin asked Seika, "Are you ready for this?"

Kirro raised his hand. "I'm not."

"You don't get a vote, sailor boy," Ji-Lin said. "Unless you're ready to abandon your loyalty to Zemyla and swear allegiance to Himitsu."

"Sure. Yay, Himitsu! Does that mean I don't have to go out there?"

"No. As a newly sworn subject, it's your loyal duty to Himitsu to help your princesses," Ji-Lin said. "You won't be in any danger. Or minimal danger. Or at least, we'll try to make sure you don't die."

"I hate this plan."

"It's your plan!" Seika said.

"So?"

Ji-Lin climbed into Alejan's saddle. Her heart was beating fast, and her palms had started to sweat. She felt like she was back on top of the Temple of the Sun, waiting for an attack, except this time she'd agreed not to fight. "It will be all about timing." As soon as the koji were in the canyon, Alejan would fly. Even if the nets didn't hold, the distraction should give him enough of a head start. He just needed to reach the cloud cover before the valravens saw them.

"Hate, hate, hate this," Kirro muttered, and Ji-Lin agreed — but she didn't see a better way. With the barrier failing, her job was to get Seika to the shrine. Continuing to grumble, Kirro climbed onto Alejan. "Should have kept my mouth shut, but no, I had to be helpful."

Seika mounted too. "We won't be anywhere near the koji. The villagers will take care of them. All we have to do is flee."

"Yeah, and if they miss? Or if the valravens escape? We'll be in the air, looking edible. What I should have said is: let's stay here until the koji go away on their own. Or let me stay."

"We'd love to leave you," Ji-Lin said, "but your father is sailing to the volcano island. You need to be there to meet him so he doesn't fire that cannon of his at the Guardians of the Shrine."

"He won't like it if a valraven eats me."

Swinging his head toward Kirro, Alejan licked the boy's

cheek with his massive tongue. Kirro squeaked, and Alejan said, "Don't worry. You don't taste good."

Looking out, Ji-Lin saw that the valravens were still on the beach. One was poking its snout into a pile of seaweed, probably looking for food. The other was pacing, sniffing the wind and stretching its wings.

She heard drumming, then crashing, then shouting and singing.

On the beach, both valravens pivoted their heads. *It's working,* Ji-Lin thought. The valravens spread their wings. One of them howled — an eerie, wolflike sound. The other echoed the howl, and then they both launched into the air.

"Be careful and be quick," one of the villagers said.

All her muscles tensed, Ji-Lin waited for the signal . . .

Crash!

That was it!

Alejan shot out of the cave. Rising in the saddle, Ji-Lin looked toward the canyon as they flew higher and higher above the island.

Kirro pointed, excited. "They caught one!"

One of the valravens had been caught in a net. The other — yes, the net was around it! It was fighting, but the villagers were pulling it down. One wing burst through the net . . .

Flying skyward, Alejan plunged into the clouds.

"Did they get the second one?" Kirro asked. "I couldn't see!"

"I think so," Seika said.

Kirro squawked. "Think so? You mean it could have gotten away? Those things don't give up. Once they've fixated on their prey . . ."

"Fly fast," Ji-Lin told Alejan.

They flew away from the island. Ji-Lin kept looking down, trying to see through the clouds. Alejan rumbled, "One is following us, but I can outfly it."

He kept flying, cocooned in clouds. Around them, all was peaceful and beautiful. Last night's storm had dissolved into a mix of white-and-gray clouds. The air was chilled but smelled fresh and salty, like the sea. "Is it still behind us?" Seika asked, anxious.

Alejan didn't answer at first. But then, "Yes. I can smell it. I'm certain it can smell me. Ji-Lin . . . I'm being heroic, aren't I? When we reach Master Shai, you'll tell her how fast and long I flew, how I outflew the valraven, how I saved you all?"

"Of course," she promised.

They kept flying.

And flying.

And flying.

Seika noticed that Alejan began to slow. His wing beats were labored, and his breath came in great puffs. Behind them, she heard a howl.

"It's closer," Seika whispered.

Kirro twisted to one side and then the other, trying to see. He whispered too. "Where is it? There are too many clouds." He was right: the valraven had to be hidden in the mass of clouds. Ji-Lin watched for any hint of movement.

"If we can't see it, it can't see us," Ji-Lin said. But she drew her sword.

"Valravens have wolf heads," Kirro said. "They can smell their prey from miles away." He was still fidgeting, straining his neck.

"Alejan . . ." Ji-Lin began.

"I am flying as fast as I can," the lion said.

Alejan flew on, each wing beat pushing them forward. The sky was silent — the only sounds were the whoosh of wind and the heaving of the lion's breath. The seabirds had scattered. Again, the valraven howled. Closer this time, below them. Ji-Lin gripped her sword harder.

And then Seika screamed.

The valraven was behind them!

Alejan veered to the right and then flew up. The valraven chased them. Its jaws were open. Its eyes were wild. *It's faster than us!* Ji-Lin thought. It hadn't gotten as tired as Alejan; it still seemed at full strength. They weren't going to be able to outfly it. And if Kirro was right about its sense of smell, they wouldn't be able to hide from it in the clouds either — it had already followed them for two hours without losing their trail. The odds of losing it in the next few minutes were very, very low.

At Ji-Lin's urging, Alejan skimmed the tops of the clouds. The koji was getting closer. *Think, Ji-Lin,* she ordered herself.

"Alejan, I'm going to try something stupid, okay? Take Seika to safety. She's the one who has to make it to the dragon, not me."

"She needs you. I need you. What kind of stupid?"

"Heroically stupid, the kind you tell tales about," Ji-Lin said. "You have to promise to let me, okay? I won't throw my sword this time."

"I won't let you get hurt," Alejan said.

"We're warriors," Ji-Lin said. "We take risks."

"Ji-Lin —"

"You swore to be my companion, to help me do what needs to be done. And this needs to be done. Just like in the tales. All of Himitsu depends on us." Leaning forward, she hugged his mane. "Please, Alejan? Promise you'll fly when I say fly?"

"I promise," he rumbled.

"Ji-Lin!" Seika cried. "What are you doing?"

Ji-Lin unhooked herself from the strap and climbed so she was crouching on Alejan's back. "Fly higher." She held on to the saddle with one hand and her sword with the other. This was why she'd trained. For this moment. It was why she was here, what she was meant to do.

"No, Ji-Lin!" Seika shouted.

"Ji-Lin, the stories —" Alejan began.

"If this works, we'll have our own story. Exactly as we always wanted. Just do as I say." Ji-Lin saw the valraven through the clouds. "Get above it!" she ordered.

Alejan obeyed, and they ramped up. The valraven twisted in the air. She saw it directly beneath her — and jumped. She landed on its back.

The monster bucked.

Rocking backward, she grabbed a fistful of feathers. It curled its body, and she slid. She felt like she was trying to ride a snake. Snarling, it bit at the air, bending its neck to try to reach her. She tried to regain her balance — it was harder, far harder, than she'd imagined. All the practice with Alejan . . . that was nothing like trying to ride a real koji who really wanted to kill her.

It flipped in the air, and she clung to its back. Distantly, she heard her sister and Alejan screaming, but she didn't have time to think about them. All she could think about was holding on. *Don't fall, don't fall, you cannot fall!*

Wind whipped around her, and she felt her stomach plummet as the valraven flipped again, corkscrewing through the air. Her every muscle strained to hold on. She squeezed tight with her legs and raised her sword with both hands.

As hard as she could, she plunged her sword between its shoulder blades. She did not pull the sword out.

The koji dove through the clouds, still bucking, but she clung to the sword hilt. She didn't think it had penetrated anything vital, just the scales, but it was enough to hurt the koji.

She yanked it to the left, and the koji flew left, screaming, to ease the pressure of the sword. She tried twisting it right — the valraven flew right. *I can steer!* she thought.

Ahead was the volcano island of Kazan, home of the dragon. The very next island! They'd nearly made it! She saw the rocky shore — far away and very, very far down. *Seika will make it*, Ji-Lin promised.

"Ji-Lin!" Seika called. They were flying beside the valraven, parallel to Ji-Lin. Wind streamed between them. "Jump on!"

"Get them to safety!" Ji-Lin called to Alejan. If she released the valraven, it would attack. She didn't have a choice. She had to ride it down. "Alejan, it's time for you to be the hero! Save my sister! Fly!"

Alejan hesitated. "Ji-Lin —"

"You promised! Fly!"

He veered away as Seika continued to shout. Ji-Lin saw her sister pounding ineffectually at Alejan's back, shouting at him to turn around, to go back for her. But soon they were out of sight, lost between the clouds. Safe.

Ji-Lin concentrated on steering the koji lower. It was going to crash. Its wings weren't working properly. She'd damaged something in its spine. It flapped, then faltered. Flapped, then faltered.

It began to spiral, and she felt her stomach flop. *Uh-oh, I need a new plan.* She yanked the sword hard, and the koji writhed in the air, close to the ocean. Waves rolled beneath them. She was going for a swim.

Close.

Closer.

Too close!

Ji-Lin jerked the sword out of the koji's back and ducked behind its wing, letting its body take the force of the hit, and then she was underwater. She kicked toward the surface, and the koji's talon wrapped around her ankle. She felt it pull her farther under. Her lungs felt tight, burning. She needed air! Now!

Swinging down with her sword, she struck at the talon. It released, and she swam up, bursting out of the waves — her sword still in her hand, as promised. She gasped in air just before another wave closed over her head.

⌒

Clutching Alejan's mane in her fists, Seika scanned the waves beneath them. "Ji-Lin!" She'd seen the valraven fall, tumbling through the sky. She'd been too far away to see Ji-Lin when they fell, but she had to be there; she had to be okay. She'd defeated the koji! "Lower," she told Alejan.

"Is that . . . ?" Kirro pointed, and then his hand fell. "No. Just a buoy."

Alejan cried, "Ji-Lin! Where are you? I did what you asked. Now please . . . let us save you! Call to me!"

He circled lower, against the wind, and Seika squinted as the spray from the water hit her eyes. The waves pounded on the gray-rock shore of the island, crashing into spectacular plumes of white foam before sweeping back out again. If Ji-Lin had landed on the rocks . . . "Ji-Lin!"

Her eyes felt damp, and she didn't think it was just from the sea spray. When the valraven fell from the sky, she'd felt as if all her insides had been ripped out. She'd wanted to cheer — victory! — but where was Ji-Lin? They'd fallen from so high!

"The tales never said that doing the right thing would feel so wrong." Alejan's voice broke into a sob.

The ocean pummeled the rocks. Seika tried not to imagine how far Ji-Lin could have fallen if she'd slipped off the koji, or how hard she could have hit the sea. She tried not to picture her on those rocks, crashing with the waves.

"The worst part is that I wanted this," Seika said. "I wanted to come. I was *happy* when Father told me we were taking the Emperor's Journey. I thought we were doing the right thing, and that if we did all the right things and said all the right words and danced all the right steps and sang all the right songs, then nothing could go wrong." So long as she did the right things, everything was supposed to work out fine, and they'd go on to be constant companions, heir and guardian. They were supposed to be together, a team, roving all over the palace, laughing at the courtiers, sneaking treats from the kitchens. Exploring the islands! Ji-Lin had said they'd explore together. There was so much they hadn't seen!

"I feel the same," Alejan confided. "I wanted this too. She

wanted this. But it wasn't supposed to feel this way! In the tales, it sounds so glorious! But all I feel is afraid and sad and small and not heroic."

Leaning forward, Seika hugged the lion's neck. She rested her cheek on his mane. Behind her, she felt Kirro awkwardly patting her shoulder.

"She'll be all right," Kirro said.

"You don't know that." Seika didn't move. Alejan's fur was comfortingly warm, like hugging the world's softest blanket. She'd been a little jealous of him when they'd first started out — Ji-Lin's new companion — but at some point along the way, he'd become her friend too. She was very glad he was here. "You saw its teeth, its claws!"

"I know her," Kirro said. "Maybe not as well as you do, but I know she won't give up."

"It's my fault. She was protecting me," Seika said. She was never going to forgive herself, even though she knew there was nothing she could have done. She wasn't the warrior. "Me. I don't —"

"She's strong," Kirro said loudly in her ear. "She'll be all right. She's probably tamed the dolphins, ridden to shore on their backs, and is lounging on the beach, waiting for us."

It was the nicest thing he could have said. She swallowed a thick lump in her throat. "You're right. She's a good swimmer. She used to race the waterfolk in the canals. Sometimes she almost won. Until the court ladies saw us, and they told

Father. She only raced one more time after that. But she won." Ji-Lin wouldn't give up. She was strong. She was—

There!

"Alejan! Down, look there!" Seika lunged forward, pointing past his face toward a shape in the water, small against the dark, deep blue.

He dove, flattening his wings against his side. She heard the whoosh of wind and felt it batter her face, but she kept her eyes open.

Below, with waves roiling around her, Ji-Lin was trying to swim. Kicking through the water, she surfaced, and then another wave crashed around her and Seika lost sight of her. "Ji-Lin!"

And then she was up again, her eyes fixed on the rocky shore, one arm reaching out. She was swimming to shore! But why was she . . . Her sword! She still held it tight against her as she swam with one arm against the waves.

Alejan extended his paws as they dove toward the water, and then he plucked Ji-Lin out, wrapping her in his paws. She struggled, clutching her sword as if it were a part of her. "Ji-Lin, it is me," he said. "You're safe."

"Seika?" Her voice was a croak.

"I'm here!" Seika called. "I'm all right. Are you okay?"

"Very, very wet," Ji-Lin said.

"You did not drop your sword," Alejan said in a proud purr. He cuddled her close to his chest, warming her.

Teeth chattering, Ji-Lin said, "I told you I wouldn't, ever again."

Seika felt her heart soar. She was okay! The koji was defeated, Ji-Lin was all right, and the volcano island was before them. They'd done it!

The fortress of Kazan. Made of gray stone, it was built into the mountainside, with many levels jutting out of the rock to create a terrace of roofs and a maze of stairs. Below it was a village, huddled against the side of the volcano, housing the people who supported the fortress. Above it, Seika could see a narrow, winding path that led to a red shrine.

This was it: the end of their journey.

And they'd made it before sundown on Himit's Day.

Nothing would stop them now. She'd talk to the dragon, the dragon would fix the barrier, and then it would be over. No more koji. No more sleeping out in the open. No more hiding in caves. No more fishing her sister out of the ocean. No more being afraid.

No more adventures, she thought. No more late-night stories under the stars. No more unicorns on mountaintops, or mer-minnows in waterfalls . . .

Alejan landed before the fortress. Guards poured down a set of steps. She should have been afraid, or at least nervous. But she wasn't. *We made it here, against odds we didn't even know were against us.*

The captain of the guard, a man in armor carrying a spear, strode toward them. He was imposingly large, with muscles that bulged against his chain mail. Stopping in front of them, he looked over Seika in her bedraggled dress, Ji-Lin wet and shivering, Kirro in his foreign sailor clothes. And then, to her relief, he bowed. "The Guardians of the Shrine bid you welcome to the island of Kazan, home of the dragon."

CHAPTER
EIGHTEEN

U GH. JI-LIN WISHED everyone would quit shouting. Her head was throbbing worse than her muscles. She felt as if she'd been pounded on with a mallet. They'd made it to the volcano island, but all she wanted to do was sleep. And get warm. And dry. *Just show me a bed.*

She'd defeated the koji. Its body should wash up on the rocks, proof of her first real victory. She should feel proud, but instead, she felt drained. Her limbs felt as soggy and limp as seaweed.

Sagging against Alejan, Ji-Lin dripped on the marble floor as they entered the fortress and were ushered into the Great Hall, a room that resembled a colossal cave, with gray stone walls, floor, and ceiling. Lanterns on hooks lit the corners. One wall was covered with a massive tapestry that depicted glorious koji battles and had a large gash across it. But the opposite wall had a hearth with a fire roaring inside the fireplace, and that was all she cared about.

Fire! Warmth!

Seika swept forward and executed one of her perfect bows. "Uncle Balez, we have come to complete the Emperor's Journey."

Their uncle stepped forward out of the shadows, and he

spread his arms. His sleeves billowed. "Welcome, my nieces! We have been expecting you. We are so pleased you've made it here safely."

Uncle Balez was beaming at them with such a friendly smile that Ji-Lin felt as if they'd come home. He looked exactly as she'd remembered. His cheeks were round and soft, his eyes crinkled as he smiled, and his white hair stuck out in wisps. She'd always thought he looked like a happy potato. Crossing to them, he kissed Seika's cheeks, then Ji-Lin's. "You are most welcome here, my dears."

Seika pushed Kirro forward. "This is Kirro, a boy from Zemyla. We hope you'll welcome him as your guest as well."

His broad smile vanished. "Zemyla! But—"

Seika interrupted him. "The story will take some time to tell. In the meantime, my sister is cold and wet. She fell into the ocean after defeating a koji over your shores." She sounded so royal! Ji-Lin wanted to cheer. And sink into the nearest chair.

"Of course. Anything you need is yours." He clapped his hands, and a man in a servant's uniform appeared. "Blankets, warm drinks, and food. Please"—he gestured to one of the chairs by the fire—"rest and be comfortable. We will see to it you are well taken care of."

Ji-Lin decided he was the best uncle ever.

"And then we wish to be brought to the shrine," Seika said. "There is no time to waste. The longer the barrier is weak, the more koji will come to Himitsu."

Really, Seika? Ji-Lin wanted to say. *Now?* Of course now. It was Himit's Day, and they'd promised. More than that, any delay meant more monsters.

She was happy, though, when a string of servants marched into the hall carrying trays of food and pitchers of water. One positioned a table in front of the hearth, and another spread four chairs around it. Food was placed on the table with a flourish. Ji-Lin sank into one of the chairs as a huge, beautiful lioness flew in through one of the larger windows.

Alejan immediately dipped his head. "Ji-Lin, it's her! Master Shai! Oh, oh, she's here! She's real!"

Ji-Lin straightened. Master Shai! "We are honored," she said. She wanted to say more, but she started shivering and couldn't stop. One of the servants placed a blanket around her shoulders. Another pressed a cup into her hands and laid a plate full of candied fruits on her lap. They bowed as they backed away.

Uncle Balez served hot kimi juice in golden cups. The sweet scent filled the air, and Ji-Lin thought of the last time she'd tasted the delicacy, after she'd passed her first exams. Flecks of spices had floated in it. The court lady who'd delivered it had said it was courtesy of her father as congratulations, and Ji-Lin had spent the entire next day hoping he'd visit. He hadn't. Here, the juice had a swirl of honey in it.

"We are honored by your presence, Your Highnesses," Master Shai said. Her voice rang as clear as a bell, echoing through the hall. She was a regal lioness, with a silken pelt and an elegant muzzle. She looked like a statue come to life, all muscle and fur. Alejan looked very young in comparison — Ji-Lin made a mental note never to say that out loud. "Your esteemed father has often spoken of you both with pride," Master Shai continued. "It seems he does not overvalue you."

He did? Both of them?

"Is Father here?" Seika asked.

"Not yet," their uncle said. "But his ship is expected at dawn tomorrow."

Ji-Lin wondered what Father would think of their untraditional Journey. Would he be proud of how they'd evaded the valravens, or upset that they'd veered off course? *We made it,* she thought. *That has to be enough.*

Uncle Balez tilted the crystal pot and filled another cup for Kirro. The sailor boy was already stuffing dried dates and caramel-soaked banana slices into his mouth. Ji-Lin set down her drink and exhaled, finally warmer. She decided she was not on the verge of death anymore. She even felt like she could stand and walk.

"Are you ready?" the lioness asked.

No, Ji-Lin wanted to say. She wasn't ready. She'd fought a koji. She'd swum through the ocean. She could have died. But that wasn't the answer she was supposed to give, the one tradition expected of her. "Yes?"

"My sister will require dry clothes," Seika said.

"All will be provided," the lioness said.

Uncle Balez clapped his hands again, and the servants returned. "Prepare them," he said. To Kirro, he said, "If you would stay and tell us your story, we would like to hear it. I'd love to hear more about life in Zemyla and how you came here." He smiled again, crinkling his eyes.

Kirro shot Seika and Ji-Lin a look. "Uh, all right. Um, I mean, yes, of course, Prince Balez."

The servants escorted Ji-Lin, Seika, and Alejan into a narrow corridor, past a study and a music room, to the bathing rooms.

The baths were cold, though better than the ocean. Ji-Lin washed with as much soap as she could as quickly as she could and came out smelling more like a flower than like a filleted cod, which was an improvement. She dressed, adding the soft leather armor she'd worn at the beginning of their journey.

And now we're at the end, she thought. She was . . . strangely sad. Her first adventure, almost done. Now that it was nearly over, she could think of it like a story, glossing over the bad parts and remembering the best.

One of the servants brushed her hair, braided it, and secured it with a black ribbon. Another affixed her sword belt around her. She thanked them, and they bowed in response.

Freshly dressed, she felt stronger. And cleaner. She strode out of the bathing area, and a flock of servants followed her. Alejan was already in the Great Hall, by the fire. His fur was damp, and he had his wings spread out for the feathers to dry.

His hero, the lioness Master Shai, sat beside him, her wings neatly folded. She was talking in a hushed voice, and he was staring at her with a dopey, adoring expression. When Ji-Lin came closer, the lioness stood and nudged her forehead against Alejan's. She then walked out past Ji-Lin, nodding once, graciously, at Ji-Lin.

Alejan sighed happily. "Isn't she magnificent?"

"You are too," Ji-Lin told him. "What was she saying to you?"

"Nice things. She thinks I'm brave for bringing two children across the islands, especially in such dangerous times. She thinks I have potential!"

"She's right," Ji-Lin said. "You're going to be an amazing imperial guardian."

"And you will be an excellent imperial warrior."

Ji-Lin scratched behind Alejan's ears. He leaned against her. "We won't be going back to the temple after this," Ji-Lin said. Their lives were going to change. *They've already changed,* she thought.

"I know. But we'll be together." He nudged her hand with his forehead. "And you'll be with your sister — after this, your father won't have any reason to keep you two apart. You're both done with training. I like her, Ji-Lin. I think we're friends now." Ji-Lin turned to see Seika walk through the hall. She wore a ceremonial dress embroidered with island birds and flowers, and she'd had her hair dressed like one of the ladies at a masquerade ball, with elaborate braids on top of her head. Her expression was a mix of determination and fear.

"Where's Kirro?" Seika asked.

"I haven't seen him," Ji-Lin said. "But you look like a true heir."

Seika's smile lit up her face. "I think that was the idea." Then her smile vanished. "Are you ready for this?"

"Of course. You?"

"Aside from a little panic. What if I say the wrong thing? What if the dragon hates me? What if she says no? But yes, I think so."

Ji-Lin wanted to say something encouraging, but before she had a chance to, Uncle Balez and Master Shai returned to the hall. Warmth and pride filling his voice, Uncle Balez said, "Please follow us, my dear nieces, and know that you carry the hopes of Himitsu with you."

⁓

Their uncle and the lioness led them out of the hall and across a stone bridge to an old road carved into the dark gray rock of the mountainside. Small stunted trees clung to the crevasses in the walls on either side, and the rocks were choked with the now-familiar irina flowers, so many that they looked like patches of snow. It was all exactly as solemn and grand and severely beautiful as Seika had hoped it would be. She loved it.

Seika glanced back and saw that others had silently joined the procession: men, women, and children from a village below the fortress. She didn't know how word had spread, but clearly it had. More came, and still more, until they led a silent procession winding up the side of the mountain.

Overhead, birds circled, and Seika watched them until she was certain they weren't more koji. Soon she'd be able to look at the sky and not worry about koji hiding behind the clouds. And soon they'd return home, and Ji-Lin wouldn't be required to stay at the temple. She could come to the palace whenever she wanted, even live there again, depending on her assignment. If Father and the masters approved, she'd be Seika's personal guard, and they wouldn't ever be apart.

Seika snuck a look at her sister, who was walking beside Alejan. The winged lion would be welcome at the palace. He'd be able to visit the other lions at the temple when he wanted to, but he'd be given rooms and invited to all court events. She pictured him in costume for a masquerade and suppressed a giggle.

"What?" Ji-Lin asked.

"I was picturing Alejan dressed as a swan."

Alejan swung his massive head to look at her with his amber eyes. "May I ask why?"

"Every season we have masquerades at the palace, special

rituals for each season. If you came to one, you could dress up as whatever you want," Seika said. It sounded less funny when she said it out loud.

"And you think I would choose a swan?" Alejan asked.

"Well, you could. You wouldn't have to."

"I would not choose a swan." Looking every inch the dignified winged lion, he lifted his tail and held his head high. "I would choose a rabbit."

Seika and Ji-Lin both smothered laughs. The lioness shot a look back at them, and Seika quickly smoothed her expression into her polite princess face.

The sky was gray to match the rocks. Behind them, a woman began to sing in a low voice. Another woman joined her, adding a higher harmony, and then a man added his voice. The song swelled, rising like the tide to sweep over them. As they reached the end, the people fanned out around them, filling the stone road. There was a simple archway of painted red wood. Orange trees grew on either side of the arch. Their blossoms were bright white against the hard gray stone. The lord and lioness halted beneath the arch and faced their people.

"Approach, Heir Seika," their uncle commanded.

Stepping forward, Seika bowed. She told herself she wasn't going to feel nervous anymore, not after all she'd seen and done, but of course her stomach didn't listen and began its familiar flopping. She ignored it. Her voice rang clear and true. "I am Princess Seika d'Orina Amatimara Himit-Re, heir to Emperor Yu-Senbi of the Hundred Islands of Himitsu."

A murmur spread through the crowd.

"Why have you come to the Shrine of the Dragon, Heir Seika?" the lioness asked.

"I have come to complete the Emperor's Journey." Was that enough? Was she supposed to say more? She tried to push down the fluttering inside. She'd crossed the islands; she could do this.

"As Guardian of the Shrine, I bid you welcome," Uncle Balez said.

The lioness echoed him. "As Guardian of the Shrine, I bid you welcome." They parted and stood on either side of the archway.

Seika hesitated. This was it. She wasn't sure why she suddenly wanted to bolt in the other direction, but she made her feet walk forward. Ji-Lin and Alejan followed her.

"Walk until you reach the heart of the volcano," Uncle Balez advised. "Look for the light — that's how you will know you are there. Sunlight touches the heart, as the poets say. The dragon has shaped the inside to suit her. Don't be afraid. You won't see any lava."

"You *will* see bones when you reach the heart," Master Shai said.

Seika swallowed hard. "Bones?"

"The dragon is fond of sheep," Master Shai said. "We

leave the bones to deter those who do not belong in the dragon's home." She paused. "Sadly, not all heed the warning."

Uncle Balez smiled reassuringly and laid his hand on her shoulder. "The dragon will hear your approach and come. Do not venture beyond the bones."

She nodded slowly.

"Do not be afraid," Master Shai said. "But do not linger either. It is not wise to linger near either a volcano or a dragon. Return as soon as you can."

Feeling less confident than she had a few minutes before, Seika walked through the archway with Ji-Lin and Alejan, and she breathed in the scent of the orange blossoms. It overlaid the faint stench of sulfur that clung to the back of her throat and became stronger as they walked toward a wide crack in the rocks.

As they moved forward, the smell of sulfur intensified until she felt as if she'd been slathered with rotten eggs. Seika looked back at the archway. The lord and lioness stood in front of their people, and they lifted their voices in song as Seika, Ji-Lin, and Alejan walked inside the volcano.

Torches lit the interior. Ji-Lin lifted one of them out of its sconce. Seika took another torch. It was heavy and smelled of burning pine, which was better than the horrible sulfur.

"Walk between us," Ji-Lin said to Seika.

Seika didn't argue. They were her guards, after all, and this was what they'd come here to do. Ji-Lin walked first, and Alejan followed last. As they descended, the sounds of the outside world faded behind them, as if smothered. Silence and darkness pressed around them.

The tunnel was as round as a tube, and the walls were rough and full of holes, like a solidified sponge. She wondered if it was natural or dragon-made — dragon-made, she guessed, based on what Uncle Balez had said. She felt the roughness through the soles of her slippers. The ground felt warm as well, and Seika was sweating in her dress. The silk stuck to the skin on her back and legs. She hoped they'd find the dragon's chamber soon. This wasn't anyplace she wanted to stay for a long time. She felt as if she were tasting rotten eggs every time she breathed. It made her throat and nose prickle and her head ache. "You know the worst part about all of this?" Seika asked.

"The koji?" Alejan suggested.

"Falling into the ocean?" Ji-Lin offered.

"The smell of this volcano?" Alejan said.

"We still don't know *why* the barrier is failing," Seika said. "Father sent us on the Journey early, which means he must have known the barrier is weak. But does he know why? Does anyone? All we know about the dragon and the barrier is from stories. And we don't even know if the stories are true. Look at Kirro's tale. It's very different from ours." *Appallingly different,* she thought.

"Two hundred years is a long time," Alejan said thoughtfully. "Stories can be forgotten. And they can change, even true ones."

"Even the tales of Master Shai?" Ji-Lin teased.

Alejan fluffed his mane. The torchlight sent shadows shivering across the tunnel walls. "Of course those are true!"

"There are a lot of them," Seika said. "They might not all be true. She's only one lion."

He huffed. "One very impressive lion. Still . . . it does not take long for a story to change or be forgotten. I know the story of your birth has been recounted multiple ways, and it was a mere twelve years ago."

Seika was startled. She didn't know anyone talked about their birth. Certainly no one ever did around them. "It has?"

"Indeed. In one version, lightning hit the palace at the moment of Seika's birth and hit the Temple of the Sun at Ji-Lin's birth and then a third strike hit your mother. In another story, your mother was not pregnant with two children when she gave birth to Seika, but when she realized she had birthed the future heir, she decided then and there that she needed a second child to guard her and so birthed Ji-Lin, giving up her own life force to create a new life. In yet another version, you were both born dead, but all the winged lions roared at once and woke you but sent your mother to death."

"I haven't heard any of those." Seika had only heard one version, from her father: that their mother had loved them very much but her body had been too weak to stay with them. She had held out until they were both born, kissed them both, and then closed her eyes. It wasn't their fault, their father said. She'd been sick. Still, he said, he missed her when he looked at them. Seika sometimes wondered what it would have been like to grow up with a mother. Luckily, she had Ji-Lin, so she was never alone, at least until they both turned eleven and Father sent Ji-Lin to the temple. "I don't think any of those stories are true."

"Or perhaps they all are," Alejan said. "A story can be true without being real."

Ji-Lin mock-punched him in the shoulder. "When did you get so wise?"

He answered seriously. "When Ji-Lin fell into the sea. I'd thought . . . I'd always thought we were meant to live lives like in a tale, that we'd be the heroes of stories that would be retold by generations, but I am thinking now that all the old stories . . . they are, at the same time, truth and lies." He paused. "I have not been having comfortable thoughts. Does that mean I'm becoming wise?"

"I think it might," Ji-Lin said.

Seika thought about the Bridge of Promises in the palace and all the conflicting stories that surrounded it. "What if there isn't a dragon at all? What if that's a lie?"

"Don't doubt it now," Ji-Lin said. "We've come too far. Besides, why would there be a shrine and a tunnel if there weren't a dragon on the other end?"

"What if she's dead?" Seika asked.

"Then I guess the barrier will finish falling, and the monsters will come." Ji-Lin sounded irritated.

Not a comforting answer, Seika thought. "And if they come? What do our people do?"

"Our people are strong now," Alejan said. "It's not the same as it was when Emperor Himitsu first came to the islands — a small, tired group. We can defend ourselves."

"But we aren't ready," Seika objected.

"Maybe we ask Kirro's father for some of those cannons," Ji-Lin said. "And people can restock the koji shelters. The lions and riders will fight."

"It would change things for everyone," Seika said.

Ji-Lin sighed. "I know."

Reaching out, Seika took Ji-Lin's hand and squeezed it. Ji-Lin squeezed back. "I don't want anything to change," Seika said.

"Things already have," Ji-Lin said.

Hand in hand, they walked into the dragon's chamber.

Dull light spilled from above — the chamber was beneath the mouth of the volcano, with a shaft that led up to the sky — but it wasn't enough to brighten the shadows. Lifting their torches, they looked around — *We made it,* Seika thought. *At last!* A vast chamber with coarse walls that looked like clumps of dried orange mud, it was wide enough for a dragon. But there was nothing here but rocks. And bones.

The torchlight flickered over an array of bones scattered throughout the chamber. Seika looked away. *Sheep bones,* she reminded herself — or at least, she hoped so. The Guardians of the Shrine were tasked with keeping people out of the dragon's home. *Except us,* Seika thought. *We're supposed to be here, right?*

It didn't feel like a place any human was meant to be.

The chamber felt even hotter than the tunnel, though she saw no hint of lava—all the rock looked as if it had cooled centuries ago. It was stained with deep colors, reds and oranges and browns. She pushed up the sleeves of her gown. Alejan was panting, his lion tongue sticking out. His wings drooped, the feather tips dragging on the rock floor. Seika licked her dry lips. She felt as if every bit of water had been sucked from her mouth and her tongue dried with sandpaper. Just breathing made her throat hurt. "Hello? Dragon of Himitsu? I am Seika d'Orina Amatimara Himit-Re, princess of Himitsu and heir to the imperial throne! I've come to talk with you!"

The tunnel seemed to swallow her words.

Seika tried again, louder. "Dragon of the Islands! It is Himit's Day, and I am Himitsu's heir. I've come to complete the Emperor's Journey! Long ago, you bargained with my ancestor. I'm here to ask you to uphold that bargain. The barrier *must* stay strong!" The words scraped her dry throat.

"Anyone hear anything?" Ji-Lin asked.

Twisting, Seika looked up the shaft, toward the mouth of the volcano. It extended to the sky, ending in a smear of light gray at the top of the volcano—the opening to the crater, far above them. She judged it was large enough for a dragon to fly through, if it wanted to. The dragon had created this chamber and the tunnels to be her home . . . but if this was her home, then why wasn't she here? "Dragon! We need you! Please, show yourself!" Her voice echoed.

The dragon didn't come.

There was no other place for the dragon to be — at least, none that Seika could see. This was where the path led. This was where she should be, the chamber that Uncle Balez had told them about. The light was here. The bones, also here. So where was the dragon? Wiping the sweat from her face, Seika called out again. "Dragon!"

"Maybe tell her a story, like the waterhorse?" Ji-Lin suggested.

"What story?" Seika asked. It was hard to think in such heat. She felt the sweat drip down her forehead and pool beneath her hair at the back of her neck. Her dress was drenched. Her eyes continued to water from the bitter air, and her lungs ached.

"Tell her ours," Ji-Lin said.

"Once upon a time, there were two princesses," Seika began. "Sisters. Born on the same day. They shared a bedroom when they were little. Shared toys in the toy room. Shared adventures in the palace. One time, Seika, the older sister, discovered a hidden passageway behind their dresser. They explored it whenever the governess was napping, which was nearly every afternoon. When the latest governess threw away the younger sister's, Ji-Lin's, favorite toy, a stuffed lion —"

"I remember that lion! Father had given it to me. Directly to me, not just through one of the courtiers. I slept with it every night. Carried it around everywhere, until the ears fell off and the tail was shredded. One of the court ladies tried to get rid of it."

"We used the passageways to sneak down to where the servants hauled the trash."

"It smelled worse than this place," Ji-Lin said. She was slumped against the rock wall. Sweat poured down her face too. Alejan looked like a wet rag. His fur was clumped, and his wings drooped.

"It did," Seika agreed. "It smelled like a hundred bathrooms mixed with cooked cabbage, plus rotten eggs. This just smells like rotten eggs. No offense meant, Dragon!"

In the flickering light, Seika could see Ji-Lin smiling. "We spent hours there, looking through the trash until we found it," Ji-Lin said. "You found it. I remember that."

Seika remembered that too. "We were so tired when we crawled back out that we fell asleep on our beds without changing our clothes or washing or anything."

Ji-Lin laughed. The sound echoed through the cavern. "We woke to about six maids plus our governess screaming so loudly that the guards came."

"You jumped out of bed, holding the lion like a shield, and put yourself right in front of me. Ready to defend me. Even then. You would have swung a sword at them if you'd had one," Seika said. "When they told Father about what happened, they left out that part. I always wished I'd spoken up and told Father that."

"We were, what, six years old? Five? Father was intimidating."

"Still is," Seika said.

"I don't want to tell him we failed," Ji-Lin said. Her voice cracked.

"Me either."

"He'll forgive you," Ji-Lin said. "He's always been proud of you. I'm the troublemaker."

"Father loves you," Seika said. "And I know he's proud of you. He talks about you, you know, about how you're becoming a warrior."

"He does?"

"Sometimes I thought . . ." Seika swallowed, though there was no moisture left in her mouth. "Sometimes I used to wish I'd been the one sent to the temple, so he could be proud of me."

"I sometimes wished I'd been the one to stay," Ji-Lin said.

"At least we're together now," Seika said.

Ji-Lin took her hand again. "Yes, we are."

Alejan cleared his throat with a rumble. "The torches."

They looked at the torches. The flame was nearly extinguished on both of them. "We aren't going to have enough light to make it back to the entrance to the shrine," Ji-Lin said. "We'll be walking in the dark."

"We can't go back yet!" Seika cried. "All of Himitsu is

depending on us. You saw those people out there." If they turned around because of a little darkness, she wouldn't be able to face that crowd. Or her father. Or any of the people they'd met on the way. "We've been in dark tunnels before. We can feel our way out if we have to. We can't fail Himitsu."

They waited. And waited. And the torches burned lower.

"Seika, we can't stay," Ji-Lin said at last. "Our light is dying."

The torches were flickering pitifully. Looking at them, Seika nodded. How long had they been here? She'd lost track of time. The stifling heat made her feel dizzy. "The dragon didn't come. We didn't complete the ritual. I promised I . . . Ji-Lin, what do we do?"

"Don't think of it as giving up. It's . . . finding another way. We'll come again, with more torches so we can explore. We'll search the whole volcano if we have to."

We're not giving up, Seika promised herself. With one last look at the silent and empty cavern, she turned her back on the rocks and the bones.

Sticking close together, they began to climb up the tunnel. When the light died, they held on to each other and kept climbing.

CHAPTER
NINETEEN

T HE PEOPLE HAD stood vigil outside the shrine. Ji-Lin saw their lights like starlight. Above, the sky was crowded with clouds, but the people stretched down the road, all carrying candles. She halted at the entrance.

She didn't want to tell them they'd failed.

Everyone was staring at them.

Ji-Lin tried to make her mouth work to say the words.

Instead, it was Seika who spoke, who took the responsibility and was brave enough to admit the truth. "The dragon did not come."

The sigh swept through the people like wind, an exhalation that was closer to a groan. The candles dipped. A few were extinguished.

Alejan flopped down on the stones beneath the archway, and Ji-Lin knelt by his side. His breathing was hard and heavy. She felt the same way, as if she'd been squeezed like a lemon. "Are you all right?" she asked.

"Tired. Thirsty. But I'll be fine. Just . . . must rest."

The lioness was walking toward them with grave, measured paw steps. "Master Shai is coming," Ji-Lin whispered to Alejan. "You might want to try to stand. She doesn't look happy." She drew herself upright and tried to look strong and responsible and brave.

Alejan's head shot up and he struggled to stand on all four paws. His legs wobbled, but he still managed to look regal. "Master Shai!" He inclined his head.

"Do not blame yourself for this tragedy," the lioness said. Her voice carried down the mountainside. "It was, perhaps, destiny."

Alejan let out a moan.

Putting her arm around Alejan's shoulders, Ji-Lin said, "We aren't giving up. We'll try again tomorrow, after we rest." They'd been through a lot today. Sleep would help. It wouldn't all seem so grim and awful in the morning.

"You cannot," the lioness said, alarm in her voice.

What? Of course they had to try again! "But . . . we have to!"

Alejan bumped against her with his head. "Ji-Lin, careful. You don't argue with a master. Especially this master."

Ji-Lin stepped away, ignoring him. She felt as if she heard ringing in her ears, as if a voice inside her were shouting, *No, no, no!* "We can bring more torches, water, food. Stay longer. Shout louder." Maybe it was the wrong time of day, or maybe they hadn't yelled loudly enough. Maybe the dragon was asleep or away or . . . *dead,* a little part of her whispered.

"That is not the tradition," the lioness objected. "Tradition is that the heir enters the volcano and bargains with the dragon on Himit's Day. There are no second chances. You have failed."

Down the path, the people began to wail. The children were crying, and the adults weren't stopping them — instead, they were joining in, keening as if at a funeral.

"This isn't about tradition," Seika said. "This is about the barrier. This is about the safety of the islands! Let us go back in the morning. We can search more, beyond the place with the bones. We'll explore farther. We'll find her!"

"It is not the way it is done," Master Shai said.

Ji-Lin balled her fists. This was crazy! Seika *needed* to talk to the dragon; the dragon *needed* to fix the barrier. "The way it's done didn't work, so we need to try a different way."

Seika was nodding vigorously. "We can't just give up! Everyone is depending on us!"

Burying his face in his paws, Alejan moaned again.

"We are the Guardians of the Shrine," Master Shai said in a regal voice. "It is our duty to see that the ritual is performed according to tradition."

"But the barrier is already falling!" Seika said.

"Yes!" Ji-Lin said. "The koji are —"

Still cringing in front of his hero, Alejan hissed, "Ji-Lin, Seika, stop! This is *Master Shai!* You can't argue with a legend!"

Ji-Lin didn't care if the lion was a legend or a hero or any of it. Master Shai wasn't making any sense. There was no rational reason why they couldn't just try again tomorrow! It was tradition, not law of nature, and the dragon had already changed tradition by not showing up. Besides, from the look of the cave, she didn't think the dragon kept a calendar. Plowing forward, Ji-Lin finished her sentence. "The koji are already here. How much worse could we make it?"

The lioness growled. "Worse. You do not understand the forces you interfere with."

Uncle Balez placed his hand on the lioness's back. Gratefully, Ji-Lin turned to him. Surely he'd see sense! "Uncle Balez, tell her we have to try again."

His friendly face looked sad and crumpled. "I am so sorry, Ji-Lin. You are welcome to enjoy the hospitality of our home, but your part in this is done. We thank you for your efforts." His voice was soft, but it was loud enough to start a new chain of whispers spreading through the crowd. The whispers sounded like a sigh, kicking off another round of keening. Ji-Lin wanted to clap her hands over her ears.

This didn't make sense! Why wouldn't they let them try again? She felt the same way she had back in the first village, when she'd been kept from fighting the koji — except this was ten times worse. The people sobbed against one another as they processed back down the stone road. Candles were being blown out, like stars fading from the sky.

At least this time, her sister was on her side.

"It's not over!" Seika cried. "It can't be!"

"When your father arrives, we will discuss the future of

Himitsu without a functioning barrier," Uncle Balez said. "Perhaps it is time for the world to change." He patted Ji-Lin's shoulder, as if to comfort her, and then he smiled — actually smiled! Why would he smile?

Both Seika and Ji-Lin began to argue, but their uncle held up his hands as if shushing them. "You have done much, children. But now it is time to rest and let others take the lead. Be proud that you tried."

"You may mourn your failure, of course," the lioness said, "for it is your burden to bear. You will gather many such burdens before you reach adulthood. We will speak no more tonight, for this is now a time of contemplation and sorrow."

Ji-Lin decided she did *not* like the lioness. And she wasn't feeling so fond of their uncle, either. Alejan was looking as if he'd had his mane shorn off. Dejected, he walked down the path with his head low and his paws dragging. She kept a hand on his back as she walked alongside him. Seika walked on his other side.

Partway down the winding road, Seika stumbled. She fell against Alejan. Shaking, she pulled herself upright. Ji-Lin was panting too. After the fight with the koji, the fall into the ocean, and now this disappointment . . .

"Ride on me," Alejan offered.

"You're tired too," Seika protested.

"Climb aboard, both of you," Alejan said. "We can sorrow together. Like the heroes who have no tales, the ones who never became heroes." He sighed heavily. "The failures."

Ji-Lin hesitated, then saw Seika's face across the lion's broad back. She wasn't going to be able to walk much longer. The heir to the empire couldn't collapse in the middle of the road. "You'd tell us if you couldn't carry us any farther?"

"Indeed. I know my limits now. But I am at least good for this."

The two of them climbed onto his back. He plodded behind Master Shai.

By the time they reached the fortress, only the original guards were still with them. The villagers had all dispersed. At the courtyard, the lord and lioness left them quickly with bows and murmured polite words, and the guards brought the princesses and Alejan inside and handed them over to a servant, who silently led them first to the baths and then to their rooms. Alejan was allowed to stay in Ji-Lin's room, and pillows had been piled near the window for him.

After the servant delivered them to the rooms, Ji-Lin heard a knock on her door. She opened it. Seika stood outside, holding a mound of blankets and pillows. Ji-Lin let her in without a word, and they set up a nest on the floor, near Alejan.

Side by side, they slept.

⟳

"Hey." A boy's voice, whispering. "Hey, wake up!"

Seika peeled open her eyes. She glanced at the window.

Outside the fortress, the sun wasn't up yet, though the sky was lighter. The moon was pale silver.

Kirro bounced into her view. "Are you awake?"

"What are you doing here? Are you okay?" Her mouth felt dry, like paste. She pushed herself up to sitting and ran her tongue over her teeth. Beside her, Ji-Lin stirred. "Where have you been?"

"Exploring. There's something you need to see."

Ji-Lin pried her eyes open. "Oh, yay, the sailor boy is back."

Standing, Seika felt the cold stone on her bare feet. She wrapped her night robe tighter around her. It was embroidered enough to pass for a dress. "What do we need to see?"

"It's important. Really important. But I don't think you'll believe me if you don't see for yourselves. *I* wouldn't believe me." He was so excited that he was practically doing a jig in front of the door. "Come on. Before everyone wakes up."

"You know, I'd just started to like you." Groaning, Ji-Lin got to her feet and pulled her leather armor on over her nightclothes. As Seika stepped into slippers, she saw Ji-Lin buckle her sword belt to her waist. "Alejan, are you awake?"

"Here." His voice came from the darker shadows of the room. He padded out into the faint moonlight. His mane was matted on one side, and his wings looked rumpled. He shook them out and laid them crossed over his back. The saddle leaned against the wall, as did their packs. Ji-Lin helped him put on his saddle and tried to untangle his mane. "Is there breakfast? There was no feast last night."

"This is better than breakfast," Kirro promised.

"I find that hard to believe," Alejan said.

Kirro opened the door, peeked out, and then slipped into the hall. "The guards are mostly at the doors to the outside, but still, be quiet."

"If my grumbling stomach gives us away, it's not my fault," Alejan said.

Seika stuck behind Ji-Lin, and Alejan crept quietly after her. It was dark in the hall. No torches were lit, and the thin predawn light filtered in through a few slits near the tops of the walls. Most of the hall was bathed in shadows. Seika was certain Uncle Balez wouldn't like them sneaking around before dawn.

"It didn't go well in the volcano, right?" Kirro whispered.

"The dragon didn't come," Seika said. Saying the words made it even more real. She felt as if a pit had opened up inside her. *We failed,* her mind whispered to her. *You failed your quest. You don't deserve to be heir. You don't deserve to be a princess.*

"What if she *couldn't* come?" Kirro whispered.

"I refuse to believe she's dead, or doesn't exist," Ji-Lin said. "I don't care what —"

He flapped his hands at them. "I mean, what if she was somewhere else?"

"Where else?" Seika asked. She glared at him, even though she knew he couldn't see her. "She's a volcano dragon. This is where she belongs."

"Besides, someone would have seen her if she left the volcano," Alejan said. "She's unmistakably large."

Seika heard a scrape ahead and grabbed Ji-Lin, stopping her from walking forward into the intersection of two corridors. They all flattened against the wall, within the shadows. Seika felt her heart beat faster.

One of the servants walked by, carrying a stack of sheets so high they blocked his face.

When he was past them, they continued. They crept down a set of stairs. Seika used a reflection in a mirror to spot a guard before they continued. After another turn, she figured out where Kirro was taking them: to the Great Hall.

The fire no longer blazed in the hearth. The room was dark, cold, and empty. Only a few lanterns were lit, enough to create more shadows. "So while you were out in the volcano — which still sounds weird, by the way — I did a little exploring. Lots of expensive stuff everywhere. And it's all kept really neat and clean and shiny. Except in the Great Hall, there's the big tapestry with the rip in it. And I thought: Why keep it there when everything else is so fancy?"

"It's an heirloom?" Seika suggested.

"They're too busy to fix it?" Ji-Lin offered.

"Or . . . it's hiding something! Like a dragon!"

Seika stared at him, then at the room. "That's ridiculous.

Why would the dragon be behind a tapestry? How would she even fit?"

"I don't know, but look." He hurried across the room and pointed at the tear in the tapestry. "This could have been done by a dragon."

"Or a sword, or . . ." Ji-Lin trailed off. "Anyway, rips happen. Not necessarily because of a dragon."

"Look behind it," Kirro said. "Go on."

Walking toward it, Seika put her hands on the woven wool. It rippled as she touched it. Keeping her hands on it, she walked to the edge and then pulled it back from the wall. Just stone. "Nothing here." Except she felt a warm breeze. "Wait—"

She pulled the tapestry out farther and slipped behind it. Instantly, she was shrouded in darkness. She felt like a little kid again, looking for a secret passageway. She walked along, one hand on the back of the tapestry and one on the stone wall—and then the wall disappeared. "Ji-Lin . . ."

"Hold on," Kirro said. "I left a light." He darted behind the tapestry, held up one of the lanterns, and lit it.

They faced a tunnel, a large one, carved directly into the mountain, receding from the fortress. Seika peered into the darkness, trying to see the end. "Kirro, where exactly are we?"

"We're in the volcano," Ji-Lin answered for him.

Seika sniffed the air—it didn't smell like rotten eggs. Or rather, it did, but only faintly. It smelled more . . . coppery, and almost sweet. "The whole island is the volcano. That doesn't mean it's all connected." She wondered what the smell was. And why the Great Hall had a hidden tunnel.

"But it does connect," Kirro said. "I heard you while you were looking for the dragon. Your voices echoed. I was going to call to you, but I was afraid I'd get caught. And I couldn't figure out how to get to you. You were above me."

Seika heard a soft noise, like a whoosh of wind, and then again, and again. They all halted. Kirro shuttered the lantern, plunging them into darkness. They crept forward.

And Seika bumped into something soft, smooth, and cool. She felt forward and touched plates of . . . metal? Not metal. But this was the source of the sweet, coppery smell. She drew her hands back. "Ji-Lin, I think . . ." She swallowed, her mouth suddenly dry. "I think I found it."

"Found what?"

"Her."

She heard a moan, like the wind low through the trees. It shivered through her bones, and she took a step back. Ji-Lin's voice was soft. "Seika?"

"Kirro, the light," Seika whispered.

He unshuttered the lantern and held it up.

And they saw the dragon.

The sleeping dragon.

She was breathing evenly, and her eyes were shut. She was stretched along the cave, with her head resting against the rocks. As the light from the lantern flickered over the dragon, Seika thought she'd never seen anything more beautiful in her life.

The Dragon of Himitsu was very long, like a snake, with iridescent scales that flashed with ruby-red, sapphire-blue, and gold. White feathers grew from her face like a magnificent crown. Her wings were small and delicate, like a dragonfly's, laid across her back.

Everything about her was elegant and powerful, from the sinewy curve of her coiled body to the feathered antlers that looked like painted flames on the sides of her head. Her scales shimmered with an array of colors on the surface of the deep red. Seika walked the length of her and then back. If the dragon hadn't been breathing, Seika would have thought she was a sculpture — the most magnificent statue she'd ever seen.

"We have to wake her," Ji-Lin said.

Seika recoiled from that idea. It felt wrong. Like scribbling over a painting. But Ji-Lin was right. The dragon needed to fix the barrier. Raising her voice, Seika said, "Please forgive us, O Dragon of Himitsu, but we must speak with you."

The dragon kept sleeping.

"Dragon of Himitsu!" Climbing over the rocks to the dragon's head, Seika raised her voice again. "Dragon? Please wake! We must speak with you!"

Ji-Lin joined in. "It's important! Wake up!"

"Shh!" Kirro said frantically. "You'll wake *everyone* up!"

"Yes! We should wake everyone! We'll get the lord and the lioness and all the guards. We'll get drums and trumpets. Together, we can wake her!" Seika began scrambling toward the exit of the tunnel.

"Whoa, stop." Kirro caught up to her. "They know she's here."

Seika stopped.

"The tapestry over the hole screams 'hiding place.'"

He's right, she thought. Of course Uncle Balez and Master Shai had to know — it was their fortress, and they were the Guardians of the Shrine. She thought of the rip in the tapestry. If they weren't hiding something, they would have ordered the tapestry taken down and repaired. Such a small detail, but Kirro had noticed it. "But . . . I don't understand. Why hide her? Why not tell us she was here? Why not try to wake her?" Their uncle and the lioness had seemed so happy that Seika and Ji-Lin were here to complete the Journey. They'd even given them advice. None of that made sense if they'd known the dragon was here all along, asleep.

On the other hand . . . they had been strangely certain that the princesses shouldn't try again and insistent that they not explore beyond the heart of the volcano. And they hadn't been nearly as upset as their people. Could they have known all along that the princesses would fail?

Before Kirro could answer, Ji-Lin said, "Alejan? Alejan, wake up!"

Seika and Kirro rushed over to her. Alejan was curled beside a bowl of meat — the dragon's dinner. A chunk of half-chewed meat was stuck between his teeth. He was fast asleep. Ji-Lin was shaking him hard. "Please, wake up!"

The lion only snored.

CHAPTER
TWENTY

Ji-Lin cradled Alejan's massive head. "Alejan? Please, wake up." He couldn't have just fallen asleep! Something was wrong. Very, very wrong. She stroked his mane and then yelled in his ear. "Wake up!"

"Shh!" Kirro and Seika both said.

He was breathing heavily, evenly. "Please, Alejan," she whispered. His tongue lolled out of his mouth, and he pawed at the stones, the way he did when he was deep in a dream. But he shouldn't be asleep. It wasn't natural. Maybe he was ill. Maybe the heat and stench of their walk into the volcano had made him sick. Or maybe the meat was old and rotten — it didn't look fresh. "I think he ate bad meat."

Seika knelt next to the food bowl. "Ji-Lin, look." She pointed to a hint of white, bright against the dark meat. "Could it be a petal? I think it is."

Ji-Lin knew those petals. "Sleep flowers." She glared at Alejan. "Couldn't you have waited for breakfast?" Or looked at the food first? Or even thought for a second with his brain instead of his stomach!

"This couldn't have been a mistake," Seika said. "You don't accidentally mix flowers in meat. This was deliberate. The dragon was poisoned!"

Ji-Lin felt anger grow in the base of her stomach. Someone had done this. No, not "someone." Uncle Balez and Master Shai. It was their fortress, their Great Hall, their tapestry with the gash. And it wasn't just that they kept the sleeping dragon a secret — they *caused* this. It was their responsibility to leave offerings, like this bowl of meat, for the dragon. They'd given her the tainted meat, and the dragon, trusting her guardians, had eaten it. "They knew. That's why they didn't want us to go back in. That's why they told us not to go beyond the bones. They didn't want us to find her, to find what they're doing to her."

"Wait, they put a sleeping potion in the dragon's food?" Kirro said. "Whoa. I mean, I knew they hid the dragon. And they lied to you about it. And I guess . . . okay, yeah, it makes sense."

"No, it doesn't," Seika said. "It doesn't make any sense at all. This is the Dragon of Himitsu. She keeps us safe. Or did, when she was awake. Why would anyone risk the safety of everyone on the islands? Uncle Balez and Master Shai are the Guardians of the Shrine. It's their job to watch over the volcano and protect the dragon. Not to . . . Not to . . ." She sputtered on the words.

"Master Shai is a hero," Ji-Lin said, feeling sick. "She fought koji. Saved a village from a lava flow all on her own and then flew the length of the Hundred Islands of Himitsu to warn the emperor — or at least, that was one of the stories." She thought of how many Master Shai stories she and

Alejan had told each other. Master Shai had been their personal hero. Alejan practically worshiped her. He was going to be crushed when he woke and realized who had betrayed them. "Why would she do this?"

"And Uncle Balez. Our own *uncle!*" Seika was pacing in tight circles between Alejan and the sleeping dragon. The lantern light bounced from wall to wall. "Father's brother! How could he?"

"Prince Balez wanted to know a lot about Zemyla," Kirro offered. "Everything. He kept me talking the entire time you were getting ready for the ritual, and then after, he wanted to talk some more. He told me to stay behind and write down anything else I could think of that I hadn't told him. He was kind of intense about it. Friendly, though. And he kept giving me snacks. To be perfectly honest, a part of me thought he was going to imprison me or chop me into pieces, but he just wanted to know about Zemyla. Like he wanted to plan a trip or something."

"It makes no sense at all," Seika repeated. "It's their responsibility to look after the dragon — protect her, care for her, see to her needs. Not put her to sleep! Why would they do this? They're the Guardians of the Shrine!" Ji-Lin nodded along with her as Seika paced back and forth in front of the sleeping dragon. They'd betrayed Himitsu, their people, the emperor, their family, everyone.

"You'd have to ask them why," Kirro said. "Except that would be really stupid, since they're the bad guys and all. I mean, they might explain, but then they'd probably drop you off a cliff or shove you in a dungeon or something. Really don't want to be in a dungeon."

"If she's been asleep for a long time, that could explain why the barrier is failing," Ji-Lin said, kneeling next to the bowl. She studied the meat again. It looked like it had been there for a while. "She's not awake to maintain it."

"Then we need to wake her up, right?" Kirro said.

There was an obvious solution. Irina flowers came in two parts: petals that put you to sleep and stems that woke you up. "We have to find irina stems. They grow in rocky areas. Should be easy to spot." Ji-Lin remembered seeing them around the fortress on their walk up to the shrine.

"*If* we can get out of the fortress," Seika said. "You saw how many guards are here — they swarmed on us when we came out of the sea. We'd have to get past them, and then back here with the flowers, without them noticing."

"We'll have to be sneaky," Kirro said.

Ji-Lin stood. "You two stay here and guard Alejan."

"You can't go alone!" Seika said.

"Stay here, and stay safe," Ji-Lin said. "I'll be right back." Without giving Seika a chance to argue, Ji-Lin sprinted through the tunnel. She left them with the lantern. As the light faded, she had to slow. She put her hand on the stone wall to guide her toward the Great Hall. As she walked, she tried not to think about what this all meant. Uncle Balez and

Master Shai, traitors. Father had to be told. *But first, we have to wake Alejan. And the dragon.*

She hurried to the tapestry — and then stopped.

Voices.

There were people in the hall.

Creeping forward, she peeked through the gash in the tapestry. Guards were standing in the hall, in front of the doors to the courtyard.

She retreated.

This wasn't going to work. She'd never be able to get out of the fortress, find the flowers, and get back without their noticing. They'd see her, and chase her. Inching forward, Ji-Lin peeked again. There was a large window across the room. She could make it if she ran fast enough, but not without being seen, which would defeat the purpose.

Ji-Lin went back into the tunnel. Alejan was asleep, and he wouldn't wake without those flower stems. And Ji-Lin couldn't do it on her own.

Seika, Ji-Lin thought.

Seika would have to get out safely, find the right flower, and handle the dragon on her own. Only a few days ago, Ji-Lin would have said she couldn't do it. She'd have said Seika was too soft, too pretty, too weak. Ji-Lin was supposed to be her sword, her shield, her strength.

But now . . . *Seika can do it.*

She went back through the tunnel to tell her sister her plan.

Seika had wanted an adventure, but this was not what she'd meant. Beside her, just behind the tapestry, Ji-Lin stretched, preparing herself to run. She was planning to carry her sword, to look more like a threat. She held it steady in one hand; then she rose onto one foot, lifted a leg, and twisted slowly, raising her arms and sword. She looked like a true warrior, Seika thought, albeit shorter and smaller than the palace guards.

She hadn't always been like this. Both of them used to be so clumsy that Master Pon, their etiquette tutor, would break down in tears. Seika remembered the time Ji-Lin had tried to climb a trellis to a balcony and had torn the trellis off the wall, landing directly in a bed of rare roses. Another time, she'd knocked over a pyramid of dates and figs, spilling them all over the marble floor. And once, she'd torn a lace gown that she shouldn't have been wearing anyway. It had been Mother's, and they'd snuck into her closet, which had been preserved exactly the way it was when she was alive. They'd tried to mend the tear themselves and only made it look worse. One of the guards had found them in the closet crying, with the dress and a snarl of thread. He'd told Father, who had been furious. That felt like a lifetime ago. *We've both changed*, Seika thought.

"Be careful," Kirro whispered.

"Stay hidden," Ji-Lin told him.

"But what if guards come? What if they see where you came from and investigate? What if they find Alejan? What if they're dangerous?"

"Call for me," Ji-Lin said. "Be loud and annoying enough for me to hear you. And then retreat into the tunnel and hide in the shadows."

He swallowed. "You're trusting me to protect your lion."

"I am," Ji-Lin said.

"I didn't think you liked me, much less trusted me."

"That's funny, because I didn't," Ji-Lin said. "But now I do."

Kirro blinked. "That's . . . good?"

"Just scream if you need me. But if you don't . . . try not to make any noise at all, okay?" Ji-Lin peeked out through the gash in the tapestry. "Five guards."

I should stop this plan, Seika thought. *Someone could get hurt.* But they had to wake the dragon. More monsters would come if they didn't. "Good luck," she whispered.

"You too." Ji-Lin squeezed her hand. And then Ji-Lin burst out of the tapestry and ran across the room. She vaulted onto the windowsill. Peeking through the gash in the tapestry, Seika saw her silhouette clear against the sky. A guard shouted, spotting Ji-Lin as she leaped outside, onto a lower roof.

All five guards rushed to the window.

Keeping as quiet as she could, Seika crept from behind

the tapestry, slinked along the edge of the room, and ran out the door. She knew what the flower looked like — the memory was burned into her brain — but it was still dark out, and she was stuck in the shadows. She hurried along the edge of the courtyard toward the stone path that led to the shrine.

She climbed the path, looking on both sides. *Little white flowers . . . little white flowers . . . little . . . There!* A patch of them were clustered in between the rocks. Kneeling, she plucked as many as she could. She piled them all into her skirt. How many would it take to wake a dragon? She had no idea. Better take as many as she could carry.

She heard more shouting and glanced at the palace.

Ji-Lin was on the spine of the roof, running. Guards were chasing her, more than were in the hall. Ji-Lin wouldn't be able to distract them forever. Soon she'd be caught — unless Seika woke Alejan.

Cradling the flowers, Seika ran back toward the Great Hall. She slipped inside.

No guards.

Good, she thought.

She ran, her slippers silent on the stone, to the tapestry. She ducked into the darkness. Stumbling, hitting her toes on the rocks, she hurried through, ignoring the pain. She saw the amber glow of the lantern up ahead. "Kirro?" she whispered.

"Here," came a whisper back. "Wait, who's there?"

"It's Seika."

"The lion is still asleep. He's drooling a little, which is gross."

She saw him near the lantern, next to Alejan. The dragon was also still asleep. Dropping down, she quickly began to peel open the stems. She scooped the innards and smeared them on the lion's lips, and then on his teeth. Kirro joined her, scooping out more stems and handing the white pulp to her.

Alejan didn't wake.

He needed to taste it.

Gathering courage, she reached her hand into the lion's mouth.

And Alejan's eyes opened. She yanked her hand back away from his jaws. "Shh," she said quickly. "Shh, Alejan. It's me, Seika. Are you all right?"

Groggily, he swung his head in both directions. "Ji-Lin."

"She needs you," Seika said. "Go. She's on the roof. I'll be all right. Help her."

Scrambling to his paws, he pulled himself up. His first few steps were shaky, but then he was running out through the tunnel, toward the tapestry. And Seika was left alone with the dragon and the sailor boy.

"How much do we need for the dragon?" he asked.

"As much as it takes," Seika said. As they continued to break open stems, she added, "I'm glad you're here."

"Really?"

"Are other Zemylans nice too?" If the dragon didn't wake, they could be meeting a whole lot more Zemylans. She tried to imagine what that would be like. She thought of the maps she'd seen in the captain's cabin: A coastline she'd never imagined. Cities. Towns. She knew Zemyla was a sprawling empire that held deserts and mountains, as well as the shore. She wondered what it would be like to see all that . . .

She realized she'd slowed and was merely holding the irina stems. *It's enough to see the islands,* she scolded herself. *You don't need any more adventure.* She peeled the stems faster.

"Some are nice; some aren't. Probably the same as here. But there are plenty of good Zemylans your islanders could help if the barrier doesn't come back. People should be told about waterhorse spit. And how to defeat a scylla. And we can show you things too — we have these really smart scientists, and they've learned a lot in the last two hundred years. You haven't lived until you've seen fireworks. We have the most incredible —"

"The barrier has to be fixed," Seika said. "It's the only way for my people to be safe." It didn't matter that she was now imagining a vast unexplored land, filled with people different from anyone she'd ever met . . . *Kirro's people have found ways to be safe,* she thought, and then she shook her head, as if that would shake the uncomfortable thoughts out.

"I just . . . If we can't fix it . . . It could still be okay, that's all I'm saying. You'd be part of the world again, instead of just hiding."

For an instant, Seika stopped peeling the stems. She stared at Kirro. "You don't want the barrier fixed, do you? If you don't want it fixed, why are you helping us?"

"Because . . . I don't know. You saved my life, all of you. And Ji-Lin said she trusted me. And this was the whole point in coming here, right? I just . . . I guess I trust you too. I know whatever you do, it'll be the right thing."

She scooped up what they had and pushed it onto the dragon's teeth, into her mouth. The dragon didn't stir. Kirro handed Seika another lump of the white paste, and she smeared more on the dragon's golden tongue.

The tongue moved, pulled back into her mouth.

Seika hopped from foot to foot. "It's working! O Dragon of Himitsu, I am —"

All words died as the dragon lifted her massive head. She opened her eyes, and Seika saw fire within them, red and amber. She stared, transfixed, as the dragon opened her jaws and spoke. "I have been betrayed!" Her voice curled through the tunnels. It filled every bit of the air. Seika felt as if the dragon's voice were clogging her head. It rolled through her and through the rocks.

"Not by us!" Kirro yelped.

Stepping forward, Seika raised her voice. "I am Seika

d'Orina Amatimara Himit-Re, firstborn daughter of Emperor Yu-Senbi of Himitsu, and I have come to renew our bargain. Long have you protected our people —"

The dragon swung her head toward Seika. Hot air huffed from her nostrils. Her eyes swirled with flame colors. "The bargain has been broken. My egg has been taken. I saw him as I fell into my unnatural sleep. I saw a man steal my unborn child!"

Seika gasped.

"I knew there was an egg!" Kirro said. "Told you!" To the dragon, he said, "The bargain was to protect the egg, wasn't it?" And then he seemed to realize he was talking to an actual dragon, and he shrank back, curling against himself as if he could vanish if he tried hard enough.

"Indeed," the dragon said, "and the bargain is now broken!" She then howled so loudly the sound drove Seika to her knees.

Seika squeezed her hands over her ears and shouted as loudly as she could, "But I'm here to renew it! I'm the heir! I came on the Emperor's Journey! Even now my father sails to join us, to celebrate the renewed bargain. He should be nearly here." She was *not* going to fail. Not now! She'd woken the dragon! Everything was supposed to be fixed!

"Without my egg, there can be no bargain," the dragon cried. "The emperor has broken his word! He failed to protect my egg! I shall have revenge!" She spread her wings, knocking into the sides of the tunnel. Rocks rained down, and Seika ducked. Kirro screamed.

The dragon flapped her wings so hard that it created a gust of wind. She then ran the length of the tunnel and burst out of the tapestry. Seika and Kirro ran after her, reaching the hall in time to see her break through the roof. Stone cracked and then split, and rocks rained down. The dragon flew into the sky as dust rose around them, filling the hall with rubble.

Three guards raced into the Great Hall, along with Uncle Balez. He halted when he saw Seika, looking from her to the rubble to the shadow of the dragon against the predawn sky. "Oh, Seika, what have you done?"

"What have *I* done? What have *you* done? She says someone stole her egg! She blames Father! Says he swore to protect it. Says that was the bargain. I think — I think she's gone to attack him!" Seika pointed to the sky — the shadow of the dragon was gone. She was already on her way, and who knew how close Father's ship was?

Uncle Balez paled. "This wasn't how it was supposed to be." He wrung his hands and began to pace across the rubble. "I never meant to endanger my brother. I never wanted to endanger anyone. I only wanted to do what our older brother failed to do: stop the earthquakes."

Seika felt as if she'd had all the air knocked out of her lungs. She thought of the story of Prince Biy and how he blamed the dragon for the earthquakes . . . but how would putting the dragon to sleep stop the quakes? That was crazy!

"*You* stole the egg!" Kirro accused Uncle Balez.

"He did?" Seika asked. Then, to her uncle: "You did?"

"Only to keep it safe while the dragon slept," Uncle Balez said.

"How could you?"

He climbed over the rubble toward the fallen tapestry. "No one was supposed to be hurt. Not the egg, not the dragon, not your father."

"Yeah, well, now people are going to get hurt," Kirro said. "Where's the egg? You have to give it back! There's an angry dragon on the loose!"

"She'll find my father's ship!" Seika cried. "She blames him for breaking the bargain! You have to tell her it was your fault." She didn't understand what could have made Uncle Balez do this, but what mattered now was that the dragon was flying to find the emperor, and Father was sailing right into her path. "Before she reaches Father!"

"I did it for the good of Himitsu!" Uncle Balez said. Kneeling, he picked up a shred of the tapestry the dragon had torn when she burst out of the tunnel. "The barrier causes the quakes!"

Hands on her hips, Seika glared at him. He was spouting nonsense. Holding the piece of the ruined tapestry in his hands, he was peering up at the sky, as if he expected the dragon to return.

"The dragon has gone to punish Father for what *you* did," she said. "You betrayed the bargain, not him. You're a traitor."

"You don't understand—I've been studying the old texts for years. The references are obscure, but I am certain of it: The barrier stresses the land. Pushes at it, deep within the earth. I thought if the dragon slept long enough, then she wouldn't be able to maintain the barrier or keep her egg from hatching. Eventually, the barrier would fall, the quakes would stop, and no one would be able to deny—"

She wanted to grab him by the shoulders and shake him. "The quakes didn't stop! If anything, they're worse!"

"Because the barrier isn't gone! It was only weakened. If the dragon were to sleep for a little while longer—"

"The dragon is awake *now* and going to kill my father. Do you want that?"

He deflated. "No. Of course I don't. He's my brother! You have a sister—how could you even think I'd want to hurt my own brother?"

"Then you need to make this right!" She put every shred of imperial command, all her training, all her self-confidence, all her strength into the words. She was the princess, and he *must* obey. "Give her back her egg!"

Uncle Balez shook his head slowly, sadly. "We were so close. Only a few days more—"

"He will die."

Something in her tone finally got through to him.

Straightening his shoulders, he met her eyes. "The egg is hidden beneath the bones in the dragon's chamber of the shrine."

She nodded. "I'll get it. Can you delay the dragon? Catch up to her on Master Shai?"

"Yes," he said. He still looked dazed, but he was nodding. He turned to his guards and ordered, "Help her." To Seika, he said, "Fly out to join us with your sister and her lion."

Following the guards, Seika and Kirro ran over the rubble and out of the fortress.

CHAPTER
TWENTY-ONE

JI-LIN RAN ACROSS the rooftop. In the moonlight, the tiles were black shadows with ridges she couldn't see. She trusted her balance to keep her from tumbling forward. This wasn't the same as running on the rooftops of the Temple of the Sun. Here, she didn't know the slopes and pitches. But neither did the guards behind her. They scrambled, crawling on hands and knees, to keep up with her.

The fortress was built on the mountainside, with many stories that jutted out of the stone. She jumped from one to the next, climbing between them until she reached the peak. From there, she looked out across the dark sea. She thought she saw a ship in the distance . . .

Yes, it was a ship. The shape of the sail was unmistakable. It was in sharp relief against the matte gray-blue-black sky. Father! But he wasn't here yet. They were still on their own until he could reach the island.

Ji-Lin heard a rumble. Looking up at the mountain, she saw that loose rocks were tumbling down one of the faces. Dirt plumed into the air. But she couldn't worry about it now. Below her, the guards were climbing higher. The closest was near enough that she could hear him puffing as he climbed.

She switched to the other side of the roof and slid down it on her feet, arms stretched out for balance. Leaping, she landed on the next level in a crouch. She heard the guards shout behind her and switch directions. Running again, she landed on the roof near the Great Hall.

And the tiles in front of her exploded.

Rocks shot into the air in a shower of debris. Screaming, she covered her head and ducked. She heard the stones hit the roof around her. Everything shook.

She saw the dragon shoot into the sky. The dragon spread her wings, silhouetted against the moon, and then let loose a cry so shrill that Ji-Lin's skin prickled.

A second later, she thought: *Where's Seika?*

Guards forgotten, dragon ignored, Ji-Lin launched herself across the broken roof. Seika had been in there! She reached the vast hole in the roof, flattened onto her stomach, and looked in to see their uncle and his guards—and there was Seika, with Kirro! She saw her sister and the sailor boy dart out of the fortress, heading toward the path to the shrine with three guards—voluntarily, it seemed. The guards looked to be leading them ... *Where are they going?*

She had to follow them. But the ground was far, very far. Ji-Lin knew she couldn't jump that distance, and she couldn't run back the way she'd come. *Alejan!* she thought. If the dragon was awake, he must be too. Standing, Ji-Lin put her fingers in her mouth and whistled loudly.

She saw the shape of the winged lion rising into the air. Waving her arms, she called, "Alejan!"

But it wasn't Alejan.

It was Master Shai.

Ji-Lin lowered her arms and began to run as the lioness dove toward her — *She's not slowing! She's going to crash!* Ji-Lin felt the rush of air from the creature's great wings as the lioness swooped past her, down into the hall, toward Uncle Balez. She hit the ground amid the rubble, executing the high-speed landing perfectly, and Uncle Balez climbed onto her back.

"Gotcha," one of the guards said, rising in front of Ji-Lin.

She dodged, leaping for another level. The guards were everywhere, swarming over the roofs. Drawing her sword, she turned. "I don't want to fight you."

One of them nodded to another, and she knew they were surrounding her. These were her people. She'd had it drilled into her: she was supposed to protect her people, not hurt them. But she might not have a choice.

A shadow passed over her, darkening the lemon-colored predawn sky, and she looked up: a winged lion, directly overhead. Master Shai or Alejan? Hoping, she jumped into the air and grabbed the lion's leg. Swinging herself up, she felt a guard's fingers brush past her foot, just missing her. She held on as they veered out over the rocks.

"Are you all right?" Alejan! It was him. Straining her arms and kicking her feet, she pulled herself up onto his back.

"Where are Master Shai and Uncle Balez?"

"Chasing the dragon," he said.

"Alejan . . ." Ji-Lin hesitated. How could she tell him that his hero might not be so heroic? "There were sleeping flowers in the dragon's meat. We think the Guardians of the Shrine hid the dragon and lied to us. Lied to everyone —"

He cut her off. "No, they wouldn't. You must be mistaken. Prince Balez and Master Shai are heroes. The stories all agree —"

"Alejan."

"Please, Ji-Lin. She's my hero."

Ji-Lin hugged his neck, burying her face in his mane. "I'm sorry, Alejan. But we have to be our own heroes now. We have to find Seika. She's gone up to the shrine." She held on, twisting so she could see the dragon flapping in a circle around the island and then heading out to sea, toward the ship. The winged lioness was following her, as Alejan had said.

Alejan flew up the side of the volcano, following the stone road. She saw the archway ahead. Closer, he flew low and she let go, landing in a crouch.

"They must have gone inside." She plunged into the crack in the mountain. Instantly, the smell of sulfur surrounded her, permeating her skin and filling her lungs.

"They took the torches!" Alejan said. She heard his claws on the rocks, as if he were kneading them in distress.

"I know. But we have each other."

"And I deeply appreciate that," Alejan said, "but neither of us glows in the dark."

The darkness felt full of monsters and dragons. She kept one hand on the wall and one hand on Alejan. "Seika! Are you there, Seika?" The heat was already squeezing in on her. She was sweating, and Alejan's fur was damp.

And then the darkness shook.

Ji-Lin was knocked into Alejan. Grunting, he fell to the side as the tunnel shuddered around them. She heard rocks crashing down, and she knew she was screaming, but she couldn't hear her own voice over the noise. Clutching Alejan, she rode out the tremor. Bits of rock rained on her, pelting her back.

It stopped, the ground quivering to stillness, but the sound of tumbling rocks went on and on. At last, the rain slowed to a trickle.

"Alejan? Are you okay?"

"Yes. And you, my princess?"

"Fine. That was . . ." She began to shake—not the ground, but her body. She clung to Alejan until she stopped trembling. ". . . bad."

"Is it going to cave in?" Alejan asked.

"No. Maybe. I don't know. Seika? Kirro? Seika!"

She heard nothing. Seika was deeper into the volcano. What if the quake had . . . *No, I'm not going to think like that*, Ji-Lin told herself. Seika had to be okay. "We have to find her, and then we have to stop Master Shai and Uncle Balez."

After what they'd done to the dragon — and accidentally to Alejan — they couldn't be allowed to roam free.

"Ji-Lin, if Master Shai and Prince Balez aren't heroes . . . then who are?"

"I don't know. Maybe there aren't any. Maybe we're all just doing the best we can." She switched to shouting: "Seika! Seika, can you hear me? Are you okay? We're coming!" Releasing the lion, Ji-Lin crawled forward, feeling her way. Rocks coated the floor. She hit them with her fingers and knees. Wincing and muttering about traitorous lords, she climbed around boulders that had fallen in the way. The tunnel could have caved in with Seika and Kirro inside. The whole volcano could cave in now with all of them inside. She tried to push the fear down hard and focus only on the task at hand. She couldn't stop an earthquake, but she could find her sister.

She hit a wall. Feeling her way, she found rubble all around, choking the tunnel, except in one place. The roof must have crumbled here during the tremor. "I can squeeze through." But Alejan wouldn't be able to make it.

"Don't go, Ji-Lin," he pleaded.

She wanted to turn around, badly. It was dark. It smelled. She was tired and scared, and she shouldn't even be here. "I have to find Seika."

"I can't leave you alone in the darkness. There could be another quake. Aftershocks. Remember in the tent?"

"I'm not afraid," she lied.

"I am," the lion said.

She hesitated.

"Ji-Lin, we are a team. You and me. Lion and rider. Don't make me leave you alone in the dark in an unstable volcano. It could erupt. It could collapse. You could get lost. You could be hurt."

"She's my sister. I'd never forgive myself if I didn't try. Not because Father told me to take care of her. Not because it's my duty. Not because I trained for this. Not because I'm supposed to be her guardian or because I want to be a hero or any of that. But because she shared an orange with me. Because we snuck out of our room together when we were supposed to be napping. Because we dumped goldfish from the fountain into the canals, setting them free, not knowing the waterfolk would eat them. Because she's known me from the beginning and will know me until the end. Because she drives me crazy sometimes, both when she gives imperial orders and when she's afraid to. Because she trusts me. Do I really need a reason?"

Alejan nudged her with his nose, and she wrapped her arms around his neck and buried her hands in the fur of his mane. "I almost lost you once already on this adventure," Alejan said, his voice muffled. "I don't want to lose you permanently, even if it means we aren't heroes, even if it means there are no stories or songs or tales about us."

"I'll be swift, bold, and unexpected," Ji-Lin promised.

"Just be careful," Alejan said. "I'll fly up to the mouth of the volcano. As soon as you reach the dragon's chamber, call out and I will fly in from above. Promise me you'll call for me."

She squeezed him once more, then released him. "I will."

Softly, he said, "Seika isn't the only one who cares about you. You *must* call me if you need me. And not because I want to be a hero. Because . . . Oh, just be careful, Ji-Lin!"

"Go," she told him. She slipped through the hole in the rocks. Alone, she continued, hands forward, feeling her way, kicking stones with her feet. Every few steps, she called, "Seika!"

I hate the dark, she thought. She felt as if she were listening with her skin. She couldn't remember how far it had been before. It had felt like eternity. She was sure it was shorter than that.

Ahead, she saw a glow — the heart of the volcano and . . . torches? "Seika?"

Softly, as if from a distance, she heard, "Ji-Lin?"

She hurried toward the glow and the voice. "I'm here! Where are you?"

"In the heart! Hurry!"

Ji-Lin heard a scrambling noise, as if hollow sticks were hitting one another. She also heard other voices — the guards? And Kirro. They were both there and okay! She ran faster through the tunnel, stumbling over the rocks, until she burst into the heart of the volcano, below the opening to the sky.

Seika, Kirro, and three guards were digging through the bones.

"What are you doing?" Ji-Lin cried.

Seika was coated in dust, with a smear on her cheek. She was kneeling in her beautiful princess skirts on the floor of the chamber. Without looking up, Seika said, "The dragon woke and said someone stole her egg. She blames Father — said the bargain was to protect her egg, and that he broke the bargain by allowing her egg to be stolen. Then Uncle Balez said he was the one who stole it and hid it here, under the bones. He's gone with Master Shai to delay the dragon until we can find it and bring it to them, to convince the dragon not to kill Father. Or whatever she plans to do."

"Given how upset she was, probably destroy the islands," Kirro said. "Or make the volcano explode . . . which would be the same thing . . . which makes me think we shouldn't be here. Can we dig faster?"

Ji-Lin stared at them both. Stealing the egg . . . Deliberately endangering the islands . . . "But . . . He . . . How could . . . That's treason! Why would he do it?"

"He said the barrier is causing the earthquakes," Seika said without stopping. "He wanted to keep the dragon asleep until the barrier fell."

Ji-Lin tried to wrap her head around it — the enormity of

what their uncle had done and what he'd tried to do. At last, she said, "Father is not going to be happy."

"Especially if the dragon eats him," Kirro said.

Both princesses glared at him.

"Sorry!" He dug faster.

One of the guards cried out, "Found it! Your Highnesses!" He pulled something out of the dust. It was emerald-green and larger than any egg Ji-Lin had ever seen — roughly the size of a human baby. The guard had to hold it with two hands. He passed it to Seika, who staggered under the weight.

"We have to get it to the dragon," Seika said as she steadied herself.

Seika was right. They had to move fast. And hope the dragon wasn't faster. Putting two fingers in her mouth, Ji-Lin whistled.

She looked up at the hint of sky, far above, at the top of the shaft. She knew he'd be there, at the mouth of the crater, waiting in case she needed him, not just because he'd promised but because that was what he always did. He was always there for her. She saw his silhouette circle the crater, black against the lightening blue sky, and then he spiraled down, lower and lower into the volcano.

He landed, and Ji-Lin leaped on. She pulled Seika, with the egg, up behind her, and Kirro climbed on too. "We're on! Fly!" Ji-Lin ordered Alejan.

With hard wing strokes, Alejan flew. Beat, beat, beat. He strained. He groaned. And then they felt a cool breeze on their faces as he rose out of the crater. The wind wrapped around them as they flew up out of the volcano with the dragon's egg.

CHAPTER
TWENTY-TWO

SEIKA SAW THE ship. It was Father's. She recognized the shape of the sails and the curve of the hull as it cut through the waves. But approaching from the other side of the island was another vessel with three white sails: the Zemylan ship. It was coming at a rapid clip, slicing through the dark waves as if it had harnessed a faster wind. It was longer and broader than Father's ship, built for power, not beauty, and it was headed toward Father's.

The dragon flew toward both ships.

Behind her flew Uncle Balez and Master Shai, faster.

All of them were going to meet at the same time.

"Alejan, we have to reach them before the dragon attacks!" Ji-Lin called. "Master Shai can't fight her alone!"

"Master Shai is a match for anyone!" Alejan said. But Seika heard the uncertainty in his voice. The dragon was larger than the scylla had been, equal to the size of both ships. The shadow beneath her covered the waves.

"We don't want anyone to fight at all!" Seika said.

Seika watched the dragon fly closer to the ships. Wind battered her face, and she had to squint. She held on tight as Alejan dipped and rose with the air currents.

From the emperor's ship, a winged lion with white fur rose into the air. Seika heard Ji-Lin's gasp. "Master Vanya!"

"Two lions!" Alejan trumpeted.

"Still won't be enough!" Kirro said.

"They are our two greatest warriors," Alejan objected.

"Alejan, about Master Shai . . ." Seika began. If Uncle Balez was responsible . . . then chances were that Master Shai knew what he'd done, perhaps had even helped.

"He knows," Ji-Lin said. "I told him."

"We don't know for certain," Seika said. "Uncle Balez only talked about himself. It's possible Master Shai didn't know." But she wasn't sure she believed that. In fact, she was almost certain Uncle Balez had used the word *we* at least once. *I'm sorry, Alejan,* she thought.

"I still love her stories, no matter what," Alejan said. "And I will still save her. We will reach them in time!" He pumped his wings harder, grunting with each wing beat.

Kirro leaned forward. "Are you sure this is a good idea? Do you see the size of that thing? I mean, I knew it was big when we were in the tunnel. But seeing it in the air . . . It could eat the lions as appetizers and swallow the ships for dinner. We'll be dessert!"

"No one hurt your egg!" Seika screamed to the dragon. "You don't have to fight! Stop! Don't fight!" But the wind swallowed her shout.

Ahead, above the ships, Master Vanya and Master Shai flew at the dragon. The dragon twisted in the air and slashed with her claws. Her tail struck fast as a whip. The two lions darted through the air. Working together, they herded the dragon higher, away from the ships, and she twisted into an *S* trying to snap at them. Her roar echoed across the sky.

But even the two greatest warriors in Himitsu couldn't stop her.

The dragon whipped through the sky, flying toward the morning sun, and then she dove between the lions, toward the emperor's ship.

The Zemylan ship pulled past the emperor's ship, and Seika saw the sailors scurrying over the deck. They were running for the weapon. A cannon, Kirro had called it. They were aiming it toward the clouds, toward . . .

Oh no, Seika thought. *They're going to —*
Boom!

"No!" Seika yelled. Suddenly, she wasn't worried about her father or the lions anymore. She was worried about the dragon.

The air shook with the blast of the cannon. With a cry, the dragon flipped sideways, and the cannonball ripped past her. Seika didn't know who she was yelling for: the dragon, the Zemylans, or Father. All of them. All of Himitsu.

"The dragon can't evade Master Shai, Master Vanya, *and* that weapon," Ji-Lin said.

"Wait!" Kirro cried. "You're worried about the dragon? I thought . . . Just tell me: Whose side are we on? Who do we want to win?"

"Everyone!" Seika cried.

Ji-Lin urged Alejan faster. "We have to save Father, the dragon, the lions, the barrier . . . Everyone must live, or we lose! All of Himitsu will lose!"

The dragon was diving again—toward the emperor's ship. Master Shai blocked her, and the dragon's teeth latched on to the lion's wing. Uncle Balez struck with his sword, and the dragon released, rearing back. Master Shai fell through the air. Seika gasped, and then the lioness righted herself and flew upward.

Seika saw the Zemylan sailors preparing their weapon to fire again.

"Drop me on my father's ship!" Kirro said. "I'll stop them!"

"How?" Seika asked.

"I'll tell them the truth," he said. "I'll tell them your story."

"Alejan, do it," Ji-Lin said.

Spray from the waves spattered them as Alejan dipped lower. He aimed for the Zemylan ship. Kirro waved his arms. "Don't shoot!" he shouted. "It's me! Kirro! They cured me!" As Alejan swooped toward the deck, Seika saw the Zemylans shouting to one another in confusion. "Father, it's me!"

Kirro jumped off as they neared the deck. His father, the captain, rushed forward and caught him. Looking up, Kirro waved at Seika, Ji-Lin, and Alejan as Alejan soared away.

In the air, the fight was continuing.

And it was getting worse. The dragon's scales were stained with blood where the lion's claws had raked her. Master Vanya's back leg hung limp behind her, and Uncle Balez was crouched on Master Shai's back. "We have to fly between them," Ji-Lin said. "Force the lions to stop! There's no winning this fight."

"The second the lions stop attacking, the dragon will attack Father," Seika said.

"Then we have to force the dragon to stop too. Simultaneously."

Seika took a deep breath and reminded herself that princesses were brave. "Drop me on Father's ship. You two stop the lions, and I'll keep the dragon from hurting Father. I'll make her listen." She held the egg tighter. The shell felt warm and seemed, oddly, to be vibrating.

"If you can't —"

"I can," Seika said.

"All right," Ji-Lin said. "Be careful."

Seika almost laughed. She was about to put herself between Father and a dragon. There was nothing "careful" about this. But it was what she had to do.

Alejan shot past Master Shai and Uncle Balez. Dipping down, he flew toward the deck of the emperor's ship. With the egg in her arms, Seika dropped onto the ship.

"Seika!" Father shouted. "What is happening? Why are you here? Why is the dragon attacking?" He was dressed in rich golden robes that pooled on the floor. His face had been painted with lightning bolts on each cheek, and he wore golden bands up his arms and around his neck. He'd dressed for a ritual — their ritual, the end of the Emperor's Journey, which would never have an end if the dragon died.

Above, the dragon roared.

Seika turned to see Ji-Lin and Alejan fly toward the dragon and the other lions. Behind them, in the distance, she saw the island. Smoke was billowing out of the mouth of the volcano. *No!* she thought.

⟡

Force the lions to stop.

Easy to say. Very hard to do. Stop *them?* Stop Master Vanya and Master Shai, two of the most famous warriors in the history of Himitsu? They were heroes! Or the stories said they were. Anyway, who was she to try to stop them from doing anything?

I'm Princess Ji-Lin, second-born daughter of Emperor Yu-Senbi, many times descendant of Emperor Himitsu, and the rider of Alejan of the Temple of the Sun. I crossed the islands with my sister. I fought a scylla and a valraven. And I can do this.

"Be swift, be bold, be unexpected, Alejan!" she shouted. "Go *between* the lions and the dragon!"

"That will indeed be unexpected," Alejan said. But he obeyed. He pumped his wings and surged forward. Above, the dragon twisted, a snake in the sky. Sunlight flashed on her scales. Closer, Ji-Lin could see that her wings had gashes — the lions' claws had struck her.

Ji-Lin raised her voice. "Dragon of Himitsu, your egg is safe! Look to the ship! My sister has it, safe, for you!"

The dragon wasn't listening. She roared. Curling her body, the dragon shot her neck forward, her jaws open, toward Ji-Lin. "Betrayers!"

Alejan dropped, and the dragon's teeth snapped shut just above the lion's head. Ji-Lin ducked fast. The two lionesses dove toward the dragon, but the dragon jackknifed, evading them. She whipped through the air, her tail flicking the clouds.

Behind the dragon, on the island, lava flowed down the mountainside, spreading over the rocks, killing trees as it touched them. Fire spread up the branches. The air tasted like ash and smoke.

Oh no! Ji-Lin thought. An eruption had created the islands. And an eruption could destroy them.

"Stop!" Ji-Lin called. "Dragon, you must stop this!"

But the dragon wasn't listening. Writhing against the sky, she cried, "My child! For two hundred years, I protected him! I kept him safe from the world, safe within his shell, safe from all, but I didn't protect him from my protectors! We made a bargain! You keep us safe, and I let you stay. Betrayers!" The dragon roared, and behind her, fire spurted from the mountain.

Master Vanya yelled at Ji-Lin. "Move aside, child!"

"Seika has the egg!" Ji-Lin shouted to the lionesses. "She'll talk to the dragon. You need to stop fighting!"

They didn't stop.

Diving toward the dragon, Master Shai swiped at her wing. Her claw tips scratched along the scales, and the dragon howled.

"If we stop, she will kill the emperor," Master Vanya said, dodging the dragon's claw and then swooping past the dragon's jaws as they closed just behind her. "You and your sister must flee to safety. This is no place for children!"

Ji-Lin leaned over Alejan's side to see Seika running across the deck toward the prow of the ship. "Seika can do it! You need to give her a chance. She'll know what to say!"

"The dragon will not listen to a child," Master Vanya said. "She won't listen to anyone. She's lost in her anger."

Master Shai commanded Alejan, "Fly away. This is not your fight."

Alejan shuddered beneath her. Ji-Lin knew he never thought he'd be in this position, facing Master Shai. She wondered if he was going to be able to say no to his hero. "Show her we're staying, Alejan. You can do it."

"You're wrong," Alejan said to his hero. "It *is* our fight. Your rider made it our fight when he interfered with the Emperor's Journey — two hundred years of tradition that kept us safe and he tossed it aside like . . . like . . . like it was rotten fish!"

The dragon roared and dove at the lions again. Master

Vanya was right — the dragon was pure rage. She gave no sign of hearing them argue around her. But Seika would be able to catch her attention, *if* the lions would stop! Ji-Lin was sure of it.

Uncle Balez shouted, "We want the same as you: to keep Himitsu safe!" He leaned sideways as the dragon swiped at them. Master Shai spiraled through the air, coming up above the dragon.

We? He was admitting this was Master Shai's fault too. *Poor Alejan,* Ji-Lin thought. "You picked a bad way to do it. Monsters are on the islands!"

As she dove toward the dragon, Master Shai shouted, "The monsters must come! The barrier must fall!" Arching backward away from Master Shai's claws, the dragon whipped her tail toward Master Vanya.

Alejan gasped. "Then it's true. You betrayed us!"

Master Shai snapped her jaws at the dragon's back leg. Her teeth grazed the dragon's ankle but did no damage. "You do not understand," the lioness said.

"You were my hero! How could you?" His voice was so broken that Ji-Lin wrapped her arms around his neck. The dragon swiped at Master Shai with her tail, and the lioness flew higher.

"The emperor refuses to believe the truth: the barrier must fall, or we are all doomed!" The lioness's voice was like a trumpet ringing across the sky. "Since he would not act, we did!"

The dragon struck at Master Vanya.

Evading the dragon's jaws, Master Vanya flew toward the other lioness. "What are you saying? Shai, what have you done? Prince Balez, explain this!"

"We have done what we must," Master Shai said. Her lips curled back into a snarl, showing all her teeth. "And if the barrier will not fall peacefully, then it will fall by force! Balez, you must use your sword. Strike for the throat!"

The dragon heard *that*. She shrieked her fury. "Betrayers!"

"We can't!" Uncle Balez cried to the lioness. "No one was to be hurt! That was what we agreed. That was what you promised. We cannot —"

"We must do this!" Master Shai said. "Do not falter now, Balez! The future of Himitsu depends on us! All the islanders' lives depend on us! Full attack!"

Alejan roared. "No!" He flew at Master Shai and Uncle Balez.

At the same time, Master Shai flew toward them, and Uncle Balez raised his sword. At Ji-Lin. No, not at her. At the dragon!

Rising up, Ji-Lin blocked the lord's sword as he swung for the dragon's wing. Metal hit metal with an echoing clang. "Out of our way, child!" Uncle Balez cried. He rose in the saddle and bore down on her. "Forgive me, but Master Shai is right. If we cannot stop the dragon, we must destroy her! It is not what I want, but it is what must be! My brother must be protected, and the islands must be saved!"

Two hands on her sword hilt, Ji-Lin held him back. Below them, she heard shouting, but it felt distant. The world compressed to just this moment: she and Alejan against the lioness and her uncle, and the lord and lioness had many years' more experience. But Ji-Lin didn't think about that. She just had to block this sword in this moment, right now —

Ji-Lin saw a flicker of movement, and the dragon's tail snapped the air with so much force that Alejan was blown backward. Knocked by the wind, Master Shai flew back, with Uncle Balez, away from the dragon. Recovering, Master Shai beat her wings, holding steady in the air. She readied for another attack.

"You had better be right about your sister's ability to stop the dragon's attack," Master Vanya said to Ji-Lin. "I am trusting you." And then she flew at Master Shai and Uncle Balez, blocking them, holding them back.

Seizing the opportunity, the dragon flew toward the emperor's ship. As she roared, fire shot higher from the mouth of the volcano.

And from the prow of the emperor's ship, Seika's voice rang out: "Stop!"

CHAPTER
TWENTY-THREE

CRADLING THE EGG in her arms, Seika ran to the prow of the ship. "Stop!" Her voice carried over the waves and was caught in the wind.

"Seika! No!" Father shouted. "It's too dangerous!"

Diving toward the ship, the dragon looked even more massive. In the east, the sun had risen, and its light caught her blood-red scales. They glowed. Seika felt fear course through her body. She locked her knees to keep from shaking, but she stayed on the prow, alone and exposed.

"Your egg is unharmed!" Seika yelled. "The bargain is unbroken! See!" She knew every eye was on her and every ear was listening to her. But she didn't let that silence her. She knew exactly what she needed to say, and she knew that she was the one who had to say it. "If you attack, you will destroy it! But if you stop, then I swear to you, on my honor as heir, on my honor as a princess, and on behalf of my people, that I will return your egg to you unharmed."

The dragon circled the ship, her tail flicking the mast. The ship rocked. "For two hundred years, my child has been safe! For two hundred years, my magic has kept him from hatching, and our bargain has kept him unharmed. But my trust has been broken. I have been betrayed by one who swore to protect me and my unborn child." Her knife-sharp claws glittered in the sun.

"The bargain can be repaired!" Seika shouted.

Joining her, the emperor said, "We are your protectors, now and always. Our fates are the same. Our home is the same."

"Don't punish everyone for the mistakes of a few!" Seika pleaded. "Don't throw away two centuries of peace for a moment of revenge!"

"Please, Dragon, listen to my daughter!" the emperor said. "Stop the eruption and look to your unborn child!"

Seika glanced at the island. Smoke was pluming from the crater. Lava was creeping down the face of the rocks, inching toward the village below it. "Please, Dragon, stop, and I will bargain with you anew!" Seika said. "We can have peace again, and safety, for your child and my people!"

The dragon fixed her gaze on Seika. It felt as if the dragon's fiery eyes were burning into her. Seika shrank back. All her instincts were screaming at her to run. But she didn't. She kept her balance on the prow as the ship rocked from side to side.

"I have felt fear," the dragon said.

"I have too," Seika confessed.

"I did not like it. The fear felt like fire, consuming me."

"But it won't consume you," Seika said. "You can live through it. You can see a new day, fresh, with no mistakes and no betrayals. Your egg is safe now! Promise you will bargain again, in good faith, as is tradition, and you may take it!" She held the egg aloft with both arms, high over her head.

The dragon considered this. Beyond her, Seika saw Ji-Lin and Alejan, with the lionesses, watching from above. She knew the Zemylan ship was nearby, also waiting, their cannon ready. Seika's arms began to shake.

"And you can guarantee this?" the dragon asked. "How can you be so certain this fear will not destroy me?"

"Because I am a princess who has made her own mistakes. I've been afraid too. And I've lived through it and grown stronger because of it. Bargain with me, Dragon of Himitsu, and you'll see!"

Seika held the dragon's glare, feeling the sweat rolling down her neck.

"Very well, Princess," the dragon said at last. "I promise we will bargain."

Behind the dragon, on the island, the fire died and the lava cooled, dimming to gray and solidifying into rock, frozen on the slopes. The unnatural eruption cooled just as unnaturally, dying fast on the mountainside. The lava was immobilized outside the village.

The emperor bowed deep and low. "Thank you, O Mighty Dragon." Seika had never seen her father bow to anyone. The emperor did not bow. He seemed rusty at it, his motion stiff.

Ash fell around them onto the ship, coating everything in gray.

"Know that I do not forgive what has been done," the dragon said to the emperor. "I will not speak with you again, Emperor Yu-Senbi. Send your daughters to me. I will parlay with them alone."

"As you wish." The emperor bowed again.

"As I have promised," the dragon corrected him.

Seika held still, not breathing, as the dragon swooped down and gently lifted the egg in her talons. Seika's arms trembled as she lowered them. Her heart felt as if it were beating louder than the drums on top of the palace spires. Her father standing next to her, she watched as the dragon flew toward the island and the now-quiet volcano. The smoke was already clearing, blown away by winds that rose from the dragon's wings. Blue sky poked through the haze.

She turned toward the emperor. He had tears in his eyes. "Father?" she said.

He laid his hand on her shoulder. "You have done well. I'm proud of you."

Before she could form an answer, Alejan and Ji-Lin landed on the deck. Ji-Lin leaped off the lion's back and ran toward her sister. Seika ran toward her. They collided in the middle of the deck and hugged each other. Into her sister's hair, Ji-Lin asked, "Did we do right?"

Seika looked over her sister's shoulder at Master Shai and Uncle Balez, who landed under Master Vanya's watchful eye. "I think so." Everyone was alive, and that was all she'd said she wanted — that was a win.

But there was still the matter of their uncle and the lioness. And the earthquakes.

Their father swept toward Uncle Balez. "Brother, what have you done?"

Uncle Balez's shoulders slumped, and his expression crumpled. "I have failed to save us. *That's* what I have done. All my life, I've studied . . ." She couldn't hear the next few words. She inched closer.

"The barrier has kept our people safe for two hundred years," Father was saying. "It is because of the barrier that our people have thrived. To risk that on a theory—"

Uncle Balez looked toward the horizon, where the barrier flickered like the air above a fire. "I have mapped the quakes and measured their effects. I've studied the old texts. The barrier should have fallen fifty years ago; the earthquakes began fifty years ago—there's a clear connection. I believe that the barrier is causing too much stress to the land, built up over the decades. Its continued existence is causing the earthquakes. And it's worsening. Eventually, the islands will be pulled apart." He demonstrated with his hands, pushing his fingers together, then yanking them apart. "We can't withstand that."

Is it true? Seika wondered. If the barrier was somehow *causing* the earthquakes . . . If the quakes were going to destroy the islands . . .

The emperor shook his head. "You have no real proof. Merely cryptic notes in old books. Our traditions tell us—"

"Didn't you hear the dragon? She kept her egg from hatching—it was supposed to hatch years ago; the barrier was supposed to fall naturally. It was never meant to stand for so long."

Seika thought of the weneb and the valravens and the scylla. There were hundreds more like them, and more koji she didn't even know the names of. "If the barrier fell for good, more monsters would come," she said.

Master Shai huffed. Even surrounded by guards, she looked regal and untouchable. "The people of Himitsu fear monsters more than they fear the trembling earth—and that is a mistake greater than any we have ever made. We feel only tremors now, but in time, there will be quakes of such magnitude that they destroy our cities, crush our people, and drown our islands." She flexed her claws and glared at the guards. "We can fight monsters; we cannot fight the earth."

The emperor shook his head. "You risk too much on a belief—"

"We can survive the koji, as the people of Zemyla have survived," Uncle Balez said. "We can adapt and learn and fight, perhaps with the Zemylans' help. We cannot survive the earthquakes."

Seika thought of Kirro and his people, the cities he'd described, the cannon the ship used. It was possible to survive the koji. He was proof of that.

"Biy knew this," Uncle Balez said.

"Biy was consumed by grief—"

"He studied the texts, the same ones I have seen! The barrier *has* to fall if any of us are to survive."

"We did what had to be done," Master Shai added. Seika heard the righteousness ringing in her voice. *She believes what she's saying,* she thought. *She thinks they're the heroes.*

Uncle Balez's shoulders slumped. "We *tried* to do what needed to be done," he corrected the lioness. "Tried and failed."

Father nodded to his guards, who closed in around his brother. "And in the process, you endangered all of us."

Uncle Balez didn't resist as his hands were bound together. "We're all in danger right now. If only I'd had more time . . . If she'd slept longer, you could have seen the truth!"

"I do see the truth: you betrayed me."

Beside him, Master Shai allowed a collar to be snapped around her neck. She held her head high and met no one's eyes. Seika couldn't help thinking of the waterhorse: *Heroes. Traitors. Both at once. We define ourselves by the stories we tell.* But which story was true: the one in which Uncle Balez and Master Shai were traitors, or the one in which they failed to be heroes?

"If you won't believe me, then ask the dragon!" Uncle Balez said, his voice desperate. "It's her barrier, and these are her islands."

The guards stepped back, uncertain whether they were truly arresting the emperor's brother and Master Shai. Seika studied her father's face — he was uncertain too. She saw it in the crinkle around his mouth. He felt doubt. Emperors were *never* supposed to feel doubt, but she read it there in his face.

"Ask her if I tell the truth," Uncle Balez pressed.

"I cannot ask," the emperor said. "My Journey was completed long ago, and the dragon will not speak with me again. Indeed, she has sworn not to."

Seika swallowed. She squeezed Ji-Lin's hand and then stepped forward, between her father and her uncle, between the lions. "I can ask."

~

The lava had cooled to solid rock. The smoke had dissipated. The ash shifted in the wind but didn't fall anew. As they sailed toward the island, Ji-Lin stared up at the now-sleeping volcano. She kept her hands buried in Alejan's mane. He was trembling but standing — he'd pushed himself harder than he ever had before, with his desperate flight to the ships. *He'll recover,* she thought. *He's strong. And so am I.*

The sailors raced around them, preparing to dock. On shore, the people of the island were clustered by the dock — they must have been watching it all unfold: the ships, the cannon, the dragon, the lions, the volcano . . . Ji-Lin wondered what they thought had happened and what stories they'd tell.

Still at the prow, Seika was waving to the crowd. *She's the perfect heir*, Ji-Lin thought. She hoped Seika realized that. All the lessons in how to be a princess . . . they'd made her strong too.

Nearby, on the other ship, the sailors were scurrying over the deck, securing the rigging and tossing out lines. Before their ship was fully docked, Kirro leaped off it and ran across to the emperor's ship. He charged up the deck, and three guards blocked him.

"It's all right," Ji-Lin called. "He's a friend!" She realized as she said it that she wasn't lying. He'd come through for them. And he didn't even seem that annoying anymore. Or at least, he was less annoying.

The guards glanced at the emperor, who nodded, and then they stepped back to allow the boy through. Kirro raced to them. "Did you see that? Wasn't that amazing? The dragon! And the lions! *You* were amazing, standing up to them like that. And Seika, on the prow, like a hero out of a tale. And the dragon — whoa, and then — oh, oh, is this the emperor? Gah!" He dipped forward into a bow and nearly fell over. Stumbling, he caught himself.

"You were great, Kirro," Ji-Lin said, "and yes, this is His Imperial Majesty, the Emperor of Himitsu, our father. Father, this is Kirro, a sailor from Zemyla."

"I just clean the decks," Kirro said. "A lot."

"Honored to meet you, deck cleaner," the emperor said gravely. He inclined his head. Ji-Lin saw the beginnings of a smile playing on his lips. She wasn't certain her father could smile. She hadn't seen him do it in years.

"My people . . . um, that is, the captain . . . he wants to talk with you," Kirro said. "He said to tell you things like 'mutually beneficial agreement' and 'trade negotiations.' Specifically, he said to tell your daughters, because he didn't think I'd talk to you, since you're an emperor and I'm . . . well, I clean decks."

The emperor's almost-smile faded, and Ji-Lin saw him glance at his brother, between the guards. "There can be no 'trade negotiations' with or travel between the islands and Zemyla while the barrier stands. But you are welcome to make your home among us. You will be the first immigrants from Zemyla in two hundred years."

Ji-Lin wondered what Kirro thought about being stuck on the islands permanently. And what about his father and the other sailors? How would they feel?

Accompanied by Master Vanya, the emperor strode off the ship at the same time the Zemylan captain debarked. Pitching his voice so it would carry to the people on the dock and the ships, the emperor called, "Welcome to the Hundred Islands of Himitsu! We are honored by your visit, grateful for your assistance, and eager to make your acquaintance."

The captain bowed. Just as loudly, he said, "We are emissaries of Zemyla, and we come in peace."

Kirro whispered to Ji-Lin and Seika. "This is pretty much

my father's dream come true — to be the first to discover the Hidden Islands. He said from now on, I'm his favorite son. I'm also his only son, but that's still good."

"Must be nice," Ji-Lin said. "I think our father has forgotten about us."

"Never," Seika said with complete certainty.

Ji-Lin wasn't so sure. She'd fought with Master Vanya and Master Shai. He couldn't be happy about that, even if he approved of the reason. Students were *not* supposed to attack their teachers; it was hardly traditional.

As if he'd heard them talking, the emperor turned from the captain and beckoned to Ji-Lin and Seika. Seika trotted toward him, and Ji-Lin followed, slower. Alejan kept pace with her.

"Captain, I'd like to introduce my daughters, Princess Seika, worthy heir to the throne, and Princess Ji-Lin, our bravest warrior."

Did Father just call her brave? Ji-Lin stared at him. She glanced at Seika, who met her eyes and mouthed, *He's right.*

"We have met," the captain said. "They saved my crew from a scylla, and then saved the life of my only son, who was dying of poison." He bowed to them, even lower than he'd bowed to the emperor.

Father smiled at them. *Smiled.*

It was more of a shock than seeing koji or finding the dragon or fighting the lions.

"Tales will be told about them," Father said. "I am proud of both of them. They have proved themselves worthy. But now they have a journey to complete."

"Yes, Father," Seika and Ji-Lin said.

CHAPTER
TWENTY-FOUR

WITH SHAKING HANDS, Seika pinned her tiara into her hair. She'd bathed, dressed, and braided her hair already. She'd told the servants that she didn't want their help. She only wanted her sister.

Sitting behind her, Ji-Lin was polishing her sword. She'd already polished it twice.

Adding another pin to hold the tiara, Seika watched Ji-Lin for a moment. The sword was gleaming, without even a shadow of dirt on it. "Do you think Uncle Balez is right?"

Ji-Lin paused in her polishing. "I don't know. Do you?"

She remembered when they were little, and Father had told them not to worry about the tremors. He'd been wrong about that — the quakes were dangerous. They'd lived through mild ones. She didn't want to face a major one; she didn't need a dragon to tell her that. "I don't know either. But I'm glad you'll be with me."

"Always," Ji-Lin promised. Putting down the polishing cloth, she sheathed her sword and stood. "Seika, I really missed you while I was at the temple."

"You know I missed you too. But now we're —"

A knock on the door. Seika stuck one last pin into her

hair and then answered it. Outside were three guards. In unison, they bowed. Seika inclined her head. Escorted, the sisters walked to the Great Hall.

Workmen had been clearing debris away, but most of the roof was still piled in chunks on the side of the hall, and dust lay over everything, as well as a thin layer of gray ash from the volcano. The tapestry had been removed to show the tunnel opening, and a picture of the red shrine had been painted around it. Torches lit either side of the entrance.

Due to the damage from both the tremor and the eruption, Father had vetoed plans to use the traditional entrance to the volcano. They were going to use the secret tunnel created by Uncle Balez and Master Shai, from the Great Hall.

"I guess it's not so secret anymore," Seika murmured.

Uncle Balez and Master Shai were watching from near what was left of the fireplace, with guards around them. On the opposite side, Kirro stood nearby, next to his father. Excited, the boy hopped up and down as he waved. Seika waved back.

By the tunnel entrance, the emperor was waiting, along with Master Vanya and Alejan. Beyond the Great Hall, through the open doors, Seika could see the courtyard. It was filled with men, women, and children who had come once again to see the Journey completed. This time, their faces were scared, and they clung to one another. No one held candles.

"Let the princesses proceed," the emperor said.

Seika walked forward, and Ji-Lin came next. Alejan followed.

At the mouth of the tunnel, Seika hesitated. "Father, I . . ."

"Go," the emperor said. "I will be proud of you, no matter what occurs."

Whatever happened, he trusted her. Them. She looked around the hall at everyone watching. All of them trusted their princesses.

It was time to act. And she was ready, wasn't she? This was what it had all led up to: the end of the Emperor's Journey. She had to finish what she'd begun.

"But what do we do if—" Ji-Lin began.

Before she could complete her question, Seika grabbed her elbow and propelled her into the tunnel. Shadows closed around them. "Father was clear. It's up to us now."

"He wasn't clear at all about what to do."

"Because he doesn't know." Seika was certain of that. She was good at reading people. He didn't know what the dragon was going to say, so he couldn't tell them what to do. "He trusts us to do the right thing."

"How will we know what the right thing is?"

"We'll know," Seika said. *I hope.*

She plucked one of the lanterns off a hook—someone had clearly left them for the princesses. Ji-Lin took one as well. The amber light bathed the rock walls of the tunnel, chasing away the shadows.

They walked forward. Inside the tunnel, the air felt

warm and wet but didn't stink like rotten eggs. In fact, it smelled a little of flowers and a little of copper — the smell of the dragon.

Lowering her voice to a whisper, Ji-Lin asked, "Do you think he believes Uncle Balez and Master Shai?"

Seika had wondered that. "He allowed them to be present."

Alejan spoke up. "But with guards. Master Shai wore a collar." Seika heard the pain in the lion's voice as he spoke of his hero.

"I think he's waiting to hear what the dragon says," Seika said. And that, in and of itself, meant he wasn't sure Uncle Balez was right.

Ji-Lin was silent for a moment. "So then it really is up to us."

"I think maybe it always was," Seika said. "This is our Journey."

They continued walking. It was becoming warmer. Pinned beneath a tiara, Seika's coiled hair trapped so much heat that her scalp itched. At last, ahead was the heart of the volcano, lit by the pale grayish light of the sky far above.

"Ah, the heir has come, as promised." The dragon's voice slithered around them. Seika saw the dragon, a hulking shadow that filled half of the cavern. Her tail was wrapped around the bones, and her front feet were curled around her egg. She stroked it with a single claw.

Seika stepped forward. "Dragon of Himitsu? We have

come to . . ." She faltered. Father had bargained with the dragon. He hadn't asked any questions. She could simply do the same, and all the people of Himitsu would be happy, safe behind the barrier. Or not safe, if Uncle Balez was right and the quakes continued.

Ask, Seika, she ordered herself. *Just ask the question.*

But if I ask . . . everything will change! Either the answer was no, and her uncle and Alejan's hero would be imprisoned and the quakes would continue, or the answer was yes . . . Seika took a deep breath. "Does the barrier cause the earthquakes?"

The dragon shifted, and the gray light skittered across her scales. She glistened in the shadows. "Ahh . . . Only one has ever dared ask that question, and when he heard the answer, he tried to strike me with his sword. Will you do the same?"

Seika said, "We won't attack, no matter what the answer." She glanced at Ji-Lin, who nodded agreement. "Please, won't you answer me?"

The dragon lifted her head, and Seika saw the swirling fire in her eyes. Her tongue flicked out between her sharp teeth. Shivers ran up and down Seika's spine. "Yes, indeed, my little princesses. The answer is yes."

She heard Ji-Lin gasp. Beside her, Alejan rumbled, a distressed noise.

"And what . . ." Seika licked her lips. She suddenly felt as if all moisture had been sucked from her mouth. *He's right,*

she thought. *Uncle Balez . . . Uncle Biy . . . They were right!*
"Please tell us, O Dragon of Himitsu, if the barrier falls, will
the quakes stop?"

"Yes."

And with that one word, Seika felt as if her entire world
shifted. "Then why don't you let the barrier fall?" She'd never,
ever thought she'd be asking that question.

Alejan let out a kittenlike whine, and Ji-Lin shushed him,
whispering, "Trust her."

Hearing that, Seika felt stronger. She stood straight and
tall, not breaking the dragon's gaze.

The dragon drew her egg closer to her stomach and
curled her tail around it. "If I drop the barrier, my child
will be exposed to the horrors and dangers of the outside
world."

"The outside world might not be so horrible." Seika
thought of Kirro. Fireworks, he'd said — they had things
called fireworks, and other wonders. And he'd mentioned
their cities, hadn't he? Cities with towers that stretched to
the sky! You couldn't have cities if you were cowering in fear.
Surely his father's ship was proof that the Zemylans had
found ways to survive, even thrive.

"He is safer in his shell," the dragon said, "though he does
not understand that. He is trying to hatch. While I slept, he
nearly did. See?" She turned the egg with her claw, and Seika
saw a crack that snaked down the side of the shell. "Only my
magic keeps him safely within."

"But he's not safe from the quakes," Seika said. "None of us are."

"I am," the dragon said. "The earthquakes will not harm me—I can fly above the shaking earth, my unborn child with me."

"We're not safe from them," Ji-Lin said.

"Why should I care if humans perish?" the dragon asked. "You are betrayers anyway."

Alejan growled.

"Not all of us," Seika said. "You must like some of us to have bargained with us for so long. Your injury—the stories say you were wounded in battle—it clearly healed many years ago. You don't need us to defend you anymore, not with the barrier up and the koji gone. So there must be something you like about us?"

The dragon was silent for a moment. "I like your stories."

And then suddenly, Seika knew exactly what to say. "Well, then . . . O Dragon of Himitsu, we have come to tell you a tale."

"Ahhh . . ." The dragon's voice was a purr.

Seika inhaled deeply, gathering her courage. She had only one chance at this. "Once, there were two princesses. Sisters. One trained to be a warrior, at the top of a mountain. She was never allowed to go home. The other trained to be the perfect princess. She was never allowed out of the palace. Until one day, when their father said they were ready . . ."

"They weren't ready," Ji-Lin admitted.

"They weren't," Seika agreed. "But they had to go, because they were needed. And their journey was more dangerous than anyone thought it would be."

"There were monsters," Ji-Lin put in. "Lots of monsters. And almost-pirates, with a dying boy. Also earthquakes and accidents."

"And there were secrets and lies," Seika said. "But do you know what happened to those two princesses, out in the world before they were ready?"

The dragon stirred, swishing her tail against the rocks. "Tell me."

"They did fine," Seika said.

"Better than fine," Ji-Lin added.

Seika felt Ji-Lin take her hand. She continued, hoping she was choosing the right words, hoping the dragon would understand. "They were *glad* they'd been sent, even with the monsters and the earthquakes and the secrets and the lies. They're *happier* because they're out into the world. They're happier out of their shells."

The dragon was silent again.

Her fiery eyes studied them, and Seika didn't move. *Please work*, she thought. *Please understand.*

"Let your egg hatch," Ji-Lin pleaded.

"Let it hatch," Seika repeated. "And let the barrier fall. We needed it in the beginning, and it served its purpose wonderfully. But it was never meant to stand for so long. We are meant be out in the world, all of us."

Still, silence.

And then, a humming—it was coming from the egg itself, as if the unborn dragon was singing.

"Please, Dragon, your child is meant to hatch," Seika said. "It can't ever fly if you don't let it. It can't ever see the world if you don't let it. It can't live if you never give it the chance. You have to let it hatch!" She couldn't tell what the dragon was thinking. She couldn't read those swirling, fiery eyes.

"What if the world is not so bad?" Ji-Lin asked. "You won't know unless you venture out into it."

"Dragon?" Seika took a step toward her. "Look at the crack in your egg—your child knows it's time to change, whether you're ready or not. It's time to make new traditions."

The humming grew louder.

Lowering her head so that her eye was even with her egg, the dragon spoke to the crack. "This is truly what you wish? I can keep you safe for centuries more."

A shard of the egg burst away.

"Oh, my child, if you must . . ."

Seika saw a talon poke through the shell, covered in shimmering goo. She squeezed Ji-Lin's hand, and Ji-Lin squeezed back. *Please let this be the right decision,* she thought. She remembered what Master Shai had said — we can't fight the earth, but we can fight monsters. She hoped she was choosing the danger they could both fight and survive.

The shell burst away as the dragonet poked its way through the goo. Its wings were folded against itself, trapped in gunk. It flopped onto the rock and then collapsed. It let out a mewing wail.

"My child!" the dragon cried. "My little prince!"

The hatchling lifted his head. His eyes, like his mother's, were tiny flames. His scales were silvery white and deep sea blue.

"What did we do?" Ji-Lin breathed.

"We did the right thing," Seika said. "I think."

"We just changed the world."

The little dragon looked up at his mother, and she lowered her head to breathe lightly on him. He made a sound like a purr. "Are you going to drop the barrier?" Seika asked.

"Yes, and it will be done correctly, without shaking the earth," the dragon said, watching as her baby struggled to his feet. He staggered one step forward before he fell onto his chin. She lifted him with a talon. "I have no choice now. My little prince will need to fly. I will remove the veil from these islands and he will soar."

"When?" She didn't know how fast dragons grew.

"Soon," the dragon said. "A few days, a few weeks at most.

Dragons grow fast, to survive. Many things hunt a young dragon. He will become strong quickly and want to fly far and wide."

After two hundred years, the barrier would be lifted in only a few days. But the quakes would stop. Himitsu would be saved—and open to the world. *Everything will change,* Seika thought. *We're not ready!*

But maybe that's all right. Maybe no one is ever ready. We all just do the best we can.

"It is time for us to bargain, little princesses, as I did with your long-ago ancestor. Here is what I ask: Your lions and riders will help protect my dragonet until he is strong enough to protect himself. And in return, my dragonet and I will protect your islands until you are strong enough to protect yourselves. You will not be left alone to enter the larger world, and neither will my child."

"That sounds fair," Seika agreed.

More than fair.

A promise of protection, and a chance to prepare. She couldn't have asked for better than that. "We would be honored to make this bargain with you," Seika said, and bowed low.

The baby dragon purred.

⟳

Ji-Lin and Seika emerged from the tunnel to find the Great Hall packed with people. Islanders had crammed inside and were perched on all the not-yet-removed rocks. The emperor and the winged lions waited as well.

Everyone was silent.

Hand in hand, the sisters stepped forward and said together, "We have come to tell a tale." And together, they told of the barrier and the earthquakes. They told of the egg and its hatching. They told of their bargain with the dragon.

All through their story, the people were silent.

The emperor listened from a throne of rubble. His hands were clasped at his waist, and his eyes were fixed on his daughters. Master Vanya stood beside him, and beside her were Uncle Balez and Master Shai. On the emperor's other side were the Zemylan captain and Kirro. They were dressed in silk robes, with golden tassels that hung from their belts. Kirro's robes were large for him, pooling at his feet, and he fidgeted as he listened. His father elbowed him until he stood still, and Ji-Lin almost laughed.

Above, the moon beamed through the hole in the roof of the Great Hall.

As they finished, the whispers began, and then the whispers grew into murmurs.

"I don't think there's a ritual big enough to cover all the changes that are coming," Seika said softly. "Even a hundred dances by a hundred firedancers won't make people unafraid."

"I know," Ji-Lin said. "But I think . . . it will be okay."

Looking out at the people, at the rubble in the Great Hall, at the courtyard beyond, she began to believe it. She heard the words: *no barrier*, and then *no earthquakes* and *no eruptions*. Their people were stronger than the emperor and Master Vanya thought.

The emperor stepped forward, and the murmurs stopped. All eyes were on him. He then smiled. *Smiled* at his daughters for the second time in less than twenty-four hours. "You have done well. Far better, in fact, than I ever dared hope. You have saved us, even though it was not in the way I expected."

"They were bold, they were swift, they were unexpected," Master Vanya said.

Smile still on his face, the emperor turned to his people. "People of Himitsu, a new era is upon us! Thanks to the wisdom and bravery of my daughters . . ." He continued, reassuring his people, warning them, inspiring them, burying his own fear deep beneath his words.

All eyes were on the emperor.

Ji-Lin saw fear, as Master Vanya had predicted. But she also saw hope.

The lioness hadn't mentioned hope when she'd spoken of the people's fear, but Ji-Lin saw it now, etched clearly in their faces, brightening their eyes and parting their lips, as they listened to their emperor. Hope, for the future, for a life in which the earth didn't break beneath their feet, in which monsters came but could be eluded and defeated.

The two princesses stepped backwards, into the shadows, and listened as their father ordered a celebration — a celebration to banish fear. Musicians scrambled into position, and the drums began. Chefs wheeled out food, piled high on carts. Acrobats and dancers swirled between the people.

"They're still afraid," Seika said softly.

"Terrified," Ji-Lin agreed. "But they'll be okay." Every word she and Seika had told the dragon was true: they hadn't been ready, but they'd had their adventure anyway. She didn't regret any of it. Their people would be all right too, even though they were scared now. It was time for all of them to step out into the world and have an adventure.

"I think you're right," Seika said.

"In that case . . ." Ji-Lin crossed the Great Hall to Alejan. "Ready to exit dramatically and heroically?" Dropping her voice, she added, "We'll be back in time for the feast, I promise."

As Alejan lowered his wings, Ji-Lin climbed into the saddle. She held out a hand to her sister. Taking it, Seika climbed on behind her.

"Wait for me," Kirro said, and scrambled into the saddle with them. As he strapped himself in, Alejan stretched out his wings. Twisting around, Seika looked at their father. He met her eyes and nodded once. Seika felt herself smiling.

"All right," Seika said. "Let's go!"

"Fly, Alejan," Ji-Lin said.

And the two princesses, the boy from Zemyla, and the winged lion flew high above the volcano, high above the sea, and looked out toward the barrier — and the world beyond.

ACKNOWLEDGMENTS

I'D LIKE TO thank my cat for not having wings, because that would be terrifying. I'd also like to thank my husband, who said, "Go for it!" when I said, "I want to write a book with a winged lion." Sadly, he did not agree to get me a flying lion, which was my follow-up question. (To be fair, our cat would have hated it.) Thank you to my amazing agent, Andrea Somberg, and my fantastic editor, Anne Hoppe, as well as all the other incredible people at Clarion Books and Houghton Mifflin Harcourt. Without you, the Hidden Islands would still be hidden. And endless thanks to my family — I love you all more than dragons.

ABOUT THE AUTHOR

SARAH BETH DURST is the author of award-winning fantasy novels for children, teens, and adults, including *The Girl Who Could Not Dream; Drink, Slay, Love;* and *The Queen of Blood.* She has won the Mythopoeic Fantasy Award for Children's Literature and has been a finalist for the Andre Norton Award for Young Adult Science Fiction and Fantasy three times. Sarah lives in Stony Brook, New York, with her husband, children, and ill-mannered cat.